T0328953

partiers
preferred

You're invited to all the best house parties at Summer Share:

CC (Cape Cod)
by Randi Reisfeld

LB (Laguna Beach)
by Nola Thacker

Shirt and Shoes Not Required
by Todd Strasser

partiers
preferred

Randi Reisfeld

Simon Pulse
New York London Toronto Sydney

Excerpts from *The Outsiders* © 1967 by S. E. Hinton. Used by permission of Penguin Group (USA) Inc.

SIMON PULSE
An imprint of Simon & Schuster Children's Publishing Division
1230 Avenue of the Americas, New York, NY 10020
Copyright © 2007 by Randi Reisfeld
All rights reserved, including the right of reproduction in whole or in part in any form.
SIMON PULSE and colophon are registered trademarks of Simon & Schuster, Inc.
Designed by Greg Stadnyk
The text of this book was set in Stone Informal.
Manufactured in the United States of America
First Simon Pulse edition July 2007
10 9 8 7 6 5 4 3 2 1
ISBN-13: 978-1-4169-0037-5

If I were to share a summer house, here's who my ideal roomies would be: the brilliant Bethany Buck, who had the original idea for the series; Sangeeta Mehta, who took this book to the next level; the agents extraordinaire, Jodi Reamer, Rachel Sheedy, and Elizabeth Harding, who all, in a game of e-phone, helped me reach my old friend, actor/producer Ralph Macchio, who reconnected me to the brilliant S. E. Hinton, who graciously allowed me to reference her classic, *The Outsiders*.

Without the contributions of these people, this book would not have been half as much fun as it is.

Thank you all so very, very much.

partiers
preferred

1

Jared's Sweet Deal

Jared Larson tingled all over. He was high on, and in, the heady hills of Hollywood. A wide smile of contentment spread across his classically chiseled face as he eased the Lexus convertible into the narrow driveway. The house it belonged to was empty and all his, all summer long. He planned to make excellent use of it. Rent out rooms, pocket a nice chunk of change, while spending the summer partying. Chicks, clubs, ka-*ching*—for a twenty-one-year-old free spirit, it doesn't get any better than that! Especially because his father would never find out. Ah, freedom: It's what this great country was built on.

Flipping his Oliver Peoples aviator shades atop his stylishly short hair, he glanced over at the familiar front door and grinned. Painted a garishly loud royal blue, it stood a few feet behind a leaf-and-vine-covered gate. Shoulder-high hedges encircled the house.

It was *so* L.A., he thought. In this town, good shrub-bery makes good (i.e, *envious*) neighbors. When you build a tall, dense fence around your crib, you force passersby to wonder: What's on the other side? Some crazy-amazing mansion? Who lives there? A star?

Jared chuckled as he started down the path of terra-cotta stepping-stones leading to the backyard. Amaz-ing? This place? In the eyes of a stoner, maybe. The blinding blue front door was only one of the odd color choices—the entire exterior had been painted a scream-ing pumpkin-orange color. Good thing this area of L.A. was considered artsy.

The neighborhood, officially Lake Hollywood, was a maze of eclectic houses on steep narrow streets that zigged and zagged so randomly, the only things you could be sure of were hairpin turns and blind driveways. A bitch to drive around, especially at night.

The part about a star living in the orange and blue monstrosity, however, was sort of true. A quasi-celebrity owned this house, an actor audiences knew by sight, never by name. Jared knew him as Uncle Robert, a char-acter actor in his forties who had, as one critic viciously sniped, "a great future behind him."

Ouch. That'd hurt. Jared's uncle, the only relative he actually liked being around, *had* weathered a long dry spell, career-wise. He'd taken roles in straight-to-DVD junk movies to pay the bills. But Rob's desert days were done, as over as yesterday's sushi craze. Robert Larson was currently making a killer comeback, in a career-defining movie. Already, there was buzz about a best supporting Oscar nomination for him. The movie was filming in Prague. When Uncle Rob packed up and left, Jared moved in.

So what if the bizarrely painted cottage wasn't like the spacious mansion Jared had grown up in?

It was funky.

"Rustic, cozy, tucked away, perched above the Sunset Strip" was the description Jared had put in the Room-mates Wanted ad on Craigslist. From that posting he'd already netted a trio of roomies. Two guys, Nick and Eliot, were coming in later today from Michigan; tomorrow, a chick named Sara from Texas would arrive. The guys didn't know the chick, and he knew none of them. That was cool with Jared—as long as they knew how to pay the rent!

Seriously, Jared was positive the two guys and the girl would work out—he needed just one more summer-share tenant to fill that last bedroom. He was confident he'd snag one by week's end, if not sooner. After all, he was charging what was, for this area, a bargain-basement rent for an amazing location. He could afford to because he had no overhead; their rent was his profit. So his dad had cut off his credit cards? Yo, every establishment he knew took cash. It was all good. Jared was born without a self-doubt gene.

He didn't need it. His father had enough doubt in Jared for both of them.

"Shabby" was the word Rusty Larson used to condescendingly describe this "shack" on "the wrong side of the hills." Why his ne'er-do-well-enough brother insisted on living there was beyond him. Of course, anything outside the three-square-mile area that encompassed the Larson family compound in Bel Air, Dad's high-rise office in Beverly Hills, and the beach house in Malibu where his bimbette of the day was stashed, was "beyond" him. Rusty Larson rarely stepped out of his Jag if an anorexic palm tree wasn't swaying gently above.

Jared agreed with his old man on absolutely *nothing*, but as he turned the corner into the backyard, his eyes widened in surprise. "Shabby" would've been putting it kindly. Forget about manicured lawn or neat patch of green. Overgrown, never-mown grass, dotted with scratchy stalks of burned-out weeds, covered what was once a decent-looking backyard.

Lucky, thought Jared, it was only a small plot of land—just enough to surround the curvy natural rock swimming pool, abutting Jacuzzi, and barbecue pit. He strode over to the pool and gaped at what used to be sparkling blue, clean, welcoming. It was a sickening greenish hue. Dead bugs and other unidentified objects floated lazily on the surface, as if they'd moved in. It was the thick coating of muck that really turned his stomach.

At least Uncle Rob's neglect could not screw up the

home's most kick-ass and valuable asset. The one thing that was free, always there, and breathtaking.

The view.

"Viewtiful," his horny teenage girlfriend used to call it. Even on a hot 'n' hazy Saturday in June, it was amazing. (Smog? What smog?)

Jared strode to the outer edge of the property and surveyed his summer fiefdom. Spread out before him, acres of lush, juicy Caliscape, The sky above, the valley below, the undulating dips and curves and turns and tiers of the hills were like surround-sound, encircling everything. Ah, the famous hills of Hollywood.

His father was a short-sighted snob. There *was* no "wrong side." Here was the heart and soul of the Southland: minimountains into which hundreds of homes neatly pressed. Some were on stilts, others carved into the rocks; all blended in with the terrain. And within eyeshot? Only the most famous of all landmarks, the *Holly-wood* sign.

Below were broad boulevards named Sunset, Melrose, Wilshire, and Beverly. At night their ginormous billboards blinked and beckoned, their hot clubs called. Down there, deals were waiting to be made, girls waiting to be flirted with, the pleasures of food and drink, all spread out before him like a never-ending smorgasbord. Ah, the possibilities. More than anyplace else on earth, Hollywood was about possibilities. They were as endless as the landscape.

This was where he belonged. This summer, he'd prove it. Jared checked his sport Tag Heuer watch—it was nearly two. The roommates weren't due for several hours, but if the inside of the house were as wrecked as the yard, he'd have to deal—quickly.

He counted the stepping-stones, knelt next to the fourth from the right, and slipped his palm underneath the terracotta stone. Wedged between the stone and the dirt was exactly what he expected to be there. The front door key.

Once inside, Jared heaved a sigh of relief. Unlike the mess of the backyard, Uncle Rob had left the house in order. Just as Jared remembered it.

The large living room was warm, welcoming, and cluttered. It was, Jared often thought, the intersection of high-end and low-brow, where expensive and rare crisscrossed with junky, cheap, and marked-down everywhere. Hippie-meets-haute. Nothing matched, and everything worked.

Dark wood beams tented a vaulted ceiling, and a worn black leather couch abutted a blue-and-orange-striped sectional sofa. A mirrored orange high-backed Moroccan wing chair and matching ottoman, which his uncle had shipped from overseas, sat by the brick fireplace.

A gallery of guitars (bass, electric, baritone, and acoustic) and other stringed instruments—sitars, mandolins, banjos, and violins—lined the pale tangerine walls, mounted like artful pieces of musical sculpture. CDs, vintage record albums, photos, and candles perched on shelves and bookcases tucked into random nooks and crannies. Between the albums, guitars, bongs, incense holders, aromatic candles, and bottles of Kabbalah water, the entire room was a hippie paradise.

Kitchen, bathroom, and a tricked-out game room completed the main floor.

Suddenly, Jared's cell phone rang. He checked the caller ID: his father.

Jared watched himself in a hallway mirror as he talked to his dad. Make that *lied* to his dad, who believed he was in summer school, making up for the disaster that'd been his freshman-year grades.

"Hi, Dad, I'm good. I'm just walking into the dormitory now . . . it's fine, I'll survive. It's Ojai Community College, not the county lock-up!

"Nope, don't need a thing. Just got done confirming my classes—they'll wipe out last semester's failing grades, like they never happened."

"Yeah, I got a private room, no pesky roommates to distract me.

"Totally, I understand why you cut off the credit cards. It sucks, but I'll have to deal, right? What's my choice?

"No need for you to visit—you've got business. It's cool, it's chill."

After he hung up, Jared raked his fingers through his

hair. He would make good this summer—that part wasn't bogus. Just in a different way than he'd told his old man.

Jared picked up a huge copper bong from the old chipped oak coffee table and stared at his reflection. Smooth-cheeked, collar up, cool and confident, clear green eyes—he did not recognize the screwup his father saw him as.

Whose fault were those failing grades anyway? He'd made it clear he neither wanted nor needed college. Rusty Larson owned Galaxy Artists, the hottest talent agency in town. Why Jared wasn't there, working at the junior exec level already, was the mystery. Whatever. He'd play it the old man's way, promising to take make-up classes, which he'd pass with flying colors. The rent-a-brainiac he'd hired to take the tests for him would see to that.

His one regret regarding his summer scheme was the secrecy involved: He couldn't tell his friends what was really up. Someone was bound to blab. In Hollywood, gossip is precious currency, and he would not chance his dad finding out. That meant house parties were out. He'd have to socialize on neutral turf: the clubs, or some girl's apartment.

Speaking of . . . he punched in speed dial. But neither Caitlin nor Julie picked up. He left messages. "Hey Cait, it's Jared. See you at Mood tonight . . . ?" "Jules, Jared here. Be at Hyde later?"

Then he made for the liquor cabinet, poured himself a Stoli-rocks, and slipped out the sliding glass doors that led to the backyard. Standing on the stone lip of the pool, he sipped the smooth vodka, refusing to let the toxic crap in the water screw with his happiness. A simple call to a cleaning service would take care of everything. As he'd told his dad, it was all chill. It'd be a funky, functional, fund-enhancing summer. Accent on the "fun" part: Jared was determined to have keggers 'o it this summer.

Inspired, he raised a toast to his absent relative.

"Here's to you, Uncle Rob—to bagging that Academy Award, and to the biggest favor you've ever done for me. Does a favor count any less just 'cause you don't know you're doing it?"

Jared knew the answer to his existential question was a resounding . . .

"Fuuu . . . !!!"

It happened so quickly he could not react—couldn't get his mouth closed before sucking in a glob of foul-smelling, vomit-inducing algae garbage. Couldn't keep his balance, couldn't hold on to his drink. He'd been pushed from behind, shoved, rendered defenseless as a girl. He heard the smash of his vodka glass hitting the poolside pavement and felt a wet film of fetid slime cover his skin. He belly flopped, face forward, into the muck.

2

Lindsay: "Didn't You Used to Be . . . ?"

Lindsay laughed so hard, she thought she'd bust a gut. The sight of Jared McPerfect—Mr. Pristine—caught unaware, blindsided, flailing, pinwheeling his arms as if he could turn them into propellers and fly . . . then, splash!, nosediving into the pool. It was too, too much. What a rush!

Shoving him had been pure impulse. She'd planned on surprising him, not turning him into the raging freak he now resembled, shaking his head furiously, like a wet dog. She clutched her stomach at the sight of Jared soaked, sputtering, and screaming obscenities as he tried to free himself from the gook-choke.

Lindsay had just arrived in Los Angeles. She'd come straight here, only to be greeted by Jared, his back to her, prepped to perfection from the tips of his alligator Tods to the top of his two-hundred-dollar designer haircut. The lad of the manor had been so engrossed in admiring his reflection in the pool, raising his glass to the splendor of himself, he'd heard neither the taxi door slam nor the thwacking of her flip-flops as she'd made her way to the backyard, dragging her wheelie behind. Jared might as well have had a target on his back.

It'd just been *too* tempting. And "temptation, resistance of"? Not a Lindsay Pierce strong suit.

"What the fu—!" Jared finally managed to splutter when he saw his stealth attacker. "Lindsay?! What are you doing here?"

She tossed back her gleaming copper hair and admonished him. "Jared Larson, this is exactly why you'd never make it as an actor. You can't keep the smile off your silly face. You want to be mad at me, but you're just too happy to see me."

He growled. "You forfeited any chance of a happy reunion by throwing me into the pool. Or should I say, the toxic waste dump?"

She shrugged. "Think of it as delayed payback. Last time I was here, it was you who threw me into the pool. Only," she amended, "it was cleaner. And we were naked."

"I don't remember you minding, especially since I jumped in after you. Anyway"—only Jared could manage a smirk while being humiliated—"we ended up in the hot tub." With that, he splashed down hard on the slimy pool surface, hoping to spray her.

Lindsay skipped backward. "I knew you'd do that.

After all these years, you're still so predictable."

He glowered, taking long, painstaking strides through the gummy water, making his way toward the steps.

"Hang on," Lindsay said. "If Uncle Rob is as predictable as his nephew, the towels will be exactly where I remember them." She flipped around, executing a killer ass-swivel—she knew he'd appreciate the move, which she'd practiced in her floaty halter top and snug, low-slung Diesels—and flounced through the sliding doors into the house.

It was good to be back, Lindsay thought.

By the time Jared had stripped off his scum-soaked clothes, taken a quick turn in the outdoor shower, and toweled himself furiously, Lindsay had settled into one of the poolside lounge chairs, fingers wrapped around a cool, fruity-flavored vodka drink. She could still read him like an IM in all capital letters: He was psyched and confused, couldn't decide whether Lindsay bursting back into his life was a good thing—or one he ought to be wary of. Given Jared's natural distrust of people (*Takes one to know one*, she thought), he was proceeding with extreme caution.

Calmly, confidently, she repeated her story, testing which parts he'd pick out as totally bogus. "Word on the street is, you're looking for tenants. You need cash, I need a place to crash. I'm back in town, I need to reconnect with friends. And who's the first friend I *bump*—oops, bad word choice—into, but you? It's bra*sheet.*" She punctuated with a winning smile.

Jared attempted a scowl but came up with a barely concealed grin. "You can't even say it right. It's *beshert*— buh-*shirt*. Not that you're even Jewish."

Lindsay toyed with her big hoop earrings and tossed her ponytail defiantly. "I'm Jewish-by-Hollywood. I lived here long enough. Anyway, Jared, I *know* what it means: We each need something the other one has. And here we find ourselves, together again. It's perfect."

"It's *beshert*," he corrected. "It means fated, that something was meant to be. It does not mean that something came up and you figured how to take advantage of it."

He'd hunkered down on the lounge chair next to hers, shirtless, just a towel wrapped around his waist, cell phone in his lap. Lindsay felt a familiar twinge. It'd been three years, and time had been good to Jared. Always a looker, he'd grown taller, tanner, leaner, and smoother, if that were possible. It was all she could do not to reach over and touch.

In the old days, her fifteen-year-old self would have practiced no such self-control. She'd have twirled that towel right off his slim waist. Jared would have been the "something" she'd have taken advantage of.

And Jared would've said, afterward, "You're amazing, Linz. Let's do this. Move in. Forget about rent." The teenage Jared she used to know wouldn't have missed a beat . . . or stopped to ask what Lindsay was doing back in California after being away so long. Three years in which she'd not once responded to his calls, letters, and, later, e-mails. Of course, being Jared, he hadn't tried very hard to stay in touch with her. Just long enough to lick his superficial wounds. Then he'd probably gone on to some other young starlet.

Today's twenty-one-year-old version of Jared peppered her with questions. The full-on interrogation. When she'd lied and said, "Word on the street is, you're looking for roommates," he freaked. Apparently, he hadn't wanted anyone he knew to find out.

He sat sideways on the chaise lounge, feet planted on the ground, hovering over her. Until she told him the truth, Jared wasn't letting his guard, or his towel, down.

"Chill out." She assured him she hadn't spoken to, nor heard from, anyone in Jared's circle. It wasn't the grapevine that'd outed him, but the *online*. Plotting her return to Los Angeles, she'd been on Craigslist every day for months, waiting and watching for a listing both location-acceptable (near the studios, where she hoped to land auditions) and financially feasible. Lindsay had money, but no intention of getting ripped off.

A match popped up a few weeks ago, worded in her native tongue, Hollywood-speak. She could have written the ad herself.

She recited it to Jared, with her interpretation. "Everyone knows a 'cozy' house means it's miniscule. 'Tucked away' is code for 'not the best neighborhood.'

And 'rustic' translates to *maybe* there'll be running water. Which reminded me of you—the prince of spin. And then I saw your cell phone number on the listing. Like I said, it's bra*sheet.*"

"*Beshert,*" he growled.

"Yeah, that." Lindsay drained her drink. Tipping her chin to the sun, she inhaled the sweet jasmine-scented air. She knew she looked . . . um . . . what was that other Jewish word? *Kvetching?* Something like that.

Jared noticed. Despite his wariness, he couldn't stop himself from admiring her. "You look . . ." He stumbled for the word.

"Luscious? Sexy? Sublime? *Kvetching?*"

A belly laugh escaped. Jared's whole body shook with obvious delight, loosening the towel. "You're somethin' else, Linz, you really are. Just off enough to be a hoot. *Kvetching* means complaining."

"You're not . . . complaining . . . that I turned up?" She pushed back on her elbows, raising herself up to face him.

The beginnings of a blush crept up his neck. Pink. It worked for him. "Memo to Lindsay," he said. "Stop trying to be such a Hollywood-speak insider. No one does that anymore. Anyway, you are quite fetching."

"Fetching? As in 'go fetch me another drink'?"

Jared sighed. "No. As in, our little Linz has grown into quite a fetching young lass."

Lindsay glowed. She'd worked hard to look this good.

• • •

There hadn't been much else to do in the middle of the Iowa cornfields, where she'd spent the last mind-numbing years, besides plot her triumphant return west. To the land of milk 'n' honey, the place of good 'n' plenty, where she'd once been plenty good, and plenty adored.

Lindsay had been a star, playing middle sister Zoe Goldstein-Wong in the long-running sitcom about a Chinese-Jewish family called *All for Wong*. She'd landed the role when she was only ten, a freakishly freckled moppet with huge golden brown eyes, a button nose, and Cupid's bow lips. Famously ticklish, she was best known for her throaty, staccato, hiccupy giggle-fits. A trait she came by naturally, alas. It always gave her away. One insensitive critic dubbed her the Woody Woodpecker of child stars.

The show had run for five years and rerun for all eternity, rendering her very public, unpretty puberty in perpetuity. She had not transitioned well—unlike an Olsen twin or the girl who'd played Rudy on *The Cosby Show*.

There'd been zits, bad haircuts, and that whole nasty "plump" thing the producers had unkindly pointed out. It didn't help that Lindsay'd been a smart-mouth, purposely ad-libbing when the cameras were rolling.

The war between Lindsay's family, under the guise of "protecting" her, and the producers—who were protecting their show—had grown bitter, and public. Good thing the tabloids weren't as out of control back then as they are now. Not that she'd ever been as big a tab-magnet as today's young stars, Lindsay, Nicole, Paris, or anyone named Ashlee or Jessica.

And there was this: The measure of her fame was not a direct connect with the measure of how much she liked being famous. Lindsay lapped up, thrived on, bloomed under every spotlighty ray of attention. She'd never gotten over the craving.

The family feud alone would likely have gotten her fired—"She's replaceable, you know," producers used to threaten—only *All for Wong* got canceled. End of feud, end of story; to Lindsay, it felt like the end of her world.

Once the gravy train stopped rolling, that is, once her income dried up and she could no longer support the family, they hauled ass back to Iowa. With her in tow. Towed her back like a broken car. Only she wasn't broken, and she didn't want to be dragged back. Grenfield, Iowa, was her family's hometown. Not hers. Never hers.

She'd spent her enforced separation from L.A. working on her looks, her ticket back. Lindsay wasn't deluded. She was far from Ms. Uber-talent, but close enough to the scene to know talent's limits. In this town, a rockin' bod combined with A-list connections were far more potent than any ability you might have.

Taking the looks route hadn't been easy. Denying herself in America's heartland, where the major food groups were corndogs, Krispy Kremes, and Dairy Queen shakes, was a bitch. Hitting the local YMCA instead of a real fitness center, working by herself instead of with a trainer, had sucked. No one helped, no one encouraged her. Not the children of the corn, as she secretly called the kids at Grenfield High, not her cretin cousins, certainly not her parents. They thought she was nuts.

"Lindsay, sweetheart," her mom (who probably felt guilty living off her all those years) kept at her, "you don't have to be skinny; you're perfect the way you are. You don't have to be judged by how you look. You can grow up normal now."

What Mom never understood? Lindsay didn't *do* normal. Not back then, and not now. She'd turned eighteen in May, graduated high school, tucked in what was left of her stomach, and headed back to Hollywood, head, tush, and tatas held high. Slim and curvy where baby fat once rolled, defined cheekbones where chubby cheeks were often pinched, she'd grown tauter, totally tantalizing. And bore ambition to match. Forget the TV "sitcomeback." Or playing some drug addict in an indie movie to prove her acting chops.

Chew this! Her goal was no less lofty than icon. Lindsay Pierce aspired to be a brand. Complete with makeup ("Get the Lindsay Pierce look!"). And fashion ("The Lindsay Pierce line is sold exclusively at Bloomingdale's!"). And major accessories ("Bracelets, scrunchies, toe rings, designed by Lindsay herself!"). Of course, there'd be a fashion doll. And a fragrance. Everyone who was anyone did perfume. She read *Us Weekly*. She kept up!

Hooking back up with Jared Larson was a means to

an end. Jared's dad owned Galaxy. Jared could get her a high-powered agent, who'd snag her star-making movie roles. Convincing her ex-bf to help? Let's just say that when she saw her ex-boyfriend's ad on Craigslist, it was a done deal.

"The truth, Lindsay—why are you really back?" Jared demanded.

Oy. Still with the interrogation. All she needed was crappy lighting and stale coffee, and this could be a scene from *Law & Order*. Why was Jared so jumpy? She attempted to peel away, if not the towel, the layers of lies he was bound to be telling. "Does Uncle Rob know you're living in his house—and renting out rooms while he's away?"

"Do Mom and Pop Pierce know where their oldest daughter is?" he volleyed back.

Lindsay laughed. She'd missed more than Jared's body: Swapping one-ups with him was one of the best parts of their relationship. They *got* each other. "I didn't run away. My folks know I'm here. Besides, I'm eighteen—legal. In case you hadn't noticed." For emphasis, she puffed her chest out, tossed her copper tresses back.

"Okay, yes, my uncle knows I'm here." Jared was pink again. Lindsay wasn't sure if her chest had caused him to blush, or he was lying.

"And Rob's okay with this?"

"Why wouldn't he be?"

Lindsay could think of about a zillion reasons but didn't press. "I take it your father doesn't know what you're up to."

"Not exactly."

"Hmmm." Lindsay narrowed her eyes. "We can safely assume Daddy Moneybags isn't financing you—otherwise, why the need to collect rent?"

Jared conceded that his father had cut off his credit cards—temporarily.

"And the crowd, our old friends? Tripp, Caitlin, Ava, MK, Julie B . . . ? None of them know the truth either?" That was a guess.

Jared held her gaze. "I'd appreciate it if you didn't tell them."

Lindsay licked her lips. *That'll cost ya*, she thought. But didn't say aloud. Instead, she closed one eye in pretend concentration. "So lemme get this straight. Your dad thinks you're at community college making up your failing grades. To be sure you don't screw around, he's cut off your credit cards. Your friends believe this hooey as well— except they assume you're plastic-fantastic, flush. It wouldn't occur to your uncle that you're squatting in his crib. Hence, you're living here for free, making money off other people. Is that about right?"

Jared's curvy lips tightened into a straight line.

"Whew! Keeping up with Jared's web of lies. Feels like old times. I love it!"

Maybe he saw the wheels in her head turning, maybe

he realized her arrival here was gonna cost him, one way or another, but Jared obviously couldn't resist lobbing one back. "I'd be careful about worshipping old times, Lindsay. You can't go home again."

She stiffened. "What's that supposed to mean? Another convenient quote from the master of deception himself?"

Jared burst out laughing again. She'd been right. He couldn't stay mad at her. He shook his head, still chuckling. "I didn't think metaphors could get any more mixed up, but once again, you prove me wrong."

"Let's try basic arithmetic. Here's the math as I see it: You want four roommates. You've got two guys coming later today, one girl arriving tomorrow—and now there's me. Add up so far?"

"You want to move in. How are you going to pay the rent?" He folded his arms over his rippley-smooth chest.

Just for fun, Lindsay uncrossed her legs.

"In U.S. currency, I mean." Jared would not be distracted.

"No problem. I'm going to get a gig. But," she added before he could chime in, "no way I'm paying what the others are! Not if you want me to keep—let alone keep track of—all your little secrets."

Jared's jaw tensed. He looked even more luscious when pissed. "That's blackmail."

"You say blackmail," she chirped, "I say quid pro quo. Which is how this town totally operates. Anyhow, it's not like I'm gunning for a free ride. I'll pay for my keep. One way or another."

Ignoring her implication, Jared said, "Do you even have an agent?"

"I'm not currently represented." She delivered the line in her best Hollywood-speak. "I thought you could help me out. I had no way of knowing about your little spat with Rusty Larson, head of the biggest talent agency in town."

Jared sighed. "We'll find a way to get you an agent."

Lindsay lit up. "I knew it! I knew we'd get back on the same track. It's bra—"

He held his palm up. "Don't even try."

"Can I try something else?" She untied her halter top. If that didn't loosen his libido . . .

3

California, Here We Are: Nick and Eliot Find Nirvana

**"Holy crap! They're gonna do it . . . right here . . .
in public!"** Eliot's bug eyes nearly popped out of his
head; the roadmap he'd been clutching slipped to the
ground. "It's not technically public if it's a private backyard, but . . ."

Nick gaped, speechless. Right in front of them, better
than big screen, more 3D than HD plasma, was the most
awesome scenic view they'd had the entire road trip. This
skinny dude—gotta be Jared, the kid who'd put the Roommates Wanted ad on Craigslist—with this *bodacious* chick,
sharing a chaise lounge in the backyard, sucking face,
pawing each other, going at it, hot and heavy. A towel
was slowly slipping off his butt and she was topless, man!
The couple was oblivious to anything else, including the
presence of the two best friends who'd driven out from
Michigan to spend the summer in L.A..

Nick felt overdressed. Clearly, dude, life out here was *waaay* more casual than in West Bloomfield. He'd have to adjust.

Eliot, unsurprisingly, was in deep distress. "N . . . n . . . ni . . . Nick . . . I think they're gonna do it!" He gulped. "We gotta let them know we're here."

"Chill, E," Nick shushed him. "These are our roommates. And you never get a second chance to get your first impression. Somethin' like that."

"This isn't right," Eliot whispered frantically. "We shouldn't be standing here. Let's go back to the car . . . until . . . uh, they're done."

Neither moved.

Nick had spent most of the three-day drive wanting to pop his best friend. No more so than right now. Why couldn't Eliot just zip it, enjoy the show? The entire trip, Eliot had whined about "things that could go wrong." He'd conjured an encyclopedia of worst-case scenarios, everything from catching Legionnaires disease if they stayed overnight in "that fleabag motel," to food poisoning from the freakin' Waffle House, to carjacking. "We're running out of gas. We'll be stranded in the middle of nowhere" was on permanent loop.

There were times he'd wanted to pull over and leave Eliot in the middle of nowhere.

You'd think by the time they'd reached Los Angeles, the E-man would have chilled out. Not so much. The shotgun-riding worrywart was sure every other car on the freeway had targeted them for a drive-by. When they pulled off the 101 at the Hollywood Hills exit, Eliot had been convinced Nick was going either "the wrong way," or "in circles." Kept whining that the car, Nick's 1997 Chevy Nova, wasn't going to make it up these steep hills, they'd be killed in a head-on with an oncoming car, just around the next hairpin turn. "This can't be the right neighborhood," Eliot whined. "We're lost. We should call Jared, give him our cross streets. He'll tell us how to get there."

Call for directions? How lame would that look?

Nick didn't need directions. Let alone nervous Nelly the nail-biter on his butt. He needed his best friend to have a little faith in him. After eighteen years of friendship, Eliot Kupferberg still thought Nick Maharis was a reckless rebel, bound for trouble. Not anymore. Nick was bound for a career as a professional model. The Calvin Klein billboards, man! His gig with a top L.A. photo agency was the first step into his bright and brawny future.

"Her p . . . p . . . pants . . . She's pulling them off!" Eliot cried, alarmed. "And she's . . . oh, shit, Nick, I know her! I recognize her, she's . . ."

"*Sweet*," Nick whistled under his breath.

The action on the chaise lounge ramped up. The make-out session got more heated. Arms and legs were wildly entangled now. Jared and the chick were bumping, grinding, breathing heavily, in their own space.

"I told you we weren't lost," Nick said.

• • •

There was nothing else to do. Nick was just gonna stand there and watch. Eliot had to take matters into his own hands. He'd noticed the cell phone that slipped to the ground along with Jared's towel. He dug into his pocket and retrieved his own mobile. During the process of renting the share house, he'd already programmed Jared Larson's number in.

The Killers' "Mr. Brightside" rang out. Which apparently was Jared's ring tone. His head jerked up. And not a moment too soon. He'd been kissing her, caressing her breasts, and was headed southward. He stopped to get the phone, just as Eliot knew he would. Hollywood playas never missed a call.

Finally! Jared saw them, standing not twenty feet away, Nick gaping, Eliot with the cell phone by his ear.

The girl, open-mouthed, flipped around, affording them a full-on topless view. Eliot nearly fainted. It *was* her.

"Jared Larson here," Jared said warily into his phone.

Huh? Who did he think was calling? Eliot was confused. Jared couldn't be that dense, could he?

Catching on, Nick shot him a murderous look.

Eliot cleared his throat. "Uh . . . Jared? It's us. Eliot. And Nick. From Michigan. We're . . . uh . . . here." Stupidly, he waved.

Jared shaded his eyes, kept a straight face, flipped the phone shut. "Dudes. You're seriously early."

Nick countered, "Nah, we're right on time. Sorry we kind of walked in on you guys."

Shit, Eliot thought: Jared had meant California time.
They weren't expected for three hours. "We're still on East
Coast time," he said by way of apology.

Wrapping the towel around his waist, Jared nodded.
"S'cool. This day has already been full of surprises."

For a guy who'd just been caught with his pants down,
this Jared character was smooth. A childhood rhyme
caught Eliot by surprise—"smooth as the shine on ya'
granny's ride." *Okay, I'm officially an idiot*, Eliot realized.

Jared pointed toward the sliding glass doors that led
into the house. "You guys go on inside. The room upstairs
with the twin beds is yours." He nodded at the girl, who
hadn't bothered to cover up. "By the way, this is—"

"Zoe!" The name popped out of Eliot. "Zoe Wong! I'd
know you anywhere. I mean . . ." He fumbled, feeling
excessively stupid, "Not that I've ever seen your . . .
uh . . . or even thought about you in that way . . . it's not
like that."

Jared swooped in for the save. "Lindsay Pierce. She
used to play Zoe on TV. Her real name is Lindsay."

And those are real too, Eliot caught himself thinking,
and turned tomato red.

Nick thought he'd died and gone to heaven. A tune
looped in his head. *I wish they all could be California
girls. . . .* Maybe they all were! He was too macho to deal
in superstitions, but this felt like a sign. Proof he'd done
the right thing, coming out here for the summer. First

thing they see? An R-rated scene, costarring a real, actual actress.

It didn't take a leap of the imagination for Nick to put himself in Jared's towel. He'd been a fly-guy in high school, a chick-magnet, teacher-charmer, trophy-winning athlete. With his dark good looks and buff bod, he was the guy other guys wished they looked like. In L.A., he'd be golden. This summer was going to rock harder than he'd dared imagine. He just needed Eliot to be there with him, not make them both look like hicks. He flexed a bicep.

Eliot nosed into the room at the end of the hallway. "Do you think he meant this one?"

Nick sighed, ran his fingers through his long, curly black hair, and elbowed his way past Eliot. "Yeah, bro, I'm pretty sure this is the room." On the second floor of the house, they'd passed an open loft area with a view of the living room, a tricked-out master bedroom with its own balcony, and another with a double bed and canopy. Theirs was good-size—twin beds against opposite walls, a couple of dressers, windows that faced the winding street.

Nick upended the bigger of his duffle bags, the one that held his weights, barbells, ropes and elastic pulleys, and a half dozen pairs of new gym shorts and matching bicep-baring tank-shirts. He was just about to shove them in the top two dresser drawers.

"Wait!" Eliot brandished a can of disinfectant like a weapon. "We have to spray and wipe the drawers clean first. Who knows what could be living in them?"

"A colony of rats? Or snakes? Maybe spiders!" Nick teased. "I'd say cockroaches, but I bet they're not allowed in this neighborhood."

"Germs! I meant germs, mold, dust," Eliot argued. "You know how allergic I am. And don't think you're immune either."

"Knock yourself out." Exasperated, Nick flopped on the bed.

Nick and Eliot had been next-door neighbors and best friends forever. They'd braved everything together, from the terror of the first day of kindergarten through cub scouts ("scub scouts," as Nick's sister Georgina used to call it), from confirmations and bar mitzvahs, braces, glasses, and zits; from the "Will I be cool?" fear of freshman year in high school through the triumph, relief, and excitement of graduation.

Didn't matter that they were so different—Nick, dark, hearty, handsome, and an up-for-anything adventurer, while Eliot was pale, shy, gawky, terrified of his shadow. Didn't matter that Eliot was a reader, a thinker, computer savvy, observant, and cautious, while Nick was all about action movies, violent videogames, wildin' out, impulse. Or that Nick was a babe magnet. Eliot? Not so much.

Early on, the two had forged an unbreakable bond, a protective shield.

No way was Nick ever going to suffer the humiliation of failing any classes. Not while Eliot had his back.

And anyone who even thought about bullying Eliot had to go through Nick first. No one was dumb enough to try.

Nick fronted that the upcoming year would change nothing, despite the fact that Eliot's grades and SAT scores had won him admission to Northwestern University in Chicago, while he (even with Eliot's tutoring) would be staying home, "stuck at State," as the Michigan saying went. If you were smart, you went to the University of Michigan in nearby Ann Arbor. If you weren't of that "caliber," a word Nick's father used, you went to Michigan State, in East Lansing. Stubbornly, Nick refused to believe that distance would cause a chink in the armor that was their friendship.

Eliot knew better.

Not that he'd dare say it out loud—'cause that'd be wimpy—but Nick sensed the real reason El had agreed to come with on this trip. Sure, the E-brain was taking classes at UCLA with some science professor. But, dude, he could have done that anywhere. Eliot was here as a last act of solidarity, of support. One final give-in to Nick, who was on a quest—his chance to make it big, to change the course of his future.

Nick had the look—and the bod—to be a model. He was five-eleven, 180 pounds of serious ripped muscle, with dark, hooded eyes—"bedroom eyes," the girls used to say—a straight nose, and pillow-soft lips. He wore his dark curly hair long, behind his ears, just brushing his shoulders, and liked to sport a few days' worth of manly stubble. Gave him a sexy, dangerous vibe.

Nick had done some modeling in catalogues for stores like Meijers and Hudsons, as well as a TV spot for a Chevy dealership. It was time to trade up. The Abercrombie shopping bag, Calvin Klein jeans, posing with some hot babe in magazine spreads. It was all about being in the right place, with a tight butt, at an opportune moment.

He could have come out west alone, he wasn't scared or anything. He just thought it'd be more fun with Eliot along.

Eliot, who was now staring out the bedroom window, declaring, "This house is one mudslide away from death."

Maybe scratch the fun part.

4

Sara: Stranger In Holly-Weird

Sara stood on the fabled corner of Hollywood and Vine, overwhelmed and underfinanced. The oppressive heat, though dry, had turned her shoulder-length, wavy blond hair into sticky, sweaty tendrils. Her loose-fitting T-shirt now clung to her. Embarrassed, she pulled at it self-consciously, and willed herself to stay calm.

Granted, she was—momentarily—lost. But she'd made it this far. She was in the heart of Hollywood, California! A place she'd spent her whole entire life dreaming about. The city that held, Lord willing, the key to her entire future. She should be tingling with excitement, not shaking with fear.

Things just hadn't started out as she'd expected, that's all.

Her dreams, fueled by magazines, movies, and the chitchat of small-town beauty pageants, had not prepared her for this chaotic city, or even this street, choked with traffic, wider than the river that snaked through her rural Texas hometown. And the people walking by—it was like a carnival of faces, tourists with cameras, bikers, hippies, skinheads, freaky folks of all shapes and sizes.

It wasn't like she believed the myth about the streets of Hollywood being paved with gold. But she had expected a town radiating glamour, glitzy stores showing off designer fashions, famous restaurants packed with stars.

Not Big Al's Tattoo Parlor. Or Bondage Babes Leather 'N' Thongs. She shuddered.

No wonder she felt less like Audrey Hepburn in *Breakfast at Tiffany's* and more like Kate Hudson in *Almost Famous*. Setting her suitcase down, she stepped off the curb, shaded her eyes from the oppressive sun, and waved tentatively, hoping a taxi would stop.

"*Mira, mira, chica*—oooh, come closer!" A man with a scruffy beard and bad skin leaned out of his car window, leering at her.

She jumped backward, her heart thumping.

"You need a ride, sexy mama?" He crooked his finger, beckoning her. "We got room for you."

"N . . . no," she managed to squeak, thankful the traffic light had changed, and the impatient car behind honked, forcing him to move on.

No, this was not the Hollywood she'd fantasized about.

Guess that's why they call 'em dreams, she thought ruefully, *and not "real life."* Sara squared her shoulders, gripped her suitcase, and plowed on. She'd taken the shuttle bus from Los Angeles International Airport into Hollywood, thinking: How far could it be from Hollywood to the Hollywood Hills? Thinking it'd be easy enough to walk.

The bus driver had dropped her off at the corner of Hollywood Boulevard and Cahuenga, advising her to grab a cab to complete her journey to the Hollywood Hills. "You can't walk it," he'd told her. "It's too far, honey. And here's a tip: No one walks in Los Angeles."

Cab fare had not figured into her carefully constructed budget, so she skipped lunch. But darn if she could figure out how you "grab a cab." In the town that made movies, hailing a cab didn't work like *in* the movies, where all you had to do was step off the curb and wave into the street. All she'd netted with that gesture was a scary man trying to lure her into his hunk-of-junk car.

She walked west along Hollywood Boulevard. The oppressive desert heat forced her sweat glands into overtime. Now everything was sticking to her, the long flowy skirt, her bra and panties, even her jewelry—a simple cross pendant and her silver purity ring.

Two long blocks later, at the crazy-big intersection of Hollywood Boulevard and Highland Avenue, she found a phone booth. The famed Grauman's Chinese Theatre, with its opulent pagoda roof, was only a few feet away; the brand-new ultramodern Kodak Theatre, home to the Academy Awards, loomed behind her.

She parked her suitcase on the curb and dug into her purse for the phone number of the only person she knew—though hadn't yet met—in Los Angeles.

Her panic accelerated with each one of the four long rings. Finally, a voice that wasn't voicemail: "This is Jared."

A long pause. Then, "Sara who? Do I know you?"

His tone caught her up short. What if the guy from whom she'd rented a room turned out to be unfriendly, or worse, a thief? What if he'd taken her money and there wasn't even a room? She swallowed hard. "Blind faith, that's what you're going on," her boyfriend Donald had said when she'd sent ahead the first month's rent. "And that's just not smart, Sara."

But Donald hadn't wanted her to go, would've said anything to stop her. And a few seconds later, when she explained herself, the voice on the other end of the pay phone softened. "Oh, *that* Sara! Of course!" Jared had told her to wait right there. He'd be by in a jiffy to pick her up. Not that he'd said "jiffy." Her word.

Heaving a sigh of relief, Sara hung up, closed her eyes, and leaned her forehead against the plastic receiver. A verse from a hymn popped into her head. *I once was lost, but now I'm found. . . .*

Yes, faith was a good thing. It would see her through. It would see her live the dream she and her mom had nurtured for so many years. And like her mom often sang, *Dreamin' comes natural, like the first breath of a baby.* . . . It would reward them for the sacrifices they'd made, for the scrimping and scraping by they'd endured for so many years. Pageants had been Sara's ticket to show business, only it'd cost a lot to enter them and make her costumes. Singing and dancing and baton-twirling lessons, it all added up! But she and her mom had persevered. Little Miss Texarcana. Little Miss Darlington County. Little Miss Country Dumplin'; Jr. Miss Bayou. She didn't always win the crown, but she usually made the top three.

Her mom was never disappointed. When she didn't win, Abby Calvin would remind her, "God has bigger plans for you. You've been blessed with talent. You're meant for better things than standing around, showing off some fancy outfit, twirling a baton. My Sara is going to be a star."

It wasn't just their silly pipe dream. Everyone at home agreed, from their friends and neighbors, to the teachers and kids at school, to so many pageant directors, she'd lost count. Becoming an actress was God's plan, her destiny.

By Sara's nineteenth summer, they'd saved enough money for one plane fare to Los Angeles, and one month's rent. The idea was to get a waitress job while calling on agents. You needed an agent to represent you, that's what all the pageant directors had said. Her first appointment was already set up by Ron Zitterman at Pageants, Inc. Sara had packed one suitcase with a few "audition" outfits. A bunch of addresses for other talent agents lay tucked into her most precious possession, her Bible.

Sara's dad believed in her, but his faith seemed to falter the nearer she got to actually leaving. Pop put the kibosh on her staying at "some sleazy rooming home, or cheap motel." He'd watched too many episodes of *CSI* to allow her to live alone.

They'd found the listing on the computer at the library. Her dad had just about grilled Jared Larson, who'd assured Virgil Calvin that the house was in a safe neighborhood, that it'd be like a college dormitory, with other girls Sara's age. Jared had mentioned that his own parents would be checking in.

"Miss . . . miss . . ." Someone was tugging on her skirt, whispering hoarsely.

How long had she been standing there, blocking the pay phone? She spun around.

"Miss . . . please . . . can you help me?" Sara's heart clutched. A child, rail thin, brown, and sweaty, thrust an open palm at her. "Please, for food," she croaked.

Sara stared down, a wave of compassion washing over her. The child's dark hair was a matted and greasy nest, her fingernails dirty, clothes ill-fitting and shabby. And she was just this little bitty thing, couldn't be more than eight years old.

"Where are your parents, sweetie?" She knelt down to

get a better look, found herself staring into big brown puppy-dog eyes, ringed with thick black eyelashes.

The child seemed not to have an answer. "I'm hungry," she finally said. "Could I have some dollars?" Her eyes now fixed on Sara's purse, up on the shelf of the phone booth.

"Of course you can," Sara said without thinking. She stood upright and scanned the street, hoping to see some adult this child belonged to.

Instead she saw the back of a husky teenager in a white tank top and backward baseball cap—peeling down the street with a suitcase. Her suitcase.

"Hey!" She grabbed her purse and gave chase.

But the young thief was fast, and the few seconds it'd taken the child to distract her were costly. Undeterred, Sara sped down the block, yelling for the kid to stop. Back at Texarcana Regional High, she'd run track, been pretty darn good, too. Only she wasn't in her tracksuit and Keds—she was hampered by the long cotton skirt clinging to her damp legs and ladylike sandals. Her calves began to ache, she felt a sharp stab in her groin. Still, she was five-nine and all legs. Sara felt certain she could have overtaken the kid. She would have, if not for the car that'd suddenly swerved onto Cherokee Street and screeched up to the curb. In a flash, the boy—and her suitcase—were inside and speeding off down the street.

More outraged than scared, she panted, waited for her breathing to slow, her heart to stop pounding. When she hobbled back to the phone booth to dial 911, the little beggar girl was gone. No doubt the kid was already in the getaway car.

She'd been set up. Scammed. Mugged.

The sobs didn't come until after she'd reported it to the police, but when they did, she shook violently. She wanted to call her mother, but wouldn't dare. What could Abby Calvin do, from a thousand miles away? Her pop would demand she turn around and come straight home. More than anything, she felt ashamed. She'd been such an easy mark—robbed by a couple of kids!

She'd just finished repeating her story to a policeman—Raimundo Ortega, his badge said—when the gleaming Lexus convertible pulled up. Its driver, a spiffy-looking guy in a bright lime-green polo shirt, crinkled his forehead worriedly. "Are you Sara? Did something happen?"

"You must be Jared. This is so embarrassing. . . ." She offered a rueful smile and told him what'd happened.

He pulled a business card from his wallet. "Officer, I'm Jared Larson. My father is Russell Larson, the head of—"

"Galaxy Artists." Patrolman Ortega, clearly impressed, finished the sentence.

"That's right," Jared said with a smile. "If you could retrieve Miss Calvin's suitcase as soon as possible, we'd be in your debt."

The cop, who'd only a moment ago advised Sara that petty theft was a low priority—discouraged her from thinking she'd ever see her belongings again—practically saluted Jared. The LAPD would get right on it! He would personally call with a status report in a few hours.

"I can't tell you how much we'd appreciate that," Jared responded politely.

What Patrolman Ortega did next could've knocked Sara over with a feather. "I know this is kinda strange . . . circumstances and all," he said haltingly, "but, if you wouldn't mind, sir, there's this, uh, screenplay I've been working on, and y'know how it goes. . . ."

Jared held his hand up. "Say no more. Just send it to my summer house in the Hollywood Hills, and I'd be happy to get it to my father right away—with a special note about how cooperative you've been."

Sara got into Jared's car numbly. What kind of strange place *was* Hollywood? "W-what," she stuttered, "was that all about?"

"Nothing that doesn't happen every day. Mr. Policeman needed extra incentive to find the thief who stole your suitcase."

She thought for a moment. "Incentive? Don't take this the wrong way—I'm grateful for everything—but wasn't it more like bribery?"

"No way. It's just how things work in this town. Quid pro quo."

"Quid pro what?" Sara was even more confused.

"You do something for me, I'll do something for you," Jared explained. "And let me tell you something—a cop with a screenplay to sell? That's just a cliché. Who doesn't have a screenplay to sell? Or a headshot to get to a casting director. A tape or DVD, a dream of fame and . . ." He trailed off, probably realizing he was about to describe Sara.

"So you really will send his script to your father?"

He shrugged. "Let's see how fast he comes up with your suitcase."

Sara was speechless.

"Anyway, at least they didn't get your money," Jared said, changing the subject. "Unless you had a cash-stash in the suitcase?"

Sara shook her head. "Something more valuable."

"Jewelry?" Jared guessed.

"My Bible."

This—*this!*—shocked him. Not that she'd been mugged. Not that he'd just bribed, and probably lied to, the police. He coughed, a poor attempt to cover up a laugh.

Sara wasn't angry. She had good instincts about people—well, if you didn't count that little girl at the phone booth—and she believed, deep down, Jared was a good person. She turned her head, sized him up as he drove. He was a looker, too, if you liked skinny boys with fancy cars who could sweet-talk their way out of any situation. They weren't her ways; she wasn't sure if they were virtuous.

But she felt safe, for the first time all day.

"You hungry?" Jared asked her now.

"No." Her stomach growled, giving her away.

He laughed. "Hang on, we're coming up to In-N-Out Burger. Best burgers in the West."

She brightened.

"With fries and a shake, that's what we'll get you," Jared was a mind reader.

"I'm on a kind of tight budget," she admitted, salivating.

"No worries, it's on me. Your trip got off to a bad start. This is comfort food—you'll feel better, promise."

He pulled up to a fast food place that resembled a glossy country diner. IN-N-OUT BURGER, the sign above it, painted fire-engine red with a blazing yellow arrow, advertised.

While they waited on the ten-car-long line, Jared informed her, "This place is a California legend. People drive sixty miles each way for their famous double-doubles."

"What's a double-double?" Sara's stomach rumbled so loud, she was sure folks in the cars behind them could hear it.

Jared just grinned.

The minute she found out, she became an instant convert. They sat at an outside picnic table for what Sara believed was the tastiest meal she'd ever had. The heat no longer bothered her, nor was she fretting about how her sweaty clothes were clinging to her. She felt sure her suitcase would be returned. Life was all about the burger—or, burgers. A "double-double" turned out to be two juicy cheeseburgers, lettuce, tomatoes, and onions stacked on a big ol' toasted bun.

She was too hungry to be embarrassed about the way she practically Hoovered it, washing it down with a rich chocolate shake. Not until she wiped her face and released a huge sigh of contentment and relief did she realize Jared was staring at her.

"Welcome to Los Angeles," he said with a wink.

Sara was charmed by the orange and blue house. "It's like a little gingerbread cottage, right out of a fairy tale . . . so colorful!"

Jared admitted he'd never quite thought of it like that.

Her appreciation grew when Jared led her into the living room. "This is just so homey!" she exclaimed. "It's like a huntin' lodge, only with guitars on the walls instead of deer heads."

A throaty, staccato laugh rat-tat-tat-tatted from behind her. Sara spun around. The cackling was coming from a pretty freckled girl with long reddish hair. Tucked comfortably in the corner of the sofa, she balanced a thick fashion magazine on her lap and held a glass filled with ice and a clear liquid.

"If you're waiting for her to stop, best sit down and get comfortable," Jared advised.

"Is she laughing . . . at me?" Sara was confused.

"Guitars instead of deer heads! That's . . . priceless!" the girl squealed, slapping the cushion with her free hand.

Jared leaned over and took the drink away from her. "Sara, I'd like you to meet Lindsay. Tragically, she is unable to help herself. She's afflicted with TAS: Tactlessly Annoying Syndrome. Exacerbated by alcohol."

Tears were sliding down Lindsay's scrunched-up face as she continued to hoot. "Hunting lodge!"

Just then the sliding glass door from the far end of the room opened, and someone started toward them. Sara gasped and turned scarlet. 'Cause this boy must have jumped down off one of the billboards on Holly-wood Boulevard. He was dark-eyed, curly-haired, and what a build! He was the hunkiest guy she had ever seen. The most naked, too. But for a teensy black boykini, he wasn't wearing a lick of clothing. She could not stop staring.

Above his swimsuit, his flat stomach formed a V-shape. He was all ripples and muscles, biceps, triceps—what they called six-pack abs. He didn't have any chest hair. And he was dripping wet.

Something went flippity-flop in her tummy. She forced herself to look away.

So it was a moment until she could respond to his greeting. He walked right up to her, held his hand out. A large hand, she noticed, with slim, well-defined fingers. "Hi, I'm Nick," he said in a big, booming voice. "You must be Sara, right? I was just in the Jacuzzi. Welcome to Casa Paradise!"

Her voice wavered. "Thank you. This . . . sure is . . . some house!"

"Too bad it could skid down the mountain in a mudslide, be swallowed up in an earthquake, or flame out in the flick of a wildfire." The worried-sounding voice drifted down from a loft area that overlooked the living room. Sara peered up into the bespeckled, round, friendly face of another boy, this one skinny and frizzy-haired, leaning over the wood railing.

"Hi, I'm Sara—and I sure hope you're not the building inspector or anything?"

Nick interjected, "He's Eliot, our resident worst-case-scenario worry-wart, and all-round pain in the butt."

Eliot. Nick. Jared. She gulped. She'd be living with three boys. Surely something Jared had not told her pop.

"You just get here?" Eliot asked. "I'll help you with your luggage. Is it outside?"

"You could say that," Jared responded dryly. "Very far outside."

A little while later Sara found herself on the low-slung striped sofa, between Nick and Eliot. Jared had settled into an easy chair, Lindsay'd fled to the black leather love seat. What surprised Sara was how friendly everyone seemed, even Lindsay—how comfortable they were with each other. And they'd only started sharing the house the day before.

What truly astounded her? She practically felt like one of

them already. Completely the opposite of how she was only a few hours ago. Settled, secure, among folks all around her age. Everything was gonna work out just fine. Maybe being robbed her first day was God's way of testing her.

"What if you don't get your suitcase back?" Nick was asking her now.

"That'd be okay." Sara pictured the little girl who'd been used as bait. "They're just material things. Those people probably need those clothes more than I do. I've already forgiven them in my heart."

"You have?" Jared was astonished.

"You're taking this really well," Eliot put in, also surprised.

This time Lindsay didn't let loose peals of laughter but leaned forward and asked, "Are you one of those teens for God or something?"

"I'm a Christian, if that's what you mean."

Lindsay smirked and pointed to the bottled water on the coffee table. "Best not drink that. It's Kabbalah water. It'll turn you Jewish."

Eliot chuckled; even Nick couldn't hide his amusement.

Jared frowned. "You're being a jerk, Lindsay."

She turned to Sara. "Only if you drink the whole thing." Lindsay found herself highly amusing, but Sara didn't get it. What'd Lindsay find so funny?

Or why, a bit later, when she innocently said, "So are you fixin' to be an actress too?" Lindsay forgot to laugh. She turned purple.

5

The View from the Jacuzzi

Jared pressed his lower back into the pulsating jet of the Jacuzzi, luxuriating in the powerful water massage. He rested his elbows on the blue marble lip of the hot tub and inhaled the sweet, orangey California air. This was his real life, not sweltering in some pissant classroom in Ojai making up his loser classes. If he cared about medieval times, he'd rent *Gladiator*, not read *Beowulf*. Advanced calculus? And God created accountants . . . why?

Jared didn't need college, he needed to fast-forward to his real life. The one where he eventually ran Galaxy, where he made business deals from the Jacuzzi, swilling Corvoisier.

The bubbly in his glass today was beer. It worked for now; he was buzzed, and flush. The hicks from the sticks, Nick and Eliot, had ponied up their share of the first

month's rent. Sara had paid for June in advance. He'd
even guilted La Lindsay into giving up some coin.

He looked at his ex-girlfriend now, across from him in
the hot tub. The Jacuzzi floozy, barely covered in a tiny
string bikini, was flirting outrageously with red-faced
Eliot, who was probably pitching a tent in his Boba Fett
boxer swim trunks.

Eliot had to know he was out of his league, but better
she cast her spell on this yokel than on Jared. He was
relieved he and Lindsay had gotten interrupted on
Friday—his resistance had been low, her persistence set on
max. He was over her, over the hurt of unread e-mails,
unreturned phone messages, unacknowledged gifts. He
could duck and weave with the best of them, but backward was not a direction Jared ever moved. It was Lindsay who slammed the door on them three years ago, and
Jared had no interest in ever opening it again. He ignored
the twisting in his gut as Lindsay playfully flicked Eliot
with water, regaling the bug-eyed yutz with tales of her
glory days playing Zoe Goldberg-Wong.

She hadn't been quite so playful last night. That
moment Sara had innocently inquired if she, too, was
"fixin'" to be an actress? Priceless! Lindsay'd gone bat-
shit. She'd taken Sara's cluelessness as a deliberate insult.
Poor Sara. She couldn't know it, but she'd cut Lindsay in
the worst possible way—a) for not recognizing her!, and
b) suggesting the two of them were equals, both trying to
break into the business.

Sara's gaffes would not go unavenged. War had been declared at that moment. But was it truly war when only one side was playing?

Lindsay had refused to share a room with Sara.

Sara had graciously agreed to sleep in the loft. It lacked privacy, but she was a total Anne Frank, and believed no one would spy on her!

When Sara realized the land-line phone in the house had been disconnected, Lindsay had refused to lend her a cell phone to call her folks.

Eliot came to the rescue, insisting Sara use his.

Lindsay wouldn't lend her any clothes to sleep in.

Sara had laughed it off. "That's all right, you're such a teeny little thing, they wouldn't fit me anyway."

That'd placated Lindsay for the moment.

Jared held out no hope for a lasting peace.

But at this moment, twenty-four hours later, all good. His third beer was icy cold, goin' down smooth. A soft southerly breeze caressed his shoulders, his hair. Neil Young's classic album *Harvest Moon* wafted through the outdoor speakers. The sun cast an orangey glow as it began its descent beyond the mountains.

Nick was stretched out on a towel next to them, letting what was left of the sun dry him. Pious pageant-girl Sara, in a borrowed pair of shorts from Nick and a T-shirt from Eliot, was sitting on the grass a few feet away, hugging her knees. And, he couldn't help noticing, totally devouring Nick with hungry eyes. Hmm . . . be interesting to see how that played out. No way had Nick not noticed blond Sara's ample curves and sweet demeanor.

Soon the housemates would be in for the ultimate Cali-sunset experience, gloriously dizzying, pinks, corals, and tangerines, a first for his newbies. Feeling generous, Jared picked up his cell phone and lazily ordered dinner from Tuk Tuk Thai for all of them. He was just about to recite his credit card number into the phone when Lindsay kicked, splashing water at him, and shook her head.

Reminding him that his credit cards had been cut off. "Wait, it'll be C.O.D. Twenty minutes? Great."

Lindsay grinned. "Have you thought about how you're going to pay for a pool-cleaning service? Or a lawn boy? It's a mess out here, in case you hadn't noticed."

Sara tilted her head. "You mean, hire someone to clean the pool? And to cut the lawn? Why would y'all do that?"

"Because that's how we roll in these here parts," Lindsay mimicked.

Coloring slightly, Sara said, "But why spend money when we can do it ourselves? There's five of us. If we all pitch in, we'll get it weeded, cleaned up in no time."

"Pitch in?" Lindsay was flabbergasted.

Sara shrugged. "I'll just go ahead and get it started. I cut the grass at home, anyway, and what's a pool if not a bigger bathtub? I can handle that. Besides, I've gotta have something to do between auditions and job hunting."

Lindsay, who'd moseyed over to Jared's side of the

hot tub, was amused. "What kind of job will you be huntin' for? And will there be a shotgun involved?"

"Knock it off, Lindsay." Jared was getting bored with her snarkiness. Lindsay's deep-seated insecurities always came out as jealousy. But of Sara? That made no sense. To make polite conversation, he said to Sara, "You said you had an appointment with an agent. Which one?"

"It's the Wannamaker Star Agency in Hollywood. I'm set up for Thursday at three. I'm hoping to have a waitress job by then so I can pay the fee."

Jared blinked. Was Sara really that naive? "Don't do that! That's a scam. No reputable agent charges up front. An agent only gets 15 percent of what you make for a job he or she has gotten for you."

Sara's face fell. "Really? Mr. Zinterman didn't say that. Guess I should cancel the appointment, then," she said dejectedly.

Just then the sound of a car horn blared. "Tuk Tuk Thai delivery!"

"Be right there," Jared shouted. As he jumped out of the Jacuzzi and made for the front door, he looked up: The sky was already painted with coral, pink, and tangerine stripes. Timing was everything.

A dozen empty Thai food containers and several downed beer and wine bottles later, the vibe was lighter, freer, the buzz shared by all as they ate al fresco, grazing, gazing into the sunset. Yeah, even Lindsay had mellowed.

Eliot, who'd settled next to Sara, sharing her towel,

was trying to cheer her up. "Maybe Jared's father can get you an interview at his agency," he suggested. "That's one of the biggest in town. Very reputable."

Lindsay was about to open her mouth but Jared clapped a hand over it, silently declaring the hot-tub a "no-insult" zone. Then he got an idea.

"That's the suckiest idea I ever heard!" Lindsay exclaimed as soon as her mouth was freed. He hadn't even finished explaining it.

"Chill, Lindsay—and listen. You both need agents, you both need jobs. I need rent from the two of you. And I've got pull at Galaxy. . . ." He was about to say, "What's the downside?" but he knew: Lindsay didn't do "competition" well, perceived or real. Sara was the enemy. Enemies don't share turf.

"What's your plan?" she asked coldly, arms folded.

Sara said nothing. Hope was written all over her face.

Jared flipped open his cell phone. First, he left a voice-mail for Amanda Tucker, one of Galaxy's senior, most respected, and most feared agents. "Hi, Mandy, it's Jared. I've got an amazing opportunity for you. That assistant position you've been looking to fill? Wait'll you hear who I got you! Call me."

Nick, Eliot, and Sara traded glances. They had a lot to learn.

Now Lindsay was grinning big. She got it. Jared was multitasking. Amanda would get an assistant with cachet, a name in this town; Lindsay would net a powerful agent. Once said powerful agent got her an acting role, buh-bye, shitty assistant job! So win-win.

Jared's next call was to Lionel Mays, a junior agent. His tone was assured. "You're gonna be kissing my butt for this one, Li—I'm sending you a fresh new talent. Every agency in town's gonna want her, and you get the first shot at repping her. You can thank me later."

Sara leapt up off the ground as if she'd been launched and threw her arms around Jared, practically burying his face in her bust. "You got me an agent? You could do that with one phone call?" she squealed. "Bless you! Bless you!"

"Down, girl," Lindsay warned, though her tone was mischievous, not malevolent. "Jared set you up with an interview. You'll have to prove yourself."

Nick put in, "But that guy you called—he has to take Sara on, right? You're the boss's son."

Lindsay grinned mischievously. "You gonna give"— she could not resist—"*Pop* a heads-up? Tell him you're sending over a proven superstar, and a chunky wannabe? Besides, isn't there some kind of disconnect between you two?"

"Nothing that would keep me from doing a favor for my friends. I'm golden at Galaxy. As always." He smiled smugly for her benefit.

Sara was beaming. She turned to Nick and Eliot. "Y'all never did say what you're fixin' to do this summer. Did y'all need Jared to make a call on your behalf?"

"I don't think there's anything Jared can do for me. I'm not what you'd call showbiz material," Eliot said, self-consciously toying with his glasses.

"Don't be hard on yourself," Sara scolded. "You can do anything you want, if you put your mind to it."

"Thank you. But both Nick and I are set. He's got an internship and I'll be at UCLA, taking a course taught by the science editor at the *Los Angeles Times.*"

"The *L.A. Times* has a science editor? What for?" Lindsay was puzzled.

"You're spending the summer in school?" Jared was equally bewildered.

Eliot explained. "I'm going for journalism at Northwestern University in the fall, and UCLA offered this great summer course—it covers natural phenomena, weather, earthquakes, that sort of stuff. Who knows, maybe I'll learn something there that can help us—if a brushfire doesn't swallow us up first."

Nick shook his shaggy mane. "Couldn't resist, could ya?"

Jared turned to Nick. "Bro, what kind of gig did you get?"

"Tomorrow I start at the Les Nowicki Modeling Agency."

Sara clapped her hands together. "I just knew you were a model! I knew—"

Eliot broke in, "He's not a model. He got an internship as a photographer's assistant." He shot Nick a look and amended, "It wasn't an easy internship to score. A lot of people applied. But once they saw Nick's portfolio and video, he got the gig."

"E's right," Nick said, "but I'm thinkin' once I get a foot in the door, I got a good shot at a modeling career."

"Definitely!" Sara's face was alight.

Lindsay took a long pull on her beer. Soberly, she said, "You do know, Nicholas, that all male models are gay. You might want to start with another part of your anatomy in the door."

Nick's jaw dropped.

It'd gotten dark out, and Jared hadn't put the outside lights on. So he could only assume that the macho Michigan model-to-be was pale as a ghost.

Jared jumped in to do damage control. "That's a sweeping stereotype, Nick. It's like saying—"

"That all actresses have to sleep their way to the top?" Lindsay stared at Sara.

Sara's jaw joined Nick's on the ground.

Eliot grew uncomfortable. "Ah, c'mon, that's such an old saw, it can't be true anymore."

Her eyes trained on Sara, Lindsay responded, "Some old clichés are still true. Like this one: In this town, to get ahead, you've gotta give some head."

"I'm sure I don't get your meaning." Sara gulped, making it clear she obviously did.

"The casting couch, girlfriend—surely even *you* have heard of that." Then Lindsay made a lewd gesture, licking her lips suggestively.

"Oh!" Sara's eyes grew big, and Jared could guess, her face red.

"Not all actresses sleep their way to the top. Why are you making her nuts?" He pinned his ex-girlfriend with angry eyes.

"Of course not all! Did I say 'all'? I meant the ones trying to break in—you know, the ones from . . . some little town in Texas . . . hoping to snag their first role." Lindsay was positively gleeful.

"I believe that I will make it on my acting talent," Sara said, no longer skittish but composed, "because I have no intention of debasing myself for any reason."

"Well, good luck with that." Lindsay rolled her eyes.

The front door bell rang. Saved! Jared wasn't expecting anyone, but was more than happy to have this conversation interrupted. So was Sara, apparently, who jumped up to answer it. A minute later he heard her squeal with delight.

She came running back around the house, one hand holding her suitcase, the other holding that of Officer Ortega. "Look! They found my suitcase!"

"We put a few of our best guys on it and got it right back. You might want to check that nothing's missing." Officer Ortega smiled proudly.

Jared went to shake the officer's hand, momentarily forgetting about the deal he'd made—until the cop handed him a thick manila envelope.

"You remember," he said haltingly, "that, uh, screenplay I mentioned? Thought you'd want to have a look at it—y'know, send it on to Galaxy."

"Of course! I'll messenger it to my father first thing in the morning. With a note about your speedy recovery of Ms. Calvin's belongings." Jared recited the well-practiced lines.

"You really gonna read that, send it to your old man?" Nick asked when the policeman had gone.

Jared shook his head no. It was Lindsay who grabbed the manila envelope and cavalierly pitched it into the pool, reciting, "I don't think this is right for Pop . . . I mean for Galaxy."

Sara, wearing Nick's shorts and Eliot's T-shirt, dove into the mucky pool to rescue it.

Lindsay was shocked.

Dripping with algae, Sara waded out of the pool clutching the soaked package. "I feel responsible. Would y'all mind if I read it?"

"Knock yourself out," Jared said with a shrug.

Much later, after everyone had gone in, Jared reflected. No one had asked him about his summer plans. He had them, all right. They involved doing exactly what he'd tried to tell his dad he could do: meet people, schmooze, network—bring Galaxy some amazing deal. He'd have to add another chore to the summer: peacekeeping. Refereeing.

More to the point: taking the knife out of Sara's back every time Lindsay plunged it in.

A full-time gig, for which he'd get *bupkis* in return: nothing. His head said, *Oh, Lindsay, what am I going to do with you?* His heart, if he let it, was already on the verge of saying something else entirely.

Is this what it would be—a battle between head and heart, all summer long? Jared hoped not.

6

Workin' for the Weekend

Lindsay Stoops to Scoop

It wasn't the smell that grossed her out. Or even the act itself. It was the way it *looked*. What if someone saw her? What if, worse, someone *recognized* her?

"Isn't that Lindsay Pierce, scooping dog poo? Eeww!" She could practically hear the snide whispers. "So *that's* what became of her!" You couldn't stoop much lower in this town, and yet, one week into her job as Amanda Tucker's personal assistant at Galaxy Artists, *this* is what she'd been reduced to—picking up after Amanda's minia-ture pinscher, George Clooney. Yes, Amanda had named it after a client she'd famously failed to land.

Lindsay flung the doggie bag into the trash. She used to have "people" who did this kind of thing for her—she wasn't supposed to *be* people. Among her other daily duties for her piddly paycheck: filling the min-pin's bowl with bottled Smart water and fetching freshly baked doggie biscuits. For Amanda, she ordered soy lattes, picked up and delivered dry cleaning and laundry, went office-to-cubicle selling Girl Scout cookies for her niece. Twice so far she'd run to the Manolo Blahnik store on Rodeo Drive, switching the gold five-inch-heeled Manolos for the black lizard four-inch-heeled Manolos, then back to the gold again.

Answering phones would've been a promotion.

"Yap! Yap! Yap!" Worse, the pesky little poo-machine on the other end of the snakeskin leash suffered from Irritable Bark Syndrome and a nasty temperament—just like his owner. He growled at little children, nipped anyone who went to pet him, and loveliest of all, tried to mount any dog he could get close to. Which was a joke, since George Clooney weighed all of seven pounds. And yet, the rat-faced runt tried to go all alpha dog, literally, on their asses.

It hadn't surprised her that Amanda kept the tiny terror in her palatial office. At her level, executive vice president of talent, she could have an alligator in there if she wanted. Lindsay hadn't thought she'd have to deal with it. Her first day, Amanda barked instructions: "Put his poo in a plastic bag. If you're not near a garbage disposal, put the package in your pocket until you find one—he gets embarrassed if you're holding it out where other people can see."

And there was this little gem: "He won't answer unless you call him by his full name."

"George Clooney, no!" she scolded him as he tried to mount a passing pit bull bearing a dangerous resemblance to its scary owner. She jerked the little rat-beast away and continued their drudge through Griffith Park. The park was huge, and way famous. It had a gazillion trails for hiking, biking, and horseback riding, places to picnic and play golf. Plus it was home to the Los Angeles Zoo and the famous Observatory, at which a very special episode of *All for Wong* had been taped. Sweet memories for Lindsay—but, hello, it was also really out of the way, high in the hills and nowhere near Galaxy's offices. On the upside, there was virtually no chance of running into anyone important. Everyone who was anyone took their Princesses and Baileys to the Hollywood Dog Park. The downside? Same thing.

In spite of her lowly chores, she was beyond grateful to have this job. Her thank-you to Jared was the air-kiss she'd blown at Rusty Larson, casually mentioning her visit to Jared at the Ojai Community College campus.

Amanda, her boss, was just under Rusty on the power chain, a classic Hollywood agent. Severely striking, short-tempered, high-strung, and prone to screaming hissy fits, she strode through the office in her Prada suits and towering heels, berating lowly junior agents and assistants, pitching pencils, notepads, and coffee cups at anyone she felt like—then doing a complete one-eighty, kissing up to casting directors, producers, directors, and studio execs.

Lindsay lapped it up, loved every second spent at

Galaxy's gleaming, curved, all-glass structure in the heart of Beverly Hills. She already felt back in the game. If she wasn't playing the part she wanted, at least she was at the epicenter of the action. Inside every office, inside every cubicle, even, the hottest scripts were being read, power meetings set up, and best of all, deals were being made. Her big break could not be far away. The assistants networked incessantly, and any juicy tidbit, gossipy or gig-worthy, got transmitted instantly.

This, as opposed to Sara's craptastic junior gofer job at *Caught in the Act*, some *ET*-wannabe TV show. At least she, Lindsay, was picking up the dog shit of a power player in the biz; Sara was probably toiling for some camera grip. And that joke of an agent Jared procured for her? Maybe he could get her an audition for third banana in a commercial. Airing on cable.

Lindsay's agent, Amanda Tucker, represented practically all of Hollywood's A-list actors. It wouldn't be long before her days of running, fetching, pooperscooping, copying, mailing, and filing were over. Besides, she had all day to eavesdrop and gossip.

What she'd scoped out so far? The gloss behind the gleaming glass structure was fading. Galaxy needed a hit. It needed a big new star, and a starring vehicle—i.e., a blockbuster movie to which it could attach its clients, producers, director, screenwriters: The Package.

Her cell phone rang. Amanda, her most frequent caller, launched into a list: "On your way back, stop at

Gelson's and pick up an order of edamame, two brown rice California rolls, and a half-caf, skim-milk, fat-free cappuccino." Another of Lindsay's chores was to remember which fad diet Amanda favored each day. "And tell them not to skimp on the wasabi—I'm famished!"

Lindsay flipped her phone shut and fished inside her purse for a pen and paper to write down Amanda's list while she still remembered it—she wasn't authorized to have a BlackBerry yet. "Sit, George Clooney!" she ordered the dog, who for once obeyed. She loosened her grip on the leash.

Bad move.

As soon as Devil Dog felt the leash go slack, he sprang into action—bolted up and away. The leash slipped right off her wrist.

Shit! Lindsay took after him, calling out his name, to the delight and bemusement of the park-goers. She dashed up a trail, around a tree, looking everywhere. Finally, Lindsay saw his tail wagging. "George Clooney! Stop!" she yelled—and promptly tripped, right into the azalea plants.

She cursed, banging the ground with her fists. She'd lost the damn dog, and with it, her job, her future, her hopes. She was doomed. She closed her eyes, lay on the ground, and thought about weeping dramatically.

"I think I have something that belongs to you." A voice—male, strong, assured—floated down from above.

Accentuated by a confirming "Yap, yap, yap!"

Lindsay opened one eye. It was level with the scuffed toe of lace-up Timberlands. Granola-guy, was her first thought.

"Miss? Are you okay? I've got your dog . . ."

She opened both eyes, allowed them to travel upward—the boot was tucked under rumpled jeans. A black Napster T-shirt came next. She was about to get to the face, only it got to her first. Scruffy cheek stubble, medium brown eyes, long dark hair. So not her type.

In bending to help her up, he dropped what'd been tucked under his arm.

She instantly recognized it as a movie screenplay.

He became her type in a nanosecond.

Lindsay poured on the grateful. "Thank you so, *so* much. I'd have died if I lost poor . . . George Clooney. He means everything to me. And he's so tiny. . . ." She trailed off, allowing actor-dude (for of course that's what he was) to lead her to a bench, where she made a great show of affection toward an obviously wary George Clooney, who growled and tried to bite her.

"So, I'm Lindsay Pierce, and you're—?"

"Mark Oliver," he replied genially.

"Are you an actor?" She nodded at the script, tucking her hair behind her ears coquettishly.

"Isn't everyone in this town?" Mark had obviously never watched *All for Wong*.

No matter. It was info, not a new fan, she was after.

What Lindsay learned: Mark, a relative newcomer

who'd been in several failed TV pilots, was represented by the Endeavor Agency, one of Galaxy's rivals. The script he was reading was for an action comedy called *Heirheads: The Movie.*

The plot involved three splashy young heiresses who use their vast resources to solve mysteries. It was Paris Hilton-as-Nancy Drew-meets-James Bond, Charlie's Angels without Charlie. As Mark described the characters, Lindsay easily saw herself as the most glam heiress, Remy St. Martin.

Mark was reading for the part of Remy's wealthy boyfriend. He didn't think the main girls were cast yet, but had heard rumors that Reese Witherspoon, Nicole Richie, and Ashanti were going to screen-test. Lindsay wiped away the drool before he could see.

She had found her first gig.

Nick Stands In

"Unzip your pants, Nicky, another inch down. We're going for more tease in this shot." The middle-aged photographer, Les Nowicki, looked up from behind the camera lens. His tan lines deepened when he frowned. "You have to learn to relax, to make love to the camera. Let's try it again."

Nick *was* trying. But relax? Not happening. Especially when a bunch of weirdos, guys, chicks, and others of indeterminate gender were staring at him, sizing him up—and down. He took a deep breath and eased his pants' zipper down another notch. An assistant turned a giant fan up, blowing his unbuttoned shirt wide open.

"That's better, that's *good!*" Les praised him through the lens while snapping his fingers. "He needs more shine!" Keith, one of Les's assistants, dashed over to rub his chest with oil. Nick tensed.

He was well into his first week at the modeling agency. The gig was not what he thought it would be. As a photographer's assistant, Nick figured he'd be hauling equipment, setting up lighting, moving props, learning by watching, getting instruction.

His goal was to get his own professional photos done, then sign with one of the major modeling agencies in town. By the end of the summer, he'd have a kick-ass portfolio—and the bucks would roll on in. Bonus? Meet 'n' greet some hot model-babes.

He hadn't bargained for spending his days, and some nights, striking seminude poses for the camera, being slathered with oils, gelled, glossed, made up, and dressed down.

Nick's primary function was being a stand-in. Before the actual models arrived for the shoot, he was the guy who posed while Les's freak-team of assistants worked on the lighting, backgrounds, wardrobe, and often, on him. There was a gal who sprayed fake-bake tans and body glitter on the models, a guy whose sole job was eyebrow plucking, a manicurist, a pedicurist, and even someone who waxed the male models. Breast carpets, considered manly by many, were verboten at the studio. It was all about slick and shiny, and especially ripped.

For hours on end Nick stood, sat, reclined, lay on his belly, squatted, leaned against the wall, the window, the bed, so the team could judge what would work and what wouldn't. Digital pictures were taken, studied by Les and his team, then retaken, with adjustments in lighting, props, and his pose. By the time the actual models arrived, the set would be positioned and the shoots good to go, swiftly and smoothly.

The cool part was when he got to wear samples of designer duds—tight D&G T-shirts, Boss shades, Zegna suits. The uncool part was that most of what he wore, he wore . . . open. Suggestively so.

Nick had been too excited when he learned he'd gotten the internship to bother checking it out, to do what Eliot called "due diligence." So he came west without the slightest inkling of what kind of modeling photo studio Les Nowicki ran. He knew now.

Les specialized in shooting models for calendars, posters, and greeting cards. Hallmark was probably not a big customer. A glance at the framed portraits lining the studio's brick walls told the tale: These models, mostly male, weren't exactly in family-friendly poses.

"Sophisticated" was the word used in his interview.

"Soft-core" was his opinion now.

"Turn your face toward the window, Nicky, rest your

left hand on your thigh," Les instructed him. "Excellent!"
He snapped away.

Nick stared outside. The studio was located on the
fourth floor of a funky building on Santa Monica Boulevard in West Hollywood, or WeHo, as Les's helpers
referred to the neighborhood.

"Boys-town," Lindsay had flatly declared.

Whatever. From his point of view, it was a bustling,
vibrant, glitzy, showbizzy part of town. Nick gaped at the
towering billboards up and down the boulevard, touting
the latest movies, biggest CDs, and slickest fashions
going. He could easily picture himself on each and every
one, especially the Calvin Klein underwear ads, Bulgari
Fragrance for Men portraits, Armani shades, Tommy Hil-
figer stripes, Izod polos, and Nautica stars. Ads he'd seen
in magazines were super-sized in Hollywood.

"Turn the other way now. I want a profile, with your
right hand on the thigh. Higher, Nicky," Les instructed,
motioning with his hand while his eye stayed trained on
the lens. "Yes, that's it!" he crowed, clicking away. "Nicky,
you're a natural!"

The compliment made him feel queasy.

"Break time, ladies," called Alonzo, another of Les's
assistants. Nick quickly buttoned up his shirt and
rezipped his trou.

"Hey, Nicky," Keith called out. "A few of us are heading
to Hamburger Mary's for a bite and a brew. Come with?"

Nick declined—politely, he hoped.

"Oh, the summer boy is too shy to go out with us," Alonzo teased, as a few others laughed. "Still hasn't warmed up, but he will."

Don't hold your breath, Nick wanted to say, but tilted his head in a friendly gesture, and headed out the door. He hated being referred to as "the summer boy." It felt condescending.

Hiding under his army green VH-1 baseball cap, he walked the several blocks to Pink's, "the most famous hot dog shack in Hollywood," according to Jared. Hungrier than usual, he ordered two man-size chilidogs and a jalapeno dog, and took his unhealthy stash to an empty table on the patio.

A leggy blonde walked by, arm in arm with a guy in a blue and maize Wolverines T-shirt, the University of Michigan football team. A wave of homesickness crashed over him. He checked his watch. It was just after 5 p.m. back home. If he'd stayed there, he'd have been finished with his shift at his dad's construction site, heading to the bar, wolfing down a brewski, flirting with the babes. He'd have been . . . home.

He flipped open his cell, about to call Eliot. Weird El, who was only here to humor Nick, was the one in pig heaven. Spending each day in a stuffy classroom in front of the computer with a bunch of other catastrophe geeks. And then coming home to feast his bug eyes on two outta-his-league babes, an actress and a virgin. Nick had just punched in Eliot's number when a tray landed on his table. He looked up—into the amazing eyes, dazzling smiles, and perky boobs of a pair of L.A. hotties.

"Is it okay if we sit here?" asked the darker-haired one.

"Go for it."

The redhead piped up, "We don't mean to pry, but you look so familiar. Are you an actor?"

"Or a model?" the other one ventured.

Nick folded the phone, and smiled a real smile for the first time that day.

Sara Gets Caught in the Act

"Sara, can you escort Cameron Diaz from her dressing room to Hair and Makeup? They're waiting for her there. And then we need you to help pre-interview Orlando Bloom—he's in dressing room three." Wes Czeny, the assistant director of *Caught in the Act*, waved a script as he passed her in the hallway of KABC studios.

"Sure thing," Sara answered brightly. "I'm on it."

A big man with bushy gray eyebrows, a bulbous nose, and the friendliest face in Hollywood, is how Sara described her new boss. Her first day, a couple of people had warned her off him. "He has an evil temper." So far, Sara hadn't seen that side of him.

"He's a teddy bear," she gushed to her roommates.

"Wait till he wants to cuddle with *you*,"Lindsay said with a smirk.

Sara had learned to let Lindsay's snide comments

slide—she was too busy to fret over them anyway. Her job took up practically all her time. *Caught in the Act* was a new show, hoping to join the ranks of such popular entertainment half-hours as *Access Hollywood*, *Extra*, and *ET*.

As a start-up, the show demanded lots of overtime. She'd been there only two weeks, and already some days Sara worked near ten hours. She did so happily, would've worked through the night if needed. It was all so new and exciting! She was getting to see everything up close, big stars and their "handlers"—her first showbiz word she hadn't learned from Lindsay and Jared!—seeing how the writers came up with ideas, watching the directors, and figuring out what all the cameras and boom microphones were for. Every single person on the set impressed her, especially the hosts of the show, John St. Holland and Susie Smiley. They were so friendly, so smooth!

"The bland, the blond, the botoxed," she'd heard one of the crew snipe about the pair. John had that kind of stony square face like it was chiseled out of marble, and Sally had blindingly white teeth, and not a winkle on her. But Sara was pretty sure viewers loved them.

She knocked on the door of dressing room one, and was soon looking into the swimming-pool-blue eyes of Cameron Diaz, who'd been relaxing on the couch, a fat fashion magazine in her lap.

"Ms. Diaz, they're ready for you in makeup whenever you are."

Cameron slipped into a pair of high-heeled slingbacks and stood up, signaling she was good to go.

The star was tall, really slim, and like so many people in Los Angeles, very friendly. To Sara's comment that she hardly needed a lick of makeup, the star insisted that all girls need all the help they can get.

Sara had to pinch herself. One of the world's biggest movie stars was talking to her . . . just like any other girl-friend. Wait'll Momma hears!

It wasn't just Ms. Diaz who'd been gracious and normal. So far, Sara had met Keira Knightley, Alicia Keys, Charlie Sheen, Ty Pennington, and several of the cast-offs from *Survivor*. A few arrived with big entourages—usually it was the hangers-on who ordered her around—but it was her job to get them lunch or whatever they wanted, to make sure they were comfortable. Some came with long lists of requirements, topics they would not discuss on camera, and at least one stormed off the set after agreeing to an interview. But mostly, she found, the big-ger the star, the nicer and more gracious they were.

The notion cheered her. When she got to be a star, she wouldn't have to pretend to be a diva, or anything like that. She could still be nice, virtuous, down-home. And she'd get there on her God-given talent, not because she'd compromised even one single value. She'd show Lindsay!

Everything that'd happened so far was due to divine providence. Jared had snared her an agent, Lionel—who she adored!—and Lionel happened to be friends with Candy Dew, the producer of the show, who mentioned they were hiring assistants. The phrase "It's not what you know, it's who you know" was turning out to be true in this world.

The point of *Caught in the Act*, she'd been told, was to present a different side of celebrities, to get them to confess their secrets—silly, sinful, salacious, or sweet; as long as it was personal, it'd do.

Candy had put it this way: "The only reason anyone comes on the show is because they have something to prove, or promote. It's our job to let them promote their latest movie, album, TV show, perfume, or whatever, prove they're not sick, or gay, or married, or too old, or crazy, and get them to spill something juicy to us. It's pretty simple, actually."

Her job? Do whatever was required, from whoever asked.

Listening to stars promote their movies got her thinking about the screenplay written by Officer Ortega. Sara had rescued it from the filthy pool because it was the right thing to do. She'd only read a few pages, but it seemed interesting. It was about this rookie cop and a runaway.

Now she picked up today's *Caught in the Act* script from Wes's assistant and made her way to dressing room three. Orlando Bloom, thin, angular, with a mustache and soul patch, was on the phone. Waiting at the door until he motioned for her to come in, she caught herself thinking, *He's not nearly as good-looking as Nick.*

When he got off the phone, he asked what she needed. That accent! It just about knocked her out.

"Would you mind if we went over the questions that Sally would like to ask during your interview?"

For the next half hour, over bottled water and fruit, they did. She found out he did not want to talk about any of his rumored romances, but he'd be happy to comment on his latest movies. And she found out, quite accidentally, that he had the funniest story to tell about his first dinner in an upscale Asian restaurant, where he mistook the heated cloth napkins for shrimp toast—and tried to eat them!

Darn if she didn't laugh as hard as anybody during the taping, as Orlando described the looks on the waiters' faces as he bit into the steaming fabric. Wes came over and put his arm around her. "Great job, Sara," he said. "You've got quite a knack for getting people to open up to you. Maybe you should consider that as a career option."

"I'm determined to try my hand at acting. That's why I'm here," she reminded him.

He snapped his fingers. "Damn! I forgot to tell you. Marla said your agent called—you should call him back. And, Sara—get a cell phone, okay?"

As soon as she could, she returned Lionel's call. And screamed so loud, the whole crew probably heard her. Sara had her first audition a week from tomorrow.

When she stopped screaming, Lionel said, "It's just a peanut butter commercial, don't get excited."

Don't get excited? How could she not? Sara practically skipped along Hollywood Boulevard that evening, thanking the Lord for her good fortune.

She was in that generous frame of mind when, passing Big Al's Bondage Boutique, she noticed a teenage girl squatting on the sidewalk, coffee cup in her hand. Sara flashed back to her first day in Hollywood. This kid was only a few years older than the child who'd scammed her—a child who was probably rotting in some juvie facility by now.

Sara strode over, opened her purse, and knelt down beside the girl. "What's your name?"

7

Jared's Spider Club Web

"'Cel-e-*brate* good times, oh, yeah'!" Lindsay, in no way a singer, belted the song at the top of her lungs. She bopped to her own beat in the passenger seat of Jared's convertible. She wasn't even drunk yet (he didn't think), yet full-on uninhibited—loud and off-key. Wasn't there a law against felonious assault of iconic bar mitzvah songs?

"'We're gonna celebrate and have a good *time*'!" She hollered out the lyrics. And had he mentioned, badly?

"Linz, take it down a thousand," he shouted.

She ducked into the oversize lavender Hermes bag at her feet—*Note to self: how'd she afford that?*—extracted a bottle of Patron tequila, and took a swig.

"Oh, no you don't." He shook a finger at her. "Put that away."

"Don't be a buzzkill, Jared," she bellowed. "'Ev'ry-*one*

a-round the world, *c'mon*'!" She danced in her seat, waving the bottle in the air.

"We're gonna get pulled over before we even get to the club!"

"When'd you turn into such a wuss? I'm precelebrating. I got my first audition next week—whoo-hoo! And besides, it's not against the law if the passenger is drinking."

"What state have you been in, besides oblivion? It's illegal to have an open bottle of alcohol in the car."

Playfully, she leaned over and licked his earlobe. "Oh, but you have a way with policemen-hyphenates. Patrolman-slash-screenwriter, officer-slash-actor-producer, cop-slash-model. Really, Jared, what're the odds you'd be stopped by another one of them?"

He had to laugh. She was so, so, so cute. And so upbeat and so damn . . . hot! Sexier than ever, stylin' to the max, wearing a shoulder-baring halter top, sprayed-on miniskirt, and slouchy high-heeled suede boots. With that pricey Hermès Birkin bag over her shoulder, the ex-girlfriend was workin' it.

He slammed on the mental brakes. He was not—repeat NOT—falling for her. And whatever playful flirting she was doing? Meant nothing. She hadn't, after all, tried seducing him again since that first day, several weeks ago. They were friends, they were cool, and tonight Lindsay was reconnecting with his—their—friends. It'd be her first night of serious clubbing since returning to Los Angeles. They were headed for the exceedingly exclusive

Spider Club at the Avalon Hollywood. Jared's posse would be there, along with a petting zoo of A-list celebrities, everyone from Ashlee to Paris.

Lindsay Pierce would blow in there and blow everyone away. She suspected it; he knew it.

Jared had been out clubbing nearly every night since the summer began. Booze and booty weren't the only reasons. This season, he had an agenda. Before Labor Day, he would make one major deal for Galaxy, his dad's agency. Using his connections, charisma, and charm, he would suss out the hot new screenplay being whispering about; which young A-list actor wanted to switch agencies; find up-and-coming new directors. In a business where information is currency, Jared would strike it rich. He would prove to his father that he was worthy. The clubs were where the connections were, where the buzz began, where the showbiz action really was. For Jared, the club scene was the motherland.

Lindsay, the distracting passenger riding shotgun, also had something to prove to the showbiz world: She was on the comeback trail.

Lindsay had repeated the story to anyone who'd listen, how she'd tipped her boss Amanda off to *Heirheads: The Movie*. Then how the high-powered agent had coaxed the screenwriter into e-mailing her a copy of the script, at the same time brow-beating her staff for not knowing about it.

Lindsay excelled at suck-up. To her boss, she modestly cooed, "If not for George Clooney, that itsy-bitsy sweetie poochie-pie, we'd never have known about *Heirheads.*"

To her agent, she was quid-pro-quo girl. She'd found it, she deserved a chance to audition. "The part of Remy St. Martin, it was written for me."

Lindsay's audition was a done deal.

Jared had tried to curb Lindsay's enthusiasm. "Amanda will totally send other actresses to audition for this. It's not you exclusively."

"They can dig up Katharine-freakin'-Hepburn and send her, for all I care." Lindsay flipped her copper tresses defiantly. "This role has my name on it."

Woe to the dunderhead who tried to yank her off the grandiosity pedestal. Jared knew when to give up.

"Besides, this script is so good, it can be the one that saves Galaxy," she'd asserted proudly.

"What about my family's firm needing saving?" That'd been a scary newsflash to him.

She repeated the office scuttlebutt: Galaxy was losing out to the biggies—CAA, ICM, William Morris, Endeavor. Galaxy had not nailed a blockbuster deal in weeks.

That'd freaked him out. In a biz fueled by "What have you done for me tomorrow?" if Lindsay was right, the situation sucked. If Galaxy looked weak, they'd soon be hemorrhaging A-list clients. His dad needed him more than ever. Rusty Larson just didn't know it yet.

A perp line-up of bare boobs, of all sizes 'n' shapes, met them at the door—the nightly brigade of girls holding their tops up, hoping to impress the bouncers at the velvet ropes of the Spider Club.

Lindsay was scandalized. "Are they auditioning for 'America's Next Top Tit-Model'?"

Jared laughed. "Things have . . . evolved . . . since you've been gone."

"You call degrading themselves evolution? Give me a break. What ever happened to the good old reliable payoff? Or the haughty 'I'm on the list' line. Or just sneaking in . . . ?"

"Like *you* ever had to! You had an all-access pass to every club in town," he reminded her as the burly bouncer, recognizing Jared, lifted the ropes and waved them in. "You may find that decadence has trumped cleverness."

"Self-degradation? Bad. Decadence? Just the way I like it," Lindsay quipped, slipping her arm around his waist.

It felt like old times.

On the trendy carousel of clubs in L.A.—Hyde, Les Deux, Mood, Rokbar, and the Tropicana came to mind— the Spider Club was the Friday night scene to make. Officially, Spider was the VIP room at the Hollywood Avalon rave hall. Realistically, only the seriously elite ever got in. Other clubs had theme nights, Spider's theme was "You know what? Don't even bother."

Inside Spider, the def-est DJs ruled. Tabletops were the preferred dance floor for sexy girls. The club was anything you wanted it to be, a rowdy drink-and-dance-fest or a discreet canoodle cradle. The red, pink, and orange

Moroccan love-den booths inspired make-out sessions *and* make-deal sessions.

Everyone was looking to score.

"Yo, Ja-*red*! Over here!" First voice he heard over the thumping beat belonged to Tripp Taylor, trust-fund son of a famous producer. The Tripster was decked out tonight in an up-collar D&G shirt and wide-brim fedora dipping over one eye, a look that was too K-Fed for Jared. He had one arm draped around slinky Caitlin Cassidy, daughter of a cosmetics empress, the other on the thigh of Ava Golightly, resident anemic-bulimic of their crowd.

"Make some room, peeps," the already inebriated Tripp ordered. "Our man with the plan has arrived. And, looky-loo, he has not come solo!"

Stacked cushy red-leather cylinders formed the back-rest of the booths, each side roomy enough to seat three or four depending on the coziness quotient, which usually went up as the night wore on.

Facing this tony trio was Julie Baumgold (or, as Jared secretly thought of her, Julie BBB—Beautiful But Bony), Austin Tayshuss, and MK Erksome. This sextet was Jared's core crowd.

Julie B. was the first to realize whom Jared had brought. She clamped one bejeweled hand over her glossed lips. "Lindsay?! Oh, my God, *Lindsay*! You look amazing!!"

Ava came in second. "When'd you get here? You look fabulous!"

Tripp extended his hand. "Jared said you were back, but he failed to mention the foxy-factor! What's in the water back in Indiana?"

"Iowa," Jared corrected him, unsure why he was annoyed.

"I knew it was one of those *I* states." Tripp clasped Lindsay's hand.

Lindsay lapped up the attention, "Thanks, you guys— it's great to be back. What're ya drinking?"

Austin, son of a socialite and an action star, rose. "Squeeze in here, Linz, we'll make room."

Jared snapped his fingers. A waiter materialized. "We need a couple chairs." Like he'd let Lindsay sit between obnoxious Austin and lecherous MK.

Once they were settled at the end of the booth, Jared was happy. Lindsay, Julie, Caitlin, and Ava traded fruity martinis and girl-talk—shopping, designers, and who-was-screwing-who gossip. Lindsay fit in as if she'd never missed a beat.

The guys, meanwhile, sucked down shots of Patron and debated cars, clubs, clothing, the Bruins, the Trojans, and who had seats nearer to Nicholson and Spike Lee for the Lakers this year. The winner should have been Jared: Galaxy owned an entire row. But since Austin's dad had a hit movie, and MK's banker-mom had just struck foreign gold, it was likely he'd be grubbing off them.

"How's summer school treatin' ya?" MK asked. "Making up those suck-grades?"

"I'm multitasking," Jared replied, "making up the grades and making deals for my dad's agency."

Hearing him lie so smoothly, Lindsay pursed her lips and playfully pinched his cheek.

Jared was about to kick her, but just then, Julie got their attention. "Guys, look who's on the dance floor! She never comes here. Must be celebrating something."

Eight heads turned. Natalie Portman and a few girl-friends were dancing to the Black Eyed Peas' "My Humps."

"She's *so* had work done," catty Caitlin sniffed. "Check the forehead."

Ava wasn't sure. "No wrinkles, but isn't she, like, twenty-two?"

"Your point?" Caitlin was clueless.

Jared chuckled. Ya gotta love superficial, especially here in Hollywood, where it goes deep.

Lindsay, quaffing apple martinis, sparkled, burbling about her coup, unearthing this amazing script *and* going for her audition next week.

"You rock, girl!" Austin cheered her on.

"That's our Linz, right back in the game. You are so my hero." Tripp waved his arms worshipfully. Bro was drunker than usual. That's what ticked Jared, not the fact that a girl Tripp hadn't mentioned once in three years was suddenly "our" Lindsay. He ordered another Patron.

Julie, suffering attention deficit disorder *and* acute affluenza, was over the actress on the dance floor and on to the Birkin bag on the floor by Lindsay's feet. She gushed, "I am so all about that Hermes! That's the ostrich leather in African violet. It's, like, seven thousand dollars, but the waiting list is impenetrable. How'd *you* get it?"

"I actually got it for free, off my agent," Lindsay said brightly, ignoring the implication.

"Amanda Tucker just *gave* you a seven-thousand-dollar bag?" Caitlin said suspiciously. "No way."

Ava arched a designer-plucked eyebrow.

"Amanda used it as a dog carrier," Lindsay breezily enlightened them. "Yesterday, the fart-faced runt took a dump in it. She was gonna throw it out. Instead, I had it cleaned." She hoisted the bag onto the table and unclasped it. "Smell anything?"

The group burst out laughing, Lindsay the loudest. Jared hugged her impulsively. Only later would he figure out how she'd "had it cleaned." She'd talked Sara into doing it.

More celebs, starlets, rappers, hip-hoppers, heiresses, and scions arrived. Lindsay kept an eye on the door, making sure everyone who used to know her saw that she was back. And in fine form!

She was flirting when Jared got up to let Austin and Ava get by—they were going to table-hop, glad-hand everyone they knew—and a stab of dread shot through him. What the hell was Adam Koenig, the kid he was paying to do his school assignments and take his tests, doing here? He was a nobody! The nobody who, if he came over to their table, could blow his cover to all his friends who believed he spent his days in summer school.

Jared stalked over to him. Best nip this little glitch in the bud, keep his secret tucked safely away.

Austin and Ava were in the deejay booth by the time he got back to their table, the dance floor was jammed, the music crankin'. A couple of semiclad women had already begun high-stepping on the tables as the dance version of Christina Aguilera's "So Emotional" came on.

Lindsay, totally tipsy by that time, massaged the back of Jared's head with her fingertips, bleating her rendition of the song into his ear. "'You are so se-*duce*-able, baby.'"

Luckily, the decibel level had shot up to deafening, so no one else heard. Jared, a little sloshed and a lot relieved that he'd taken care of his problem—Adam and friends were gone—gazed into her smoked-glass eyes and touched her soft dusty-pink pillow lips. She licked his finger and giggled. "'Yes, just *so* se-*duce*-able, baby . . .'"

"Linz!" Julie bopped up on the booth cushion and hoisted her skinny bod onto the thick glass table-top. "Come dance with us."

Caitlin followed, and soon the two of them were shimmying to Rod Stewart's "Hot Legs." Lindsay was into it. Her skirt, Jared couldn't help noticing as he helped her up, was awfully short.

As if magnetized, their table was instantly surrounded by a dozen guys. "Shake ya tailfeathers," someone yelled out, clapping as the music morphed seamlessly into tunes by Mariah Carey, Akon, Kanye West.

"Go, ladies! Go, ladies!" MK stuck two fingers in his mouth and whistled.

Outkast's "Hey, Ya" came on, and a girl atop a table across from them shouted, "Hey y'all—what about us? Can we get some love?" She and her girlfriend, in matching booty-shorts and sky-high Jimmy Choos, bumped hips together as the room egged them on and the song encouraged. *Shake it, shake it, shake it like a Polaroid picture, shake it, shake it!* And to the guys' delight, the dancers did just that.

"Oh, yeah?" Caitlin crowed. "Watch this!" She, Julie, and Lindsay did a highly suggestive bump and grind.

"Chick dance smackdown!" someone yelled.

From the far side of the room, another trio wanted in on the action. The group on the dance floor didn't want to be left out. For the next frenzied half hour, Spider Club became an elite rave scene with the whole crowd sweatin', singing, doing shots, and mostly dirty dancing at the urging of dance club favorites like Gwen Stefani. *Go, Hollaback girrlll! Go, Hollaback girrlll!*

Lindsay was having a blast. Her rat-ta-tat-tat howl pierced the room.

God, Jared had missed her.

Out of nowhere, a lace thong flew through the air. He grabbed it. Linz—? But no, it belonged to Julie, now crooking her finger in a come-to-me motion.

Never gonna happen, he thought, pitching the panties to Austin, who'd come back to support his "team."

Caitlin had ripped off her bra and tossed it into the air. MK caught it and hung it on his ear, like a doofus. Lindsay wasn't wearing a bra. Jared hoped she wasn't drunk enough to—

"Your ex-girlfriend is smokin'!" raved Tripp. "Just how ex is she?"

"What do you mean?"

"I mean," Tripp leaned in, "can I have a go?"

"No!" Jared exploded.

Tripp held his palms up. "Whoa, sorry, bro, no need to get your boxers in a knot. I thought you two were over—"

"We are!" Jared shouted over the music, "But . . . she's . . . plastered! I don't want her taken advantage of, that's all."

"Help me up, you guys!" It was Ava, a little late to the dance party, now wanting in on the tabletop action.

If he hadn't been so pissed at his friend, Jared might've thought twice about the wisdom of four girls on one glass table. Ava, it turned out, didn't "go lightly" at all.

A half second later, she was up.

The table? Not so much.

A loud crack blasted through the room, accompanied by panicked screams. The table split in half, as if someone had karate-chopped it down the middle. Shrieking, the four girls slid to the center, crashing into one another. Julie's heel hit the halved glass first and hardest, sending shards flying in all directions. Her left leg folded under her and she grabbed at the air, trying to stop plummeting. But Caitlin had already fallen on top of her, pushing her down further. Ava grabbed at Lindsay's hair, causing Linz to holler even louder and topple right into the Julie-Caitlin tangle.

Amidst the flying legs, arms, and butts were martini glasses, since the girls had been toasting themselves while dancing. Splinters of colored glass sprayed the room, nicking them even as Jared, Tripp, Austin, and MK rushed to extract the girls without embedding any glass into their skin.

The Spider waitstaff rushed over. They got Ava off first, then Lindsay, Caitlin, and finally Julie, who was sobbing hysterically. "My leg! I broke my leg! Get an ambulance!" Between sobs she managed to insist she'd only go to Cedars-Sinai, not St. John's.

Caitlin and Ava, suffering cuts and bruises, would accompany Julie in the ambulance. Cait was already demanding plastic surgery because a few splinters had scratched her face. Ava, feeling guilty that she'd caused the landslide, wouldn't stop crying long enough to see if she'd actually gotten hurt.

Lindsay was strangely subdued. Wrapped in Jared's jacket—her clothes had ripped to shreds, seemingly the worst of her injuries—wobbly on her feet, she refused medical care.

Jared was truly worried for her, but the best she'd let

him do was carry her to the car. He seat-belted her in and took off. Spider had insurance, and there were enough "names" there to deal with any consequences. His didn't need to be among them.

"You sure you're okay?" he asked every few blocks.

Lindsay leaned back against the headrest and closed her eyes. He wanted to warn her that her head would start to spin if she closed her eyes. But when he glanced over, she was . . . smiling? "Some comeback," she mused.

He felt himself relax. "Some girls just know how to make a lasting impression. No one's ever gonna forget your first night back on the scene."

"Jared?"

"Yeah?"

"I really, really, *really*—"

"You really what?"

He signaled left at the light at Highland and went to face her, but Lindsay had turned her back to him. She was leaning out the open window. Hurling her guts out.

"Oh, my God, Linz, why didn't you tell me to pull over?"

After a few heaves, she turned back—wiping her face on his jacket sleeve. "I really am happy to be back."

It was the sloppiest smile he'd ever seen. "I am too, Linz," he said softly. And it was true. She had him at hurl-o.

8

Full House

"What were you *thinking*?" Jared's voice scaled up an octave as he leaned in over the poker table. "Bringing a homeless person into this house?" His disgust and fury were aimed at the one person *least* likely to cause controversy: Sara.

It was Lindsay, martini glass in hand, who giggled, "A homeless ho. Does that make her a ho-ho?" She slapped the table with delight; her pile of poker chips went flying.

No one amused Lindsay more than herself, Eliot realized.

Unamused, Sara raised her finger to her lips. "Shush! She has a name. It's Naomi Foster, and she can hear you!"

And no one was more righteous than Sara.

Eliot shuffled the deck of cards. The housemates, who'd been together just under a month, had fallen into weekly Thursday-night poker sessions. Lindsay had started it, which was ironic, since she was the worst player. And that was quite an accomplishment, since Sara had never played in her life.

Linz could not keep a straight face. When she had a good hand, she got so excited, the table shook. When she was trying to bluff, the giggles began. Signaling raises all around.

Eliot dealt two cards facedown, then an exposed card to each of them.

Jared's jack of diamonds was the high card, but his focus was squarely on Sara. "I want her out. End of story."

"You gonna bet?" Nick motioned.

Jared tossed a one-dollar chip into the center of the table. "And I don't care if she can hear me!"

"Well, you should," said Sara, coolly studying her cards. "I raise you a dollar."

"I raise both of you!" Lindsay, who was showing a lowly three of hearts, declared.

"Check." Nick tossed in enough chips to stay in the game.

Not Eliot. He wasn't getting into this pissing contest. He had crappy cards, and the chances of winning this hand were on par with those of the homeless girl staying at the share house.

Sara had brought home a "stray," as Lindsay callously declared. Jared may have been loudest in his censure, but truthfully, no one was thrilled.

"Naomi," Sara said steadily, as Eliot dealt another

round of cards, "is goin' through a rough patch right now. A little Christian charity wouldn't hurt any of you."

Charity, Eliot could have said, wasn't just for Christians. It was part of every religion. In his house at the Passover seder, the silver cup symbolized that the door was always open to anyone in need. But in his experience, it was theoretical. No homeless person ever came to his table.

"Charity?" Jared said. "Fine. We'll give her money"—he threw five dollars' worth of chips into the center of the table—"then she can leave."

Sara pressed her ruby lips together and raised Jared again. "Money isn't what she needs. She needs someone to care about her, help her get her life together. Why can't y'all see that?"

"We do." Nick stepped into the uncharacteristic role of peacekeeper, a role no one else, including El himself, wanted. "Jared has a point. This girl, this Naomi, could be a criminal. She could steal from us, or worse, hurt us."

Sara smiled. "Have y'all seen her? She's tiny. She hasn't had a hot meal in weeks. I couldn't just leave her out there."

There were many things Sara could just not leave. Like cleaning the house. The tall, shapely pageant beauty believed it was wasteful to spend money on a maid, so she assumed the responsibility.

No one *wanted* to help, but Eliot and Nick couldn't stand by and watch her go Cinderella. So they pitched in. Between them, they'd gotten the backyard lawn mowed, the garden weeded and replanted. Draining the entire pool and scrubbing that mother had taken a full weekend.

Jared and Lindsay? They were all about creating chaos. It never occurred to Linz that *she* was supposed to pick up after herself. The diva never had to. Where she tossed a towel is where it stayed. Where she left a dirty martini glass? It waited for someone else to pick it up.

It would've been easy for Eliot to dismiss Jared and Lindsay as clichés, spoiled, self-absorbed rich kids. But Lindsay'd spent her entire childhood working, and even now, in her drone job, she never missed a day at the office.

True, it'd turned all kinds of ugly the night Linz revealed that she didn't get the role in *Heiress: The Movie*, even though she'd rocked her audition. When Amanda informed her that the role had gone to "it" girl Sienna Miller, Lindsay'd been outraged. A pissed-off Lindsay put the "mean" in demeanor.

It soothed her wounds only a little upon learning that Sara hadn't been chosen for the peanut butter commercial, despite her brilliant reading of "Go crunchy, go smooth, go organic!"

But Lindsay was a trooper. A day later, she'd licked her wounds and gone on high alert for her next chance at an acting role.

Jared was another story. Eliot had already figured out that he was supposed to be taking summer school courses but instead spent his days on the phone, playing agent, attempting to make deals, collecting rent while house-sitting for his uncle. It was obvious to Eliot the kid was busting to work—in Daddy's company.

Nothing that'd happened so far had scuffed the shine off Jared McSmoothy. Until now. He raked his fingers through his hair and admonished Sara, "What gave you the nerve to bring her here—without even asking me?"

Eliot could've answered that one! What gave Sara the nerve was her sense of extreme righteousness.

Naomi—who couldn't be more than, what, sixteen?—had been in the kitchen slurping down a bowl of ramen noodles when Nick and Eliot had come home earlier in the evening. Nearly lost in Sara's fluffy terry robe, she'd stared at them with frightened saucer eyes—the biggest, roundest violet eyes he'd ever seen outside of a velvet painting, or an anime cartoon.

"This is Naomi. She'll be staying with us for a while." Sara had introduced her before the Michigan boys picked their jaws up off the floor

Nick had offered his hand. "Hi . . . uh . . . do you come from around here?" A stupid question, but at least he had manners.

Eliot hadn't been able to stop staring at her sunken cheeks, pierced eyebrow, and dark wet hair dripping onto the collar of the robe. Though Sara insisted otherwise, it was clear to Eliot that the girl was homeless, a beggar. Or a hooker.

Naomi had been asleep in the loft when Jared and Lindsay came home. They'd been arguing about her ever since.

Nick searched for a compromise. "What if we did a background check? If she doesn't have a police record, maybe it'd be okay for her to stay with us a few days."

"That won't be necessary, since she's not staying even one night." Jared glared at Nick.

This was one of those moments when Eliot totally hated himself for being such a wimp. But he couldn't help himself. "There are knives in the kitchen, Nick. . . ."

Lindsay put in, "What's she need knives for? She could take a guitar off the wall and bash your head in while you're sleeping—"

Sara slammed her cards down on the table.

Lindsay kept it up. "Or bring her bad-ass friends into the house. Rob us at gunpoint—"

Sara cut her off with an angry look.

It took a lot to piss off Nick.

He'd reached "a lot." "Lindsay—shut up! Sara, you said you befriended her on the corner of Hollywood and Highland. Seriously, what do you know about her?"

Sara tipped her chin up. "She's a human being. She's hungry and cold, and has no one. What else do I need to know?"

"How about"—Lindsay deliriously raked in the pot of chips, which she'd just won—"the location of the nearest homeless shelter?"

"Good idea." Jared flipped his cell phone open.

Sara reached out and swiped the phone from him. "Better ask if they have two beds available. If you kick her out, I go with."

A long pause. Finally, Jared muttered, "You're being ridiculous." But he didn't take his phone back from her.

Sara dealt the next round. She played five-card stud. Nick took three cards, Eliot, two. Lindsay insisted that because she had an ace, she was entitled to four. Jared tapped his cards on the table, meaning he'd play the hand dealt him.

Sara, also playing her original five cards, softened a bit. "I'll take full responsibility for her."

"What does that mean?" Jared demanded.

"I'll keep an eye on her. She can come to work with me, and here in the house, she can help me with the cooking, cleaning, weeding the garden—you know, the stuff you and Lindsay are too good to do."

Jared didn't have an answer.

They played the round of poker, Sara raising the bet three times before the foursome stopped challenging her.

Then Sara turned over her hand: full house.

"California is the calamity capital of the world." Eliot, who'd never so much as mowed the lawn at home (being allergic to pollen, mites, and dust), found himself in the backyard late Saturday morning, on his knees, sharing gardening duty with Nick, Sara, and Naomi. Armed with something called a weeding trowel, he was trying to uproot a stubborn dandelion—and more important, yank his housemates' heads out of the sand.

"Between floods, fires, earthquakes, mudslides, and riots, more disasters have happened here than any other place," he told them.

"At least there are no hurricanes," chirped Sara. She was planting seedlings, determined to clean up the backyard, and pretty it up, too, with a new garden.

"The rains sometimes lead to massive floods, which can become landslides. I don't have to tell you that homes like this one"—Eliot paused to nod at theirs—"are at big risk for that."

Three sets of eyes stared at him: vacant (Nick), wary (Naomi), and the worst, indulgent (Sara, humoring him). Gamely, he plowed on. "I know you think I'm being paranoid, but—"

"You? Paranoid?" Nick, working an edging spade in the ground, quipped. "Why would we think that? Just 'cause you're wearing a gas mask and gloves to weed the yard?"

"It's not a gas mask!" Eliot pulled the surgical mask down to his chin. "It's for my allergies, but you all should be wearing them. Who knows what kind of poison might be in the ground? I don't want to breathe it in. And you all should be wearing gloves."

Sara said soothingly, "We're not making fun of you, Eliot."

Naomi, who'd tried to settle in as unobtrusively as possible, giggled.

He blurted, "We're all in imminent danger!"

"Danger, Will Robinson! Danger, Will Robinson!" Nick cupped his hands around his mouth like a megaphone and did his best *Lost in Space* voice.

Sara squealed with delight.

That wasn't even remotely funny. Eliot scowled at them.

Nick poked him in the ribs with his edging spade. "Okay, we *are* making fun of you. But the alarmist thing is wearing thin, dude."

"I'm being a realist. This is science."

"My bad, man—I forgot that course you're taking at UCLA. What's it called, Disasters-R-Us?"

Again, Sara giggled. But when she looked up at Eliot's serious mug, she stopped. "Eliot, sweetie, come on. Nothing bad has happened here in a long time."

He could not help it. "Well, only if you consider nineteen ninety-four a long time ago—one of the worst earthquakes hit just a few miles from here. Fifty-five people were killed."

That's when Eliot noticed a flash of something—fear? memory?—scud across Naomi's heart-shaped face. He was moved to ask, "Are you from California, Naomi? Were you here when that quake hit?"

She paused, and shook her head. "We traveled all over the country, so I'm not exactly from anywhere."

Eliot totally didn't believe her. Nor did he challenge her.

"Fifty-five people?" Nick was back on the earthquake subject. "That's nothing compared to hurricane deaths, or tsunami devastation. I'll take my chances at fifty-five."

"You wouldn't say that if one of those poor souls was someone you loved," Sara pointed out. "But I believe in my heart we'll be fine."

Eliot kept on point. "A range of natural disasters, from brushfires to rockslides, collapsed bluffs, and earthquakes, have all hit L.A. at one time or another. The next time could be any time!"

Sara put down her watering can, folded her long shapely legs under her. "If we really are in imminent danger, do y'all think my momma would have allowed me to come out here?"

What Eliot thought: Her momma was a zealot waiting for her own life to begin when Sara got famous. What El said was, "I think we need to take this seriously, so we can be prepared if something does happen."

"You cannot fix what you refuse to see," Naomi mumbled, brushing her jaggedly cut jet-black hair out of her eyes. "I heard that somewhere."

Eliot gave her props. "There! I couldn't have said it better."

"So what have they been saying in that class you're taking?" Naomi, sitting on the crabgrass, pulled her knees in close to her body.

"The natural disasters we're seeing—mudslides, brush fires, earthquakes—are gonna keep happening."

"Oh, stop it," Sara said. "You're just tryin' to scare the pants off us." Catching Nick's smile, she turned a deeper shade of red.

"What does your boyfriend back home say about your being here?" Eliot demanded. "Has he ever heard of the San Andreas fault line?"

Sara looked wounded; Eliot felt like a heel. "I'm not sure what Donald has heard of," she said quietly. "He didn't want me to come."

"Hey, I'm sorry, that's none of my business. I just . . ." Eliot reached out and took her hand.

"I understand. You're worried something bad's gonna happen. And even if we don't agree, we're friends, and we should listen."

Nick stood up and peeled off his tank top. Eliot caught Sara's reaction. Look up "lust" in the dictionary: That'd be her picture.

He stuttered, "The . . . the . . . thing about wildfires and floods is that you have some warning. Earthquakes can tear your life apart, without warning."

Naomi suddenly bolted up, wordlessly, and headed inside the house.

Eliot continued, "Like I was saying, the nineteen ninety-four earthquake was a six-point-seven magnitude—it was one of the most destructive disasters in U.S. history, and it would've been way worse if it had hit during the day, when people were at work, out shopping, in school, if more cars had been on the road. As it was, the tremor toppled chimneys and shattered windows all over southern California—it was worst in Northridge, which isn't far from here; it's in the Valley. A dozen people were killed when an apartment building collapsed. An entire highway was destroyed; a freeway overpass collapsed in a busy intersection."

"But if there's no warning, what can anyone do?" Nick asked.

"Be ready. I'm putting together an earthquake preparedness kit—I bought a transistor radio, flashlights, gloves, gas masks, bike helmets, and a first-aid kit."

"Transistor radio?" Sara asked.

"We'll lose electricity in an earthquake—no TV, internet, nothing. It's the only way we'll have of knowing what's happening, when help is arriving."

"What's with the gloves? In case of snow?" Nick teased.

"Not snow: glass. It'll shatter all around you. You don't want it embedded in your hands when you're trying to crawl out."

"You bought all this stuff already? Where is it?" Sara asked.

Eliot smiled. "I'm putting it all in the kitchen cabinet by the microwave. One more thing: Nick, you gotta get Jared to show you where the main gas line in the house is. We'll need to shut it off at the first tremor."

He got them to agree to everything, except to practice drills like ducking under something sturdy, a heavy table or doorframe, and getting as far away from windows or anything made of glass. But Eliot was happy with the progress he'd made. At least they were listening. "It's possible the next one will be, like, an eight on the Richter scale—that's what they're calling 'the big one.'"

"Who's got a big one?"

Lindsay, and her scathing wit, materialized. Leave it to her to make a crack that'd arouse *and* annoy them. Eliot shielded his eyes from the sun and looked up, hoping no one saw his face: the combination of lust and livid was embarrassing. Lindsay was luscious, bedecked in bangles, hoop earrings, toe rings, and ankle bracelets—and not much else. Her red string bikini was as tiny as a Kaballah bracelet. She'd come outside to sun herself, and deigned to stroll over to the garden.

"We were talking about earthquakes." Eliot's voice squeaked.

"Not that you couldn't cause a few quakes, looking like that," Nick noted.

Delighted, Lindsay dropped anchor—her towel and her barely covered butt. "Is Eliot making everyone nervous?"

Not as much as you are, he thought . . . nervously. "I'm just explaining—"

She cut him off with a dismissive wave. "Native Californians don't worry about that stuff. So-called experts have been going all alarmist, predicting massive death and destruction for decades. Chances are, hurricanes will destroy the Southeast before we get even another tremor. We just get all the press."

Native Californians . . . Eliot thought about what she'd said. People like Jared and Lindsay thrived on calamity—drama queens and princes *lived* for life on the edge. To them, it's like a disaster movie they've been cast in. They really did live in a dream world.

Lindsay interrupted his musing. "Anyway, if you're so sure of impending disaster, why don't you leave? What's keeping you here?"

Another question he'd asked himself.

Nick answered for him. "El, leave?" He looked meaningfully from near-naked Lindsay to shapely Sara, and shook his head. "Snowball, meet hell. This place is as near to heaven as my boy is likely to get."

Lindsay chuckled. Sara laughed nervously.

Eliot colored but didn't dispute his friend. He got up and strode into the house for a cool drink. He knew the real reason he'd stay. It wasn't about the hot babes living under the same roof. Eliot had no shot with Lindsay, no matter how much she flirted with him.

And despite Nick's encouraging him to go after Sara, she was a real long shot, what with the boyfriend back home and the way she looked at Nick. Besides, she'd confided in him about some purity pledge she'd taken, had shown him a ring that symbolized her commitment to stay a virgin until marriage. So no, Eliot wasn't staying in the hopes of getting lucky. What kept his feet glued to the shaky California terrain was Nick. Something wasn't right with his friend.

"You okay?"

He spun around. Naomi was settled in the corner of the striped couch, with what looked like a screenplay splayed over her knees.

"Yeah, I just came in for a cold drink. Can I get you something?"

She shook her head and returned her attention to the script.

Out of curiosity he asked, "Are you trying to break into showbiz too?"

She didn't look up.

9

Naomi: Fear and Fireworks on Independence Day

Crack! Boom! Pop!

The house rumbled beneath her. It sounded like the deep growl from the belly of a beast—or was that her own body? Naomi was quaking, shivering, despite the blanket she was snuggled under. She hugged her knees, squeezed herself further into the corner of the sofa between the pillows. As if that could protect her.

She tried to focus on the dialogue of the script Sara had given her to read, hoping to blot out the loud commotion just outside the sliding doors. Why Sara insisted Naomi read it, she couldn't figure out. It wasn't a part Sara was up for; this was some random story about a policeman and a runaway. Sara probably thought Naomi related to the plot: That's how little Sara, or anyone, knew.

The story wasn't half bad, but the part of the

runaway, Moxie, was not one she related to at all. Naomi had not run away.

She put her head back into the script, but it was no use. The blasting fireworks panicked her, brought up memories she'd worked hard to forget. As for the burbling buddies in the backyard hot tub, they just distracted her.

"Awesome!" She heard Nick reacting enthusiastically to the fierce display of a Fourth of July sky pageant. "Oh, man, that *rocked*!"

"Look at the those stars, those colors!" Sara marveled.

"That's what it's like every time Jared and I hook up," Lindsay teased Sara. "The earth *moves*, we see stars! You should try it." Word had spread quickly through the share house about Sara's moral convictions. Naturally, Lindsay took every opportunity to taunt her.

"Quit it, Linz," Jared interjected. "Sara Calvin will be our first virgin movie star."

Naomi knew Jared was still furious that Sara had brought her into their house. And since the high and mighty Jared was chief pooh-bah, it was a wonder Sara had prevailed. There were moments, like now, she wished Sara had not. It wasn't for lack of gratefulness. She was plenty thankful to Sara. She just wished she didn't have to be.

Pop! Pop! Crack!

Another chorus of fireworks exploded, louder. Naomi jumped. Whoever was launching these was close to the house. Too jittery to sit in one place, the formerly home-less girl sprang off the couch and strode over to the sliding doors, where she could now see, as well as hear, the show going on outside.

It was after nightfall on July Fourth. The five house-mates had squeezed into the hot tub. She could almost see the fireworks reflected in their shiny, happy faces, their unscarred eyes. From this rarefied perch high in the Hollywood Hills, they did have an amazing view of spectacular light shows, above and below them.

There was room for her in the hot tub. Sara had offered her a bathing suit.

No way. The idea of hanging out with this bunch freaked her out.

The feeling was mutual.

They tolerated her. It'd been a little over a week and she hadn't assaulted anyone, stolen anything, smoked or snorted any illegal substances, nor snuck any lowlifes into their house. Moreover, she helped Sara with the chores. Didn't mean she was now welcome.

It was easy to know what Jared thought of her. Garbage. Trash. Human debris. Not that McSmoothy said as much to her face. His act was neutral, but he wasn't much of an actor. Jared still wanted her out. Lindsay wanted what Jared wanted, and gave him all he asked for—and judging by the frequent noise from his bedroom, they were making each other very happy.

Jared and Lindsay, too impressed with themselves for words, were glued at the hip in the Jacuzzi, lasciviously feeding each other bits of sushi. Lots of tongue action, putting on a show for everyone to see.

Eliot was mooning after Sara, who was lusting after Nick, whose dark eyes were focused only on the spectacle in the sky. Naomi chuckled. The pious girl was havin' all sorts of trouble with that temptation law, or commandment, or whatever it was. Every night, during her prayers before bed, she kept praying that she wouldn't fall into temptation.

Naomi didn't think He was listening. Not that she believed much in God, or in any higher power. Maybe she had once, a long, long time ago. But that belief had long ruptured, had gotten buried beneath the rubble of what was once her life.

Compared to what she'd been through, the little domestic dramas playing out here were laughable. These five had no idea how lucky they all were. Naomi checked herself: She'd been pretty lucky too, that Sara had come into her life when she did.

The good-hearted country girl was the real deal, a rare deal, a true believer. Doing the humanitarian thing, befriending Naomi instead of what most people did: avert their eyes and walk by the beggar girl, or toss a few coins in her cup and continue walking. Worse were those who wanted something from her.

Sara didn't want anything. She wasn't trying to proselytize, pimp, or procure her services in any way. Sara never pressed her to find out what had happened to Naomi, why she was on the streets. The tall girl with the wavy blond hair was naive enough to just want to help.

Still, no way would Naomi have come home with her. But the day she finally said yes was the day the street had gotten too dangerous: Some low-life skinheads had threatened her, and she'd been terrified.

And despite the roommates' resistance, things were okay so far.

During the day, she went to work with Sara on that *Caught in the Act* TV show. No one asked her who she was or why she was there. They just took her for another lowly intern and piled drone stuff on her—Xeroxing, filing, fetching coffee, taking notes. She was too smart to get comfortable, though.

Her "pay" for working on the TV show with Sara and helping around the house? Food, clothing, shelter. Naomi had her own room of sorts: the basement of the share house. The most important compensation, however, was safety. For now, Naomi was safe. And now was all she, or any of them, really had.

Naomi put the script down and wandered back into the kitchen, where a sink full of dirty dishes awaited. She didn't really have to, but she needed to keep her shaking hands busy, so she began to scrub and dry each glass, spoon, fork, dish, and coffee mug.

Her eyes wandered out the window over the sink to the backyard. Nick was slurping down a Bud Lite from the bottle, leaning against the back of the hot tub, eyes closed. He had that model pose down. He was harmless, she thought, sweet, dumb, and meaty. He'd been friendly from the start, and now regarded her as a mere curiosity. He didn't ask a lot of questions or stare at her relentlessly like his roommate.

El-geek, as she secretly thought of him, peppered her with "kind" questions. She was supposed to think he cared, but she saw right through him. In his mind, she was some runaway, a poor, pitiable soul who'd come to Hollywood looking for fame and fortune, falling instead into a life of drugs, prostitution, homelessness, hopelessness. A cliché.

If only they really knew.

She'd give the himbos from Michigan one thing: They were devoted to Sara. Whatever the tall, tawny Texan asked, they'd do. Like hauling a couch from the game room to the basement, clearing and cleaning an area for her to sleep.

Sara brought out the best in those boys.

And the worst in that Lindsay creature.

Around Sara, Lindsay was snotty, superficial, jealous, and bitchy. Putting her down at every opportunity. Lindsay was supposedly trying to mount a big "comeback," but so far, she hadn't gotten any acting parts. The only thing that cheered her was that Sara hadn't either. Chuh! Even the homeless girls on the streets were more supportive of one another.

Sara had another audition coming up this week. Naomi had been helping her rehearse.

"You're up for the role of who?" Lindsay's loud question pierced the air. Instinct kicking in, Naomi stealthily made her way back into the den and opened the sliding doors so she could see what was going down. She wanted to be there, in case Lindsay's claws came out. "How come I don't know about this?" she charged. "Are we keeping secrets now?"

"Tomorrow I'm reading for a guest role in *Heroes*. Didn't I tell you?" Sara's tone was even.

Boom! Crack! A thunder of fireworks spilt the sky, and Naomi flinched.

"How'd you even find out about it?" Lindsay wanted to know.

"Lionel, my agent, sent me up for it. It's just a little bitty guest role, only two scenes. That's probably why you didn't get sent for it. It's not important enough for you."

Appeased, Lindsay relaxed, shrugged her bare shoulders.

Naomi's eyes went wide. Lindsay bought that? Geez, she's so high on herself, she can't see through the bull-shit clouds.

Sara should have left it at that. But she didn't. "Got any tips for me?"

"Yeah." Lindsay tilted her head back, poured a shot down her throat, and wiped her mouth with her arm. "Lose twenty pounds. You'll never work in this town lugging around that much weight. Real women have curves, but there's nothing real about Hollywood. Girls who get work in this town look like Nicole Richie at her boniest."

10

Sara's Body Works

The muscles in his stomach crunched tightly, then smoothed out again, tightened, then relaxed. Nick Maharis, lifting weights while doing knee bends in his bedroom, was almost more than Sara could stand. And yet that's exactly what she was doing, standing in his doorway, afraid to breathe, watching those abs and quads tighten on the down motion, then biceps, triceps, and pecs stretch across his dark, hairless chest when he straightened up.

Breathing out as he pushed down, breathing in as he came up. Up, down, his gym shorts riding up his thigh, his biceps bulging. She was hypnotized.

The crunch of his muscles when he dipped down, the smooth pecs when he stood upright. Crunchy, then smooth. Like peanut butter. Licking it off his chest, how tasty would that be? That's the ad campaign they should have gone with.

She gasped, clapped her hand over her mouth. How could she have thought that?

Nick flicked his dark eyes toward her. "What's the matter?"

"No-nothing . . ." she stammered, swallowing hard.

"You made a noise like you saw something scary."

In her head, she was hearing her boyfriend's admonitions: "Don't fall for any slick lines, Sara. All those guys out there want only one thing from you."

"Anyway, welcome to my makeshift gym." Nick grinned.

The night Lindsay made the rude comment about Sara's weight, she'd been more startled than hurt, but it'd led to a shouting match. Eliot argued that Sara didn't need to lose any weight; Jared agreed with Lindsay that maybe her "heft" wasn't helping during her auditions.

"That's crap," Eliot had said heatedly.

"What do you know?" Lindsay had challenged. "Ever been an actress? I don't think so." She'd turned to Sara. "You have three choices. Starve yourself, throw up after every meal, or snort coke. Ask any model or actress—that's how we roll in this town."

"No way! Don't you dare!" Eliot had been scandalized. "Either of you!"

Nick had genially offered to show Sara a workout

routine. "To tone you, keep you in fighting form—that's all you need."

Too quickly, she'd said yes, please, and thank you.

Now that she was here? In sweatpants and her brother's old cut-off T-shirt? Now that her eyes were glued to Nick's glutes? Her thoughts sinful? Sara Calvin knew this was a bad idea.

She was going to do it anyway.

Nick's workout equipment consisted of a set of weights, a barbell, ropes, and a huge red rubber ball that reminded Sara of a giant inflatable beach ball.

"Not exactly state of the art," Nick conceded, "but it'll have to do for now. Can't afford membership in an L.A. gym."

"Not yet. But when you're up on a billboard modeling for those famous designers, you'll be able to buy your own gym."

When he laughed, his eyes crinkled up so all you could see were those long, thick black eyelashes. All she could feel was her tummy tumbling.

She should leave. Now would be a good time.

"So how do you want to begin? Stretching? Aerobics? Curls? Lunges? Weights?"

Donald's voice popped into her head. "Once you start, it's impossible to stop—you just keep falling down the well. Remember your purity pledge. Remember me. I'll be waiting when you get back."

She didn't want to go back. She'd been in California

over a month, and so far, though she'd only been on one failed audition, she loved her job, she loved the people she'd met, she was learning so much!

But she only had until the end of August. Then her mom's money ran out, her job ended, she'd have to give up the house-share and move someplace cheaper. Or move back home, defeated. Back to Donald, who didn't want her to succeed.

Her voice wavered. "Nick, do you think Lindsay's right? If I don't lose weight, I'll never get any acting jobs?"

Nick shrugged. "I'll tell you what I know. Those skanky types who starve themselves? Not hot."

"Not attractive?"

"No way. Guys like girls with a little meat on their bones, you know? Working out isn't about getting all skinny. Exercising helps shape and tone you. It's good for your heart, lungs, everything. But if you wanted to lose weight—and I'm not sayin' you should—anything that increases your heart rate burns calories."

Could he not hear her heart racing? She could lose weight watching him.

"We'll start with some simple stretches." He bent over at the waist, so his fingertips touched the floor.

She watched.

"This is a great stretch for the back of your thighs, glutes, and lower back."

She bent over, wondering what he thought of her glutes.

"Do you feel it?"

"I think so." To tell him what she really felt would incriminate her.

Nick demonstrated stretches for the calves, inner and outer thigh muscles, arms, and shoulders. It was when he came up behind her, putting one arm gently around her waist, bending with her, to show her an abs stretch that Sara felt her legs turn to jelly.

He laughed. "Balance. That's what half of working out is about."

Next was weight lifting, for underarm toning. He demonstrated first.

"Okay, Sara, your turn." He came up behind her and proffered two small barbells. "These are fifteen pounds. Might be a little heavy at first."

He stood behind her. Very close behind. He lifted her right arm and placed the barbell-shaped weight in her hand. "Here, curl your fingers around it. Take the other one. . . . Now pretend like you're Popeye, showing off your muscles."

She laughed nervously and did as told. Tried to, anyway. She couldn't do it more than once; after that, the weights pulled her arms down to her sides.

From behind, Nick bolstered her arms. "Try again. Don't be discouraged. Just do as many reps as you can. You'll improve, you'll see."

He was so close, she could practically feel the beads of sweat transfer from his body to hers. She inhaled him. Sweat and soap: The combination was intoxicating. She had to do something. Say something. Conversation would take her mind off what her body was saying. "How's your modeling going?"

"Slow," he admitted. "Not exactly the way I thought it would." He explained that he, too, had a deadline. Three months to make it before he had to concede defeat, go home. Just like her.

"When's the audition for *Heroes*?" he asked, demonstrating lunges.

"Friday." She tried to follow, taking a long stride, bending her knee, stretching forward at the waist.

"Nervous?"

She was hyperventilating for other reasons entirely.

"Lunges are good for keeping your thighs taut and your butt tight," he explained. He continued to demonstrate, unaware that his shorts rode up even higher with each stride.

Her tummy and butt tightened without her moving a muscle.

"Do you feel it in your thigh?"

When he cupped her quads, she jumped.

"So what exactly is the part in *Heroes*?" he asked, amused at her nervousness.

"It's for a girl named Victoria, a friend of the cheerleader's, out to betray her."

"A bad girl, huh?" He tilted his head and rubbed his chin. "Not exactly how I'd cast you."

"You see me as the good girl." She laughed uneasily.

"I guess I do. But that's why they call it acting, right? You make the audience believe you're something that you're not."

"You be a good girl," Donald had reminded her. "Don't let them change you out there. Don't compromise your morals."

Keep talking. Stop thinking. Stop feeling. Any topic would do. "Nick, do you remember that script written by the policeman who found my suitcase?"

"The one you rescued from the pool?"

"I've been reading it. I admit I don't know much, but it's every bit as interesting as the ones the stars talk about on *Caught in the Act*."

"The cop's is better? No kidding!" Nick seemed genuinely surprised.

She'd just about finished it, and was having Naomi read it too. It was called *Hide in Plain Sight*, and it was about a girl forced to go into witness protection with her mobster parents. She runs away, the bad guys go after her, and this young cop gets involved.

"Sounds cool," Nick agreed. "Why not give it to Jared?"

"I'm not Jared's favorite person right now, remember? He'd probably make fun of me. And really, what do I know?"

"As much as anyone, I'd think."

"Maybe you want to read it?"

"I'm not much of a reader. If not for Eliot, I might not have made it through high school."

"I don't believe you. You ever think of acting?" Sara asked. "You've got the looks for it."

"Me? I have no talent whatsoever—and I think you need more than looks to make it in this business. And someone like you, you've got both—you're a knockout and a natural talent."

She blushed. He thought she was a knockout? "There are so many beautiful people here, I'm nothing special." He thought she was a knockout! "What I have is grit and determination."

"And me."

"You?" Sara's heart went into serious flutter.

He grinned and rolled the huge ball toward her. "With the help of my rockin' training, and this balance ball, you'll snag the next role you're up for."

She laughed. "I was wondering what that ball was for."

"It's for stretching, pull-ups, and stomach curls. Come on, I'll show you." He rolled it into the center of the room. "Lay faceup on it."

She giggled. "I'll fall off."

"I'll hold you steady, don't worry."

That's exactly what she was worried about.

Cautiously, she followed his instructions, draping her back on the ball, legs slightly apart, touching the floor.

"Arms straight out," he said. "Now use your stomach muscles to pull yourself up, just enough to curl yourself."

Nick stood over her.

She couldn't move.

He took her hands. "Use me as resistance, and pull."

She did as told. Maybe a little harder than he'd expected. Because she pulled him right down on top of her.

"I have good news, and bad news. Which do you want first?" Lionel, the sweetest man ever, Sara's agent and friend, called her at work.

"Might as well be done with the bad news first."

"You didn't get the part on *Heroes*."

She swallowed nervously. "Is it because I was too . . . big?"

There was a pause on the other end of the phone. "Not big enough of a name. They went with Nicole Richie."

"I'm ready for the good news, Lionel."

"You sitting down?"

"You know I'm not. Go ahead. Lay it on."

"Just got word that they're doing a remake of *The Out-siders*."

Sara's eyes widened; she squealed. "Oh, my gosh, I just love that movie!"

"It's a classic," Lionel agreed. "Made names for Tom Cruise, Matt Dillon, Ralph Macchio, Rob Lowe, Emilio Estevez—they all went on to bigger and better after that. There's one important female role, Cherry Valance. It's pivotal, it's perfect, it'll make a star out of whoever gets it."

Sara flashed on a scene from that movie. "Cherry. Was that Diane Lane who played her in the original?"

"Good girl! You know your classic movie history. You have a week to prepare. This is a biggie."

"You really think I have a shot? I haven't gotten anything so far—not even that dang peanut butter commercial."

"All the better, my smooth and crunchy one," Lionel quipped, and Sara's belly flip-flopped.

"They want an unopened jar. An unknown, a fresh, talented looker who'll blow 'em away. In this case, not having any credits is a definite plus."

"Just what we knew would happen," her mama crowed when she called with the news. "See, I told you, Sara, every time you tried for something and didn't get it? It's because you're bound for real stardom. I know this is the one."

Lionel sent "the sides"—a few pages of the script with Cherry's scenes—by messenger that afternoon. By evening, both she and Naomi had read it and had shared the news with Nick and Eliot.

Eliot was pumped. "That's my favorite book from junior high! I'll go online and order the original for you from Amazon."

"It was a book?" Sara asked.

Eliot booted up his laptop. "Required reading."

"In our school?" Nick scratched his head. "I don't remember it."

"That's because I did your report." Eliot was on the Amazon site. "You had to say if you'd rather be a greaser or a soc. You picked greaser."

"S. E. Hinton," Naomi murmured. "She wrote it when she was sixteen."

Eliot complimented her. "That's right."

Naomi had offered up nothing about herself. Sara wasn't sure the girl even had an education. "I guess it was required in your school too?"

Naomi shrugged. "I guess."

Eliot was all about it. "You *have* to read it, Sara. You'll understand the character better and ace the audition."

"I'll go out and get the DVD. We'll help you rehearse," Nick offered,

Sara was overcome with emotion. Everyone wanted to help her! She threw her arms around Eliot. "You have no idea how much this means to me. Y'all are . . . my best friends." She started to cry, and Eliot stroked her back, holding her tightly. She wasn't sure, because she was crying, but she thought Eliot whispered into her ear, "You smell sweet."

Sara wept. Eliot grabbed a tissue and blew his nose. Even Nick, notorious noncrier, sniffled. They'd settled around the big oak coffee table in the living room, lit candles, ordered dinner in, and watched the DVD of *The Outsiders.*

"Johnny Cade gets to me every time," Sara said between sobs. "His life was so sad, and he was a hero. And Ponyboy, you just can't help loving him. . . ."

Nick leaned back on the couch, stretched his arms out. "Forget about them. It's Dallas Winston—Dally—that Cherry is supposed to be in love with."

"No she isn't," Eliot corrected. "She says she *could* love him—"

Naomi picked up the pages of the script from the coffee table. "Should we start helping Sara rehearse, while it's fresh in our minds?"

Nick volunteered to read Dally's lines, Eliot shoved his hands in his pockets, doing Johnny. Naomi played Ponyboy.

Sara alternately sat, stood, walked around—and eventually, after several readings, lay down on the carpet to stretch her back and her imagination. She wasn't real happy with any of her readings, and wanted to try again.

" 'What's a nice, smart kid like you running around with trash like that for?' " She sounded like a sweet, syrupy kindergarten teacher. That wasn't right.

Naomi responded as Ponyboy: " 'I'm a greaser. Same as Dally. He's my buddy.' "

Eliot clapped. "Naomi, that was good!"

Nick added, "Dude, if you were a guy, you could totally nail this."

Naomi ducked her head down, embarrassed, and mumbled, "Let's keep going. Sara? Do Cherry's next line."

She did, and tried it completely differently.

"That was better," Eliot decided.

It was just okay. Cherry was a complicated girl—she could be sensitive and sweet, but also sarcastic and confrontational. She didn't have that many scenes in the movie, but she made you remember them.

"Let's go over the part where Dally brings her a soda at the drive-in," Nick suggested. He read Dally's line, pretending to hand her a drink. "'This might cool you off.'"

Sara recited, "'After you wash your mouth and learn to talk and act decent, I might cool off too.'"

Darn, that was bad. Sara closed her eyes.

Eliot tented his fingers. "In this scene, Cherry's being sarcastic, Sara. You need to read it . . ." The room went silent.

Naomi spoke up finally. "As if you were Lindsay."

"That's right, like this," came another voice, oozing with snarkcasm: "'*After* you wash your mouth . . . and learn to talk and act decent, I *might* cool off too.'"

Sara, prone on the floor, looked up just in time to catch the full impact of the ice-cold Pepsi flicked in her face. She was aghast.

The pointy toe of Lindsay's boot was on her stomach before she could get up. "By the way, Cherry throws the soda at him *before* she says the line."

Lindsay turned theatrically and whirled out of the room. Exit, stage left. Jared, clutching a few pages of a script marked "The Outsiders," wore a dumbfounded expression. He followed her.

11

Jared Plays House, Lindsay Plays Games

"Why is *she* auditioning for Cherry?! That role is mine, and I want her off!" Lindsay was steaming, stomping around the elegant, expensively appointed great room at the Larson family mansion in Bel Air, waving her cell phone around like a weapon.

"Put the phone down, Linz. You can't call Amanda; you're not calling Lionel." Jared, resting his elbow on the marble fireplace mantel, tried to dissuade her. "You got the audition too. And we're not asking them to cancel Sara's audition."

Lindsay pouted. "I thought you were on *my* side."

Jared reached for her, drew her into his arms, and kissed her tenderly on the neck. "Always, baby, always." He stroked her hair, reassuringly. "But—"

"But what?" She pulled away. "You think she's better than me?"

"Of course not! Linz, listen. Every young actor in Hollywood is up for a role in *The Outsiders*. It stars seven guys—"

"And one girl," she pointed out. "The one who'll be remembered over everyone else."

"It has the potential to be a star-making role," Jared conceded.

"Or the comeback role of a lifetime! No one will ever think of me as Zoe Wong again. Cherry is my Charlize in *Monster*, my Scarlett Johansson in *Lost in Translation*, my Kirsten Dunst Mary-Jane moment in *Spiderman*. Sara, who's never done anything, cannot get that role!" In frustration, Lindsay grabbed a pillow off the Armani/Casa sofa and threw it at Jared.

Jared caught it, then caught her in his arms again. "Linz, look at me."

She tried pulling away again, but he gripped her tightly.

"Seriously, babe, you have to hear me."

The sun filtered down through the tinted skylights, reflecting like kaleidoscopic glints in Jared's emerald-green eyes. A girl could get lost in them trying to find his soul, Lindsay thought, if she let herself. He parted his lips, and something inside her softened. His kiss was sweet, sensual, not overpowering. It didn't have to be: Lindsay understood.

Jared had spirited her away for the weekend. His dad, Rusty, was on a business trip. The twins, Brooke and Brynn, were on a spa/shopping weekend somewhere in

Santa Barbara. Glynnis, their mom, hadn't lived with them in years.

Which left the mansion on Stone Canyon Road in Bel Air empty, but for the staff. They were thrilled to see Jared, had happily placed his order for a huge bouquet of white calla lillies, had delightedly sprinkled the majestic staircase leading upstairs with a blush of rose petals.

He'd done this for her. He'd taken her for a few stolen days of luxury away from the funky—and crowded—share house in the hills, a weekend's break from her crap-tastic job and the ever-more-contentious roommates. Jared had been neither romantic nor sensitive when they were together the first time. Either someone had given him lessons—or, this time, the boy was just a goner for her.

Lindsay didn't want to think about the second thing. Her focus had to be on her career—that is, on *having* one. Slowly, she extracted herself from his embrace and sank into the enormous Italian leather armchair.

"Jar, I so totally appreciate what you're doing for me. The house, this weekend, it's . . . amazing. It's just that getting this role is imperative."

"Why this one? Acting gigs are like buses—you miss one, the next comes along."

"This one is here now. It could redefine me, show the world my real talent. But first, I have to eliminate—"

"Sara?" he interjected. "Give me a break, Linz. She's one of dozens of actresses in Hollywood going for this role, why obsess about her?"

"In some ways, she's exactly what they're looking for," Lindsay explained. "Sara's as unknown as unknown gets. She's got that corn-fed, freaking Oklahoma thing down. She's tall, blond—"

"Cherry's a redhead," Jared reminded Lindsay, "more like you. I don't think Sara has any shot at this."

"Can we make sure of that?" she said in a whisper.

"No, we cannot. And we should not."

Despite his unwillingness to cooperate, Jared's confidence made her feel better. More so when he reached into the bar and poured her a raspberry Stoli.

"Anyway . . ." Lindsay licked the rim of the glass, inhaled the flavoring, and closed her eyes. Mmmm, it was good. "Cherry Valance is a soc. I'm a soc. I can look down my nose at anyone!"

Jared grinned and settled on the wide armrest of her chair. "Yes, and that's what I love about you. But—"

"What but? No buts!" She sipped her Stoli.

"In this script, Cherry's not a typical soc. She sympathizes with the greasers, too."

Lindsay pulled away from him. "So what are you saying? Miss Proud-and-Pious does sympathy better than I do?"

Rhetorical much? Jared drained his scotch and soda. Wisely, he kept that thought to himself.

"I'm an actress. I can do anything. She hasn't proved she can do anything, besides win Texas beauty pageants!" Lindsay sniffed.

"Then why are you worried about her?" Jared slid into Lindsay's chair so their thighs rubbed against each other's. He put his arm around her, drew her even closer. "You know how to do this. Make the part yours. Forget Sara, and everyone else going up for it."

She knew he was right. But she needed this role. She was running out of time—and maybe even faith in herself. A little.

If she didn't get it?

It would prove she didn't have the chops, the talent to stretch beyond being in a dumb sitcom.

It would mean her family was right: She ought to have stayed fat and barefoot in Iowa, not tried to claw her way back into the biz.

Her whole life, all she'd be remembered for was Zoe Stupid Pimply Wong. And that giggle.

If she lost to Sara? Unthinkable, the ultimate humiliation. She'd be laughed out of the share house, hooted out of the hot clubs, kicked out of her crowd, ridiculed out of Galaxy. Worst of all? She'd be pitied.

Lindsay tucked herself into Jared's chest, looked up at him with big, sad eyes. "You really think I have a chance?"

Jared refused to humor her. "Here's what I know: You are Lindsay Pierce, and what Lindsay wants, what Lindsay goes after, Lindsay gets."

This time, she initiated the kiss. There was nothing slow or sweet about it.

It was his smile, she thought when they pulled apart,

not his eyes. If you could read that smile, you'd know Jared Larson. You'd see the vulnerable boy inside the slick exterior, the insecurity and yearning behind the McSmoothy facade. She had hurt him by ignoring his letters, e-mails, gifts. She was capable of hurting him again. She didn't want to—especially not at this moment. But what did it say about her that she couldn't account for tomorrow?

"Listen, baby," he was saying. "This weekend, we'll work on the sides, we'll do Cherry's scenes together. After we pamper ourselves with room service, massages, movies, and ultimate pleasure."

The rose petals were meant to lead them upstairs, to Jared's posh bedroom. The twosome never made it off the armchair. Good thing it was sturdy.

Lindsay swung her leg over his, turned her body toward him. Jared encircled her; he parted her lips with his tongue, and they kissed passionately. He pulled her onto his lap, let his hands wander under her T-shirt. "God, you're beautiful," he whispered between caresses, soft squeezes, and more kisses.

Gently, Lindsay loved him back, lightly massaging his chest, kissing his shoulders, his neck, blowing little puffs in his ear. She knew what he liked. And what would come next.

First she unzipped him while continuing to stroke his chest, then he repaid the favor. Their caresses were practiced, familiar, and tender, his on her thighs, hers on his abs, her fingertips skimming his belly just beneath the elastic band of his briefs.

They knew each other's rhythms, and though they were sweaty, excited, and panting, they moved with deliberate, delicious slowness, each more interested in the other's pleasure than in their own. He licked her neck, she bit on his earlobe, drew little circles around his nipples, while he let his fingers travel the length of her body.

Jared was quiet in his lovemaking; Lindsay, not so much.

Would they have heard the car pull up, the door open, and the footsteps entering the room if she'd been a quieter lover?

Moot point.

Rusty Larson probably had cleared his throat loudly, maybe coughed a few times as he caught sight of their naked, entwined bodies on the Roche-Bobois double-arm chair. And Lindsay wasn't really sure how many times he'd had to shout "Jared!" before they looked up.

"Yummy! Mr. L, these garlic noodles rock!" Lindsay, slurping the tasty cellophane noodles, was beyond pumped. And the savory lunch, which also included Dungeness crabs and tiger prawns, courtesy of Rusty Larson, was really only part of the reason.

"Nice to see you enjoying yourself, Lindsay," Jared's dad said, winking.

Someone else's dad, in someone else's mansion,

walking in on his son in a compromising position with an ex-girlfriend, likely would have reacted somewhat differently than Rusty Larson had. The powerful Hollywood mogul was neither horrified, embarrassed, furious, shocked, indignant, nor bewildered. He didn't shout "How dare you?" Or "What the hell do you think you're doing?" Or worse.

Rusty Larson was bemused.

Instead of recriminations, there was a reward: lunch! And a lovely spread it was, catered by the trendily precious Crustacean of Beverly Hills, and served al fresco on the patio that overlooked the koi pond in the Larsons' Bel Air backyard.

Oh, sure, there was an obligatory exchange about the awkward situation. Jared acted chagrined. "Man, I'm so sorry you had to walk in on that."

Rusty did the "understanding dad" thing. He chuckled, "That dorm room at Ojai isn't exactly the way to impress Lindsay. Not very comfortable, I imagine. And you assumed you had the house to yourself. I get it. If I were you, I'd probably have done the same thing."

That's when Lindsay got it. In some twisted alt-reality, walking in on them reaffirmed Russ's belief that Jared really was spending the summer as he'd promised, making up his courses, living in the dorm. Why else would Jared seize the opportunity to sneak back to the mansion when he believed it empty?

"By the way," Rusty said, "I heard from your uncle the other day."

Jared tensed. "How's it going over there in . . . where is he again?"

Smooth, Lindsay thought. *Like Jared doesn't know.*

Rusty confirmed that Uncle Rob was in the Czech Republic, and likely to be there through September. "I hear the buzz is strong on his performance," Rusty added. "Maybe this one will finally be his big break."

"Yeah," Jared added snidely, "an Academy Award does wonders for family relationships. Maybe you'll finally stop looking down your nose at him."

There's no shit like family shit, thought Lindsay, as Jared and Rusty went into the same verbal tussle she'd heard years ago. Jared absolutely believed Rusty saw him as a slacker—just like his uncle—an unworthy heir who'd practically flunked out of college. A son who needed to be taught a lesson: a tough-love summer spent at school with no credit cards.

Without planning to, by getting caught, they had just lent credence to his dad's assumption. How weirdly wonderful was that?

Indeed, Rusty was abnormally ebullient, nothing like the gruff, all-business head of the agency she saw at the office. His reddish hair was graying at the temples, he had the look of a tanned, fit, supersuccessful mogul totally down. No one would guess from his demeanor that he was at all worried about the future of Galaxy. No one who wasn't an insider.

Over forkfuls of roast lobster and shot glasses of sake,

he was relaxed, expansive, confiding. "I give you credit, Son. I had my doubts you would stick school out. I figured you for a week or two before you'd start asking me to cut you a break. But I promise, you do things my way, make the best of it, it will pay off."

If Jared snared a deal, as he'd been trying to, maybe this summer would change Russ's opinion of his son after all, Lindsay mused. And hey, if there was a little sumpin' sumpin' in it for her, so much the better!

She smiled sweetly. "Take my word for it, Mr. L, Jared's totally made the best of things." Her hand strayed under the table, stroking Jared's thigh.

Rusty regarded her. "Jared didn't tell me you two were back together."

"The secret's out now," she conceded, moving her fingers beneath the hem of his shorts, drifting up his thigh, rendering him excellently silent. To his dad, she gushed about how she commuted to Ojai on the weekends, just to see him—but the "shlep" was so worth it.

Jared dropped his napkin. Purposely. In diving under the table to get it, he managed to fish around Lindsay's lap. Which is the reason she squeaked, sounding like a chipmunk, when answering Russ's question about where, exactly, she was living this summer. "With fr-friends!"

She started to laugh. The Lindsay laugh. Lightly, she smacked Jared in the head as he came back up from under the table.

"Ah, the Zoe giggle. Who could forget that?" Rusty's eyes crinkled when he smiled.

Lindsay sobered up swiftly. "Actually, Mr. L? I'm hoping everyone will. . . ."

He looked at her quizzically.

She took a deep breath, ignored Jared kicking her. "I don't know if you're aware, but I'm up for Cherry in *The Outsiders*."

"Are you?" His eyebrows arched. "That's terrific. Amanda is sending you out?"

On this subject, Lindsay could no sooner be coy than she could bluff at poker. She hammered her point: "Can you do anything to help me get the role?"

Jared warned, "Linz, don't go there . . ."

But Rusty chuckled. "I like a woman who just comes out with it."

"She's not asking you to do anything underhanded," Jared put in.

Lindsay kicked him hard now.

"I know," his dad agreed, "but, Lindsay, you understand that I don't have any real influence over who gets the role. That's a decision made by the director, and the producers."

"Well, can you at least tell me who else is going up for Cherry? I heard that Ashlee Simpson and Nicole Richie campaigned for it. Is that true?"

Before his dad answered, Jared jumped in thoughtfully, "Isn't the director of *The Outsiders* with Galaxy? Maybe you could just ask her a few questions—y'know, what they'll be looking for at the auditions."

Rusty leaned over and mussed Jared's hair. "Okay, I like your thinking, Son. No dirty pool, just something to help your lady. Hang on. . . ."

Rusty stood up, flicked open his cell phone and punched in the speed dial for one of his star directors. After a minute, they heard him say to the big-name female director, "Sweetheart, how's it going? No, I'm back on the West Coast—yeah, got in early. So listen, about *The Outsiders*. You start casting this week, right?"

Lindsay bounced up and down in her chair, completely unable to contain herself. A couple of times during the conversation, Jared put his palm over her mouth to keep her from squealing.

"Spill! Spill," she shouted as soon as Rusty hung up.

"They're testing some of the teen stars for Ponyboy—kids like Jesse McCartney, Zac Efron. I'm hearing everyone from Tom Welling to Justin Timberlake to Tobey Maguire and Jenson Ackles for the greasers."

"And Cherry?" She prodded.

"They're only seriously looking at unknowns."

Lindsay bit her lip. "Or someone making a comeback?"

He studied her, pressed his fingertips together. "Sure, Lindsay, that's possible."

"Dad," Jared said, "anything you can tell her, any insider tips that you know—it'd be a real favor. More than anyone, Lindsay's helping me get through my classes. She's been so supportive, helping me with my papers and stuff. That oughta be worth something."

Rusty looked surprised.

Lindsay melted.

"I asked for the entire script to be sent over. If you read the whole thing, you'll see what they're going for— an updated version, not as close to the book as the nineteen eighty-three movie was. They want the greasers tougher, more like hip-hop kids, and the socs to have a little more meat to them, not so one-dimensional. As for Cherry, they're thinking of a sexier type, more sultry than syrupy. And instead of mourning her boyfriend Steve, she's making an obvious play for Dally. But anyway, it should all be in the script."

Lindsay's heart soared.

Jared said, "Dad, this is . . . really cool of you."

Rusty said, "I gotta warn you, Lindsay, all the insider info in the world won't help if some actress just comes in and blows them away. Scripts change all the time. It'll be up to you to win the role by yourself."

"Oh, don't worry, Mr. L. I will. I will so get this on my own. It's . . . *beshert.*"

"Hi, Sara." Lindsay was in leaning over the kitchen counter Sunday morning, sipping coffee and pretending to read the *L.A. Times.*

Sara, wearing some heinous puffy-sleeved thing out of the Frederick's of Purity catalogue, regarded her warily. "What are you doing up so early?"

"Early? It's after nine." Lindsay acted borderline chipper.

"And yet this is the first time I've seen your face before noon on a Sunday." Sara slung her fake leather bag over her shoulder.

"I couldn't sleep. I'm nervous about the audition next week." Which wasn't entirely a lie.

"Me too," Sara acknowledged.

Lindsay turned toward the fridge. "So, I'd offer you coffee, but you don't do caffeine, right? How about some o.j.?"

"Thanks, but I don't have time."

"Off to church, huh? And I guess your little shadow isn't going along."

"No, Naomi doesn't go to church." Sara headed toward the door.

"Hey, Sara, wait up. Mind if I come with?"

Sara's clear blue eyes went wide—then quickly narrowed. "Why?"

Lindsay heard Jared's voice in her head. *Do not pull anything with Sara. Take the high road. Win the role because you're the one best for it.*

Lindsay shrugged. "Because it's Sunday. And I'm feeling"—she pressed her lips together—"well, a little prayer couldn't hurt, right? A little inspiration?"

Sara hesitated. Clearly she didn't believe a word of this hooey, but no way would Sara refuse. Especially after Lindsay greased the wheels: "We can borrow

Jared's car. Beats the walk and the bus. You'll get a front-row pew."

A few moments later, after Lindsay had changed into the longest dress she owned, only a couple of inches above her knee, she carefully backed out of the driveway and headed down the hill toward Cahuenga Drive. "You know, Sara, I've been thinking—"

"About getting religion so you can get a role in a movie?" No mistaking it: Sara's tone was sarcastic. Lindsay guiltily wondered who she had to thank for that: her influence, totally.

"Didn't take you very long to get jaded," Lindsay remarked.

Chastised, Sara mumbled an apology.

Lindsay laughed. Waiting for the light to change at the corner of Sunset Boulevard and Doheny Drive, she admitted, "Anyway, I do have sort of a confession to make."

Sara eyed her suspiciously. "Save it for church."

"I think *you'll* find this confession useful. With all due respect to the higher power."

Sara crossed her arms, distrustful.

"Here's the thing: I had lunch at Jared's family's house yesterday. His father, Rusty Larson, was there."

"Mr. Larson, who owns Galaxy. You asked him about the movie," Sara guessed.

"I got insider info."

"And you're taking this opportunity to share it with me? Even I'm not that much of a hayseed. Not anymore, anyway."

Lindsay exhaled slowly. Here it was; Sara would either buy this or not. "Hear me out before you turn me down. Rusty—I mean, Mr. Larson—told me that dozens of actresses are going for it, but they need to make a decision within the next three weeks. So I had this brilliant idea. Why don't we work together in this first round of auditions, eliminate the competition?"

"How are we going to do that?"

"By using the rest of the info he gave me."

As All Saints Baptist Church came into view, Lindsay launched into her plan to give Sara the wrong info.

"They're totally playing it old-school, a faithful adaptation of the nineteen eighty-three Francis Ford Coppola movie. So you should watch it again, totally imitate Diane Lane's performance, but sweeten it up. They want Cherry to be so sweet, she could cause an insulin attack. Really sensitive. Really moony for her dead boyfriend, Steve, and for Ponyboy."

A small pang of guilt stabbed her. And surprised her. Why should she feel guilty? Hollywood was cutthroat. Better the girl learned it now. Still, she was feeling borderline crappy now that she was totally turning Sara the wrong direction. Lindsay forced herself to swallow the guilt, and stay on point.

Sara still didn't trust her. "You're saying you know this

because Mr. Larson got it straight from the director, while you listened in?"

Lindsay wavered. Sara was staring at her with her big blue eyes. She pushed on. "Can you keep a secret? Jared and his dad have . . . issues. And Rusty kinda thinks that I'm a good influence—"

Sara chortled. "*You're* a good influence?"

Lindsay was miffed. "Believe it or not, there are worse influences than me. It's not like I'm some doped-up loser, like your little friend Naomi."

Before Sara could defend the homeless girl, Lindsay said, "Rusty cares about Jared's well-being, and helping me is his way of helping Jared. It's all good."

Even Sara could see the logic in that.

"So will you work with me? We get rid of the competition, and when it gets down to the two of us, as it will, the best one will get it. That's fair." Lindsay pulled up to the church and shifted the car into park. She held out her hand. "Deal?"

Sara hesitated, then took it. "It's not fair at all. But it's Hollywood."

"When do services end? I'll pick you up." Lindsay gestured at the imposing stone structure

Sara was puzzled. "Aren't you coming in?"

Lindsay waved her hand dismissively. "Not necessary. I made my confession. I feel so much better. My soul is cleansed, knowing we're in this together. Besides, Barney's is having a sale."

12

Nick and Eliot Get Really Nervous

Nick felt nauseous. It wasn't something he ate, more like something he'd bought into. This whole deal. Except for the part where he got to live in a cool Hollywood place with sexy roommates, the summer was turning out to be one serious bust. He stared at the pot of coffee sitting on the burner at Nowicki studios. No one had brewed fresh; this'd probably been sitting here since the weekend. He poured himself a cup anyway, tasted the grinds in his first sip. His stomach lurched.

It was the end of July, and he didn't even have a portfolio yet, let alone appointments with reputable modeling agencies. Which Nowicki's was not. The stuff being shot at his studio was so not his cup of bitter coffee. No matter how you sweetened it.

"Nicky—"

God, he hated being called Nicky. Especially by the boys here.

"Nicky, darling, they're waiting for you in the back room. They've got the camera set up. Chop, chop." Alonzo, one of Les's personal assistants, clapped his hands.

"Be right there," he called, tossing the coffee into the garbage.

They were shooting a calendar called "A Year of Boys," and Nick was on stand-in duty for the twelve models, one pictured for each month. The poses were all, needless to say, shirtless and suggestive.

Yesterday, he'd posed as Mr. January: naked except for fur-lined briefs. When the real model came in, they'd had to stuff the briefs—at least Nick hadn't suffered that humiliation!

Today, they were doing Mr. February.

"Nicky, Nicky." It was Les, summoning him to the set they'd created, the facade of a fireplace. Nick would be posed lying on his side on a fluffly rug, bracketed by long brass fireplace tools. Les frowned when he saw him. "Didn't anyone tell you? We need you stripped down."

Stripped down?

Alonzo advanced, thrusting a cardboard cutout of a red heart at him. The Valentine's Day prop. "This is all you're wearing, Mr. February."

Nick gaped. The prop was just big enough to cover

him . . . maybe. He shook his head vehemently. "No way. I can't do this one."

Keith, the one member of Les's posse Nick could deal with, strode into the studio and assessed. "What's wrong?"

"Nick is being shy. And we're running late." Alonzo taped his wristwatch.

"Find someone else. I'm not standing in front of everyone—"

"Hang on a minute," Keith said. "I'll be right back." When he returned, he was holding a beige thong. He grabbed the cardboard prop from Alonzo.

"Here, man," he said to Nick. "Go behind the screen over there, put this on, and use the heart to cover yourself. No one will see anything."

Nick grimaced. He hated every second of this. But at least Keith had been cool.

Impasse overcome, the rest was routine, if no more comfortable. He lay on his side, stretched out on the carpet, propped himself up on one elbow, cupped his chin. In his other hand, he held the red heart in front of him, positioning it wherever Les told him. "A little to the right. No, a little lower. Try it higher." Wearing the thong, girly as it was, helped. He felt somewhat secure. Even as Les bellowed, "Wait, what's he got on? He's supposed to be naked. It's in the shot."

Keith reminded him. "Don't worry, Les. The real model won't be wearing it. Forget it's there. Let's get the lighting right and be sure he's positioned where we want him."

Nick breathed a sigh of relief.

Short-lived, as it turned out. Les decided his faux model needed shine, a full-body layer of gloss. Alonzo and Alain—privately, Nick thought of them as the Twinkle Twins—raced to apply it. No fans of Nick, who'd refused every one of their social overtures, no matter how innocent, they did everything possible to make him squirm.

They slathered it on with long, sensual strokes. He tried to bat them away. "Cut it out," he barked.

"Oh, but we're not done," Alonzo purred. "Les wants you slicked up good."

Nick'd had enough. He took a swing at Alonzo, who ducked just in time.

"Oooh," Alain squealed, "a rough one!!"

Keith strode over. "Cut the shit," he ordered Alonzo and Alain. "You two are done here."

When the shoot was over, as a way to say thanks, Nick invited Keith to lunch.

Keith Sternhagen, Nick learned over pizza, subs, and beer, had come to L.A., as he had, from the Midwest. "Racine, Wisconsin. Nice city."

"Hoping to be a model?" Nick asked.

"An actor," the young man confided. "But it's a hard nut to crack. I left right out of high school, had no connections, and my savings didn't last very long. I needed to get a job, and I was lucky that Les took me on. I've been with him, making a good buck, for going on seven years now."

"So you just gave up on the acting? You don't go out on auditions or anything?" Nick took a bite out of his ham and cheese sub.

"Not lately. My last agent dropped me. It's disheartening. You keep putting yourself out there, only to keep getting rejected."

Nick understood. He lived with it. Sara and Lindsay—who had plenty of connections—had been striking out. Last week, they'd gone for their *Outsiders* audition: Neither had heard a word since, and both were on pins and needles. It wasn't fun.

"With Les," Keith was saying, "I got a steady income, a trade, a family. I might not be famous, but I'm not getting rejected every day."

Nick gulped his soda. He gathered his courage. "Keith, can I ask you something?"

"Sure," Keith put his pizza down.

"I'm not . . . I don't want to offend anyone. Y'know, I'm cool with live and let live. But that's not my lifestyle—"

Keith threw his head back and laughed. "You're kidding! You've made that very clear, my friend."

Nick blushed. "Sorry, I'm just . . . this is hard for me. It's a new situation. I thought maybe with time, it'd get easier, but it's the opposite. I'm thinking about quitting." There, he'd said it.

"Don't."

"Why not? I'm . . . man, I'm miserable here."

"Look, you came out here to be a model—"

"Not that kind."

"Dude, everyone starts somewhere. And no matter what you think of Les, or the studio, it really can lead to that billboard up there." He pointed through the restaurant window to the billboard of a man and woman posed sexily for Armani cologne.

"You think so?"

"You've got the look all right, you've got the determination, and the work ethic. You need to pay your dues, and then you need a break. From where I sit, you're on the right road."

Nick considered. "So you think this internship, this summer, could really lead to something big? I should stick it out?"

Keith's brow furrowed and he leaned in over the table. "Do you mind if I give you some advice?"

"Mind? No, I'd really appreciate that."

"You need to get closer to Les. You do that, he'll shoot the portfolio for you, and he'll hook you up with the best agencies in town. I've seen it happen. But right now, you're not exactly making friends at the studio, and that influences Les."

Nick's stomach clenched. Was Keith saying what he thought he was? 'Cause no freakin' way, man.

Keith continued. "You're a lust magnet. I'm not telling

you anything you don't already know—why else would you be here? You made it this far, you put yourself in the right place, right time. Now you gotta play it for what it's worth. Otherwise, you can take those pretty pecs and sculpted abs back to Michigan. Open a gym or something."

"That can't be the only way to break into modeling," Nick groused.

"It's your call," Keith said carefully. "No one will ever force you to do something you don't want to. But you know that famous saying, 'The lady doth protest too much, me thinks'—and you know what that means."

Nick had no freaking idea what that meant. He put his cards on the table. "Look, Keith, I'm not gay. And I'm not gonna do anything . . . like that. If making friends with Les means what I think it does, forget it."

"You'd just as soon go home a failure, huh?"

Nick swallowed hard.

"Let me ask you something. Been dating a lot since you got here?"

"Why do you ask?" In fact, he hadn't dated at all since getting to L.A..

"Haven't seen you with any girls, you haven't talked about anyone. Just curious, that's all."

"Well, don't be. I could get any chick I want. . . ." He trailed off, and for some reason, began to sweat. "I've just been really busy this summer. I haven't had time," he mumbled.

Keith shrugged. "How much time do you need? All I'm saying is, don't close the door on something you've never even tried. At the very least, it might be a means to an end. At best? You might like it."

Nick went all drill sergeant on Sara that evening, just hammering away as she grunted and panted through her push ups. "I want to see ten more reps!" He was angry, and knew it was wrong to take it out on her, but couldn't seem to stop himself.

"No, not . . . possible," she moaned. "Too hard." She flopped on the floor.

"Let's get those arms toned—let's try twenty-pounders." He brought over the weights.

Sara sat up. "Nick, is everything okay?"

"Why wouldn't it be?" He attempted a smile, but missed. "We've been working out for three weeks; it's time to ramp things up. That's how it works."

"Okay, let me put my hair up in scrunchie, and we'll do weights." She pulled a ribboned one from her pocket and pulled her wavy hair into a ponytail.

"Here." He gave her a titanium barbell-shaped weight.

Instead of taking it, Sara slipped her arm around him. "I can tell when something's wrong, Nicky."

He tensed. "Please don't call me that. Now, come on. If you get a callback for *The Outsiders*, you want to look lean and mean."

Sara took the weight.

"Pump it up," he coached. "Come on, up, down, up, down. Feel the burn?" he asked as she struggled with the barbell.

"All I feel is burning tired. Nick, this is too hard," she grunted.

"No pain, no gain," he recited, feeling like a heel but unable to stop.

"These weights are too heavy," she complained. "I can't do it."

"Sure you can. Build up that muscle."

"I'm gonna pull a muscle first." She dropped the weights on the floor.

He exhaled. "Let's do aerobics, then. Here's a jump rope. Think you can manage that?"

"Why are you being so mean?" Sara began to cry as she took the rope and started the routine he'd taught her.

"I'm being real. You're being too sensitive," he growled. "You gotta toughen up in this biz, or you'll never get anywhere. I thought you learned that."

Ten minutes later, Eliot walked in. He grabbed a water bottle from the nightstand and handed it to Sara. "Nick, give the girl a break. She's sweating bullets here. What are you trying to do?

"I'm helping her. She's gotta tone those muscles if she wants to make it."

"It won't help if she's dead."

• • •

After Sara had left to take a shower, Eliot confronted Nick. "What was that all about?"

Nick dropped down on the bed, kicked his sneakers off. "What?"

"Why were you pushing her so hard?"

Defensively, Nick replied, "I ramped up our workout. What's it to you?"

"The girl was practically in tears, Nick. What'd you say to her?"

"Get off it, Kupferberg. If Sara's got an issue, she's a big girl, she can tell me. Or do you speak for her now?"

Eliot's jaw dropped. "What's going on, Nick? This is not you."

"When did you appoint yourself expert on me?" Nick said defensively.

Eliot scratched his head, then turned to leave. "When you're ready to be normal, I'll be outside in the hot tub. Sara and I are going to rehearse there."

Five minutes hadn't gone by before Eliot stomped back into the room, slammed the door, and accused him, "You like her. That's what it is. You want her for yourself."

Nick bolted up. "What the—?"

Eliot pointed his finger accusingly. "You're hot for Sara. Only you can't have her, so you're being nasty to her, and to me, instead. I'm right, aren't I?"

Suddenly, Nick burst out laughing. Leave it to Eliot

to take a situation and bring it to a whole new level of ridiculous.

Eliot's face turned beet red. "Nice to see your mood shift, but I wasn't aware I was being so funny."

Nick got off the bed and threw his arm around Eliot. "Sorry, man. For everything. I just had a really rotten day at work, and I guess I was taking it out on Sara. And you."

Eliot was unconvinced. "You know I like her. . . . I mean, I really like her, Nick."

"Well, go for it, bro. The coast is clear—except for, uh . . . well, there's Donald." He ticked off his fingers. "There's the purity pledge. And there's"—he looked skyward—"the big guy upstairs. I don't think she's giving it up for anyone."

Eliot smiled wanly. "She looks good when she's sweating."

Nick grabbed a comb from the dresser and looked in the mirror. "Got a question for you. This guy at work said some mumbo-crapo about some lady is protesting too much. Like I was supposed to know what he meant."

"What guy at work?"

"What's it matter? Just tell me what it means. If you know."

"'The lady doth protest too much' is a line from *Hamlet*. You remember a little of tenth-grade Shakespeare? It means that if you keep saying no to something, the opposite is true. Like if you keep insisting, over and over, that you're not into Sara, the opposite is true. You really *are* after her."

And how'd we get back there? Nick was confused. He was not after Sara.

"Why not?" Eliot broke in like a mind reader wielding a sledgehammer. "How could you not be attracted to her? She's sexy, she's gorgeous, she's sweet . . . she's the whole deal. I'm having a hard time just being friends."

Nick worked hard to not let his panic show. Sara was hot, anyone could see that. So was Lindsay. Yet he wasn't really interested in either of them. Was it possible that the job was changing him? Turning him gay? Could someone turn gay?

Carefully, he said to Eliot, "Look, bro, I know you like her. And even though I think she's a challenge—Religion Girl's got baggage, like we just said—I'm just stepping out of the way. Not to sound, you know, obnoxious, but I can get any girl. I don't need Sara."

"Good," Eliot said. "Step far out of the way. 'Cause if she does decide to ditch Donald, I want to be the guy, y'know? And even though I'm not that great-looking, I think I have a chance with her. I really do."

All Nick could manage was, "Keep the faith, dude."

The following Thursday night, everyone except Naomi settled around the poker table in the game room. It'd been ten days since Lindsay and Sara had auditioned, a fact Lindsay made everyone aware of . . . every minute. "I so know that phone's gonna ring," she burbled, getting up to refill her glass and Jared's with vodka. "It's gonna be Amanda. And she's gonna say, 'Call back tomorrow, Linz, for your second audition for Cherry. The casting directors love you!'"

She gaily winked at Sara. "And then, Eliot's phone is going to ring—that's the number they have for you, right?"

Nick growled, "Can you just deal the cards, Lindsay? We're here to play poker, not be the audience for your nightly monologue."

Lindsay smiled sweetly as she carefully dealt a card to each person. "And Eliot's gonna answer his phone and go, 'Sara, it's for you. It's Lionel . . . you've got a call back, you're still in the running for *The Outsiders!*'" With a flourish, she threw a dollar into the pot. "Who bets I'm right?"

Jared raised her a dollar. "I bet you lose this hand."

"I hope you're right, Lindsay. I raise both of you," Sara said with a grin.

Eliot won the round. He chose his next words carefully, having planned this for a while. "I have a wager. I bet not a single one of you will know what to do when an earthquake hits. And I'd like to—"

Jared rolled his eyes. "Would you stop with this already? It's August. You'll be gone in a month. Then you won't have to worry."

"You wouldn't either, if you knew what to do," Eliot responded sagely. "I'm going to teach you."

"Like hell." Jared pushed his chair back, went to refill his glass.

Lindsay hopped up too. But she was too stoked, in too good a mood to be annoyed. She strolled behind Eliot's chair, draped her arms around his neck, and playfully kissed the top of his springy hair. "As long as we can keep playing cards, I say, let the El-man go all 'Earthquakes for Dummies' on our asses."

Eliot flushed copiously.

Jared whirled around from the bar, gave her a look.

But he wasn't gonna mess with a deliriously happy Lindsay. And Nick wasn't gonna bother putting a cork in the Catastrophe Kid, either. When El was on a tear, nothing was going to stop him.

Over several hands of Texas Hold 'Em, five-card stud, and high-low, Eliot gave detailed preparedness instructions. "First, there are over three hundred and fifty earthquakes a year in L.A.."

"That's like one a day—no way," said Nick dismissively.

"They're just so small you don't feel them, except for maybe a gentle wave in the middle of the night. That's the other thing: ninety percent of earthquakes happen in the middle of the night."

"Why's that?" Lindsay, suddenly interested, asked.

"There's a theory about seismic activity triggered by geological temperature changes that happen at night."

Lindsay snickered. "I can see why temperatures definitely rise at night."

Eliot got flustered. Damn, that girl could make pure snow blush. He plowed on. "There are generally two kinds of quakes. The first is a rolling quake; it rolls through in a waving motion and you feel like you're on a boat. That's the ground bending. The buildings actually sway and move. The wave rolls through and is gone in about four or five seconds."

"What's the second?" Sara asked nervously.

"The shaker. It hits like a bulldozer. You feel like you got slammed by a WWE wrestler. The shaking is so intense, windows blow out and buildings pancake—implode. The nineteen ninety-four quake lasted over forty-five seconds!"

"Doesn't seem like that long," Nick noted.

"It will when you're going through it," Eliot responded. "Anyway, we won't have much warning, but if you start to feel a wave beneath you, get moving. Whoever's closest to the kitchen, grab the preparedness kit and distribute the contents. Then get out of the kitchen fast! It's one of the worst places to be during an earthquake. If you're downstairs, duck beneath this table; it's the sturdiest one in the house."

Jared was astonished. "You weighed it?"

"I didn't have to. It's made of solid cherry wood, and we'd all fit under it. Unlike the low coffee table in the living room."

Lindsay grinned wickedly. "But it'd be cozier under

the coffee table . . . and there's water there." She looked at Sara. "Oops, it's Kaballah water—you can't drink it. You'll have to go Jewish, or stay parched. 'Cause everyone knows in the event of an earthquake, don't drink the tap water."

Nick started to scold impish Lindsay, but Sara put her hand up. "It's okay. In case of an earthquake, I think I could make an exception. Anyway, what if you're upstairs when . . . I mean . . . if it happens?"

"Bend over and kiss your ass good-bye?" Nick suggested playfully.

"Stay upstairs," Eliot said. "The stairs could collapse, and falling debris could hit you in the head. Stand in a doorway, or against an inside wall. And wherever you are, get away from all windows. By the way, Nick, did you ask Jared where the main gas line is?"

Nick had not.

"Okay. We can check it out tonight. We have to know how to turn it off. Where's it located, Jared?" Eliot asked.

Jared threw his hands up. "How am I supposed to know? This is my uncle's house. And somehow, the subject of the freakin' gas line never came up."

Eliot banged his fist on the table. "Well, it should have. We've got to find it. Unless, in the event of an earthquake, you want to take the chance of being blown sky high."

"Whoa, chill out, E. After the game, I'll find it," Nick said soothingly.

"How will you know where to look?" Sara asked.

"My old man's in construction; I'll figure it out. And," he added, with a stern look at Jared, "I'll show you, in case the subject does come up."

Jared pressed his lips together. "You guys are taking this way too far. This is ridiculous."

Eliot shrugged. "Dude, you want our rent money? There's a few things you're gonna have to deal with—we should have figured this out back in June. Since we're talking about your life too, maybe you want to take it more seriously."

"You go, E-man!" Lindsay, borderline sloshed, clapped her hands.

Jared decided to push Eliot's buttons. "What makes you so sure it'll be an earthquake, anyway, not a wildfire? Or a tsunami?"

"I'm not sure," Eliot responded. "I bought gas masks for all of us, and helmets, in case of that. They're in the cabinet with the earthquake preparedness kit."

It was all Jared could do to keep from pissing his pants. Tears of laughter rolled down his face. His question had been facetious.

Eliot was steaming.

Lindsay put her forefinger to her lips and tilted her head. "Eliot, when's your birthday?"

"What's that got to do with anything?"

"I bet you're a Leo. 'Cause, baby, you are a passionate one. You roar, boy! Am I right? Are you a Leo?"

"His birthday is August twelfth," Nick said.

Lindsay squealed, "Oh, my god! I was right! And that's next week—we are so having a party." She jumped up and pirouetted around the room, "Par-*tay*! Par-*tay*! I say—par-*tay*!"

"Lindsay, sit down and deal the cards. It's your turn," Jared said.

"Only if you say okay to a party." She plopped into Jared's lap and kissed the tip of his nose.

No way could Jared resist Lindsay. Who, Eliot wondered, really could? So when, as dealer, she insisted on a "new game," they all went along with it.

"Here we go," she grinned maniacally. "Only one card each. I deal it face down. You can*not* look at it!"

They indulged her.

"Now," she said. "I want each of you to take the card—don't look—and stick it on your forehead so everyone can see what you have, only you can't."

"You're making this up," Nick said skeptically.

"I am not!" Lindsay protested, "It's called Schmuck Poker. Am I pronouncing it right, Jared?"

Jared was laughing too hard to speak, but he nodded his head as he pressed his card, a five of clubs, on his forehead.

"Come on," Lindsay urged, "everyone do it."

Eliot shook his head in disbelief. Lindsay had a jack of spades; Sara, a seven of hearts; Nick, a queen of hearts. He had no idea what he had.

"Now we bet," Lindsay declared.

"On what?" Nick asked incredulously.

"On our cards, silly," she answered. "This is poker. Jared, you start."

"I bet five dollars." He tossed his money into the pot.

Which sent Sara into a whirl of laughter.

"You think you have me beat?" Jared challenged, "with that piddly card on your forehead?"

"I raise to ten dollars!" was her feisty response.

Lindsay, sure she had the table beat—'cause after all, she was Lindsay—capped the betting at twenty-five dollars—but not before everyone had dissolved into hysterics and finger-pointing. By that point, Nick, Eliot, and Sara had folded, believing Miss Thing the probable winner.

Which is how Lindsay scooped the pot away from Nick and Eliot, who, it turned out, both had her beat. She'd bluffed.

Triumphantly, she crowed, "I win! I win! Now we have to have a party. We'll celebrate Eliot's birthday, and call-backs for the audition. Sara's and mine."

Sara, giggling at Lindsay's antics, finally managed to say, "You're gettin' ahead of yourself. No one's called—"

Precisely at that moment (she could not have staged it better), Lindsay's cell phone rang.

A half second later, so did Eliot's.

13

Lindsay and Sara: Two Auditions

Pumped or pissed. Lindsay couldn't decide what she was more of. Getting the callback meant she'd made it to the next round of auditions, trounced hundreds of Cherry-wannabes. Yesss! She was smokin'! Lick fingertip, raise it high in the air!

But so—*damn*—had Sara! What was up with that?

For the benefit of the housemates, she'd fronted "knowing" they'd both get callbacks, when naturally, she knew nothing of the sort.

Wait . . . take that back. She did know one thing: She'd kicked *ass* at her first audition. 'Cause that's the kind of thing, as she'd joyfully recounted to Jared, you just "know" when you're doing it, and get confirmed by the looks from the casting directors when you're done. They lean over, whisper in each other's ears, write on their note pads, nod encouragingly, and say—this is key—"We'll be in touch."

As opposed to the dismissive "Thanks for coming." The English-to-Hollywood translation: "You sucked." Forget about a follow-up. Only good news nets the phone call.

So when Amanda herself rang during the poker game, Lindsay shot off her chair as if she'd been launched.

When Eliot sang out that Lionel was calling for Sara, Lindsay crash-landed, her good mood up in flames.

How'd *that* happen? She'd personally seen to it that Sara gave the wrong kind of audition. Told her to do the reading all sugary and saccharine when the full script confirmed they were going for Cherry Bomb, not Cherry Vanilla.

So what'd happened? Had Sara had only pretended to believe her, and gone balls-out the way the casting directors wanted? Or worse, had Sara read Cherry's lines dripping with toothache-inducing sweetness, and won the judges over anyway?

The second scenario was Lindsay's total nightmare.

'Cause if that'd happened, it meant the girl from nowhere had "something"—the indefinable unquantifiable charisma. The "thing" that must not be named.

The dark art Lindsay had no defense against.

She couldn't share her insecurities with Jared. She'd sort of not told him about deliberately trying to undermine Sara. Jared played by Hollywood rules—winning at any cost, that is—but there were some things he was stupidly stubborn about.

Like wanting Lindsay to win the role fairly. Like it was okay to procure the script and insider info, but not okay to screw up someone else's chances. Especially when that someone else was rent-paying Sara?

Lindsay had played her own game. It'd backfired. Somehow, Sara Calvin, a nobody from nowhere, now had the same exact chance of nailing this role as Lindsay had. Where was the fair in that?

Lindsay's stomach churned. She really, really didn't want to lose out to her own housemate.

The first round of *Outsider* auditions had taken place in the casting directors' offices in Beverly Hills. It'd been a cattle call, the waiting area jammed with dozens of would-be Cherrys. They came in all stripes: blondes, brunettes, redheads, African Americans, Asians, Latinas, tall, tiny, short, stocky, curvy, stick-thin. Some wore cowboy hats (did they think this was a remake of *Bonanza*?), others decked out in prim 1960s dresses. More than half the girls had anxious stage mamas and papas at their sides. Several paced, others perched, many couldn't decide how to calm their stomach-churning nerves. Silently or out loud, all were going over the audition scenes in their heads—and overtly or covertly, wishing the worst to every other person in the room.

They waited an excruciatingly long time to be called in, one by one, for their tryout. Then they got five minutes to make a lasting impression on the casting directors with a stellar reading. And then, coming out, one by one, by turns hopeful, dejected, deluded.

Two weeks had passed since the heinous cattle call, and the field had been whittled down considerably. According to reliable sources—i.e., Galaxy office gossip—there were now about twenty girls in contention. Eighteen others besides Lindsay and Sara.

This second round of competition took place at the Warner Brothers studios in Burbank in front of the movie's director and producers. The crop of actresses who made it through would then have a final audition for the studio boss. Rusty Larson had a weekly tennis game with the head of Warner Brothers studios. Should Lindsay be Galaxy's only client in the finals, she was in.

She had to make it through this round. Two obstacles stood in her way: the director, Katherine McCawley, and Sara Calvin. She didn't know the director at all, didn't know what card to play to win her over. She knew Sara all too well.

To better her chances with the first, she'd rented the DVD of the director's first movie, and rehearsed a gushing suck-up speech about it.

To better her chances of beating Sara, she planned to sneak into the girl's audition: Whatever Sara did in her tryout, Lindsay had to do it better. Slipping in unnoticed was the easy part. She needed one piece of luck: for Sara to be called before her.

"Lindsay Pierce, you're up first!" A clipboard-clutching assistant summoned her. Clue number one that the good luck goddess might not be smiling on her plan. Sara, from across the room, gave her a fingers-crossed signal. Which was, she had to reluctantly admit, sweet of her. Which Lindsay had deliberately not been toward her. She prayed the karma gods weren't out today.

Her stomach churning, she managed to wave back.

Gamely, she followed Assistant Lady from the waiting area to the set, which turned out to be the one used for TV's *Smallville*. Made sense, Lindsay conceded, as that show took place in small-town America, as did *The Outsiders*. She smiled inwardly: Being tested in this setting reinforced her instinct about what to wear. In the 1983 movie, Diane Lane had done most of her scenes in buttoned-up blouses and skirts. Today's Cherry, at home in this setting, would be clean-cut, prepped up, in Lucky jeans, midheel boots, layered pink polo, carrying a Kate Spade bag.

Lindsay Pierce? Check!

She'd used a curling iron to give herself long, loose waves, brushed her bangs to the side and clipped them back with a ribbon bow—her one homage to the beribboned actress in the original.

The casting agents, director, producer, and random

assorted assistants huddled in a row several feet from the stage, to which Lindsay had been asked to ascend. Huge spotlights from the overhead beams lit the area, an instant reminder of her days spent on a stage not unlike this one, as Zoe Wong.

Her stomach settled. She no longer worried about the good luck gods. She waved at her audience. "Hi, I'm Lindsay Pierce, and I'm a big fan of—"

"We know who you are," one of the producers interrupted her. "We know how thrilled you are to be here, and we're running late."

She gulped. Okay, so they'd heard this all before. Whatever. She lifted her head confidently, and smiled graciously.

"We're going to do two scenes," he told her. "We'll start with Cherry and Dallas at the drive-in movie, then we'll move on to Cherry and Ponyboy. Are you ready?"

She drew a breath. "Locked and loaded."

He called the actor who'd be standing in for Dallas Winston: Lindsay was caught off guard. He was tall, scruffy, rugged . . . omigosh! The boy from the park! What was his name—Mark? For a moment, she forgot herself, gave him a huge smile, and started to ask how he'd done on that other movie. The young actor saved her from what would have been a huge gaffe. He got his Dallas on immediately.

Caddish, cocky, sexy, he pretended to offer her a soda. His reading was half sneer, half come-on. She knew the lines, knew when and how to toss the soda at him . . . she also knew she'd gotten flustered. Had screwed it up. She'd meant to play it haughty, righteous, and cool. Instead, she knew she came off unsteady, unsure of herself.

Mark-as-Dallas did his next line.

Cherry's comeback to him was supposed to be flippant, a one-up. Only she didn't do it right! Another half-assed reading—Lindsay was starting to panic. Where was her inner nasty when she needed it most? Lindsay so wanted a do-over. Otherwise, based on that stinky reading, it'd be *all* over.

"Okay," called the casting director, "now we'll do a Ponyboy scene." The actor called on to read with her this time turned out to be Tom Welling, the actor who starred in *Smallville*. Lindsay didn't know him, was surprised he was reading for Ponyboy: He was much too pretty for the part.

She did the line pointing out what an original name Ponyboy was. She did it without any sarcasm. She then told him everyone called her Cherry because of her hair color. She'd planned on tossing it, but didn't.

The next scene they were asked to do was further on in the script.

A strange sensation came over her as she read with the handsome young actor. Gazing into his chiseled face, his jade-green eyes, she saw not an actor, but . . . but . . . Jared? She didn't have time to think about it. Instinct said: Go with it.

And she forgot, just forgot—she'd later say—how

she'd planned on reading Cherry's lines, how the script called for a mean girl. Ponyboy smiled Jared's smile, and she knew in an instant that no matter what the script called for, no matter what the director's "vision" was, it was wrong. It wasn't Cherry. The key to finding the character wasn't in the book, the movie, the screenplay, or insider info. It was right there, inside her all along.

Cherry wasn't some random cardboard snob, no matter what era the movie took place in. She was a teenager—impetuous, flirty, feisty, but also sweet, soulful, and sensitive. With enough foresight to understand she was stuck in a world that wasn't fair to the greasers or the socs.

Some of Cherry's characteristics fit her, Lindsay, like a glove. Others were such-the-Sara. She ended up doing the reading as neither: She did it as Cherry.

Her last line of the reading was, "Just don't forget that some of us watch the sunsets, too."

The actor gave her a surprised look. She thought: I can't believe I did that. I did exactly what I shouldn't have. I blew it. I blew—

"Lindsay—is that your name?" The director spoke first. "That was an interesting take."

The casting director coughed. "What happened between the first reading and this one? You went in an entirely different direction." Translation: "If I knew you were going to read this way, you would not have been called back."

Lindsay had nothing to lose. "I didn't plan it. I'm not

sure what came over me. I think it was just . . . that's Cherry. It's who she is. It's who I was at that moment. I know that's not the way you wanted it. I'm sorry, but . . ."

The director stood up, her round face made pretty with a genuine smile. "Lindsay, I know you were in a sit-com several years ago. But today? You blew me away."

Lindsay lit up like the Las Vegas skyline.

"Of course," the casting director quickly threw in, "we have more actresses to see. But I think it's fair to say you will be hearing from us."

Lindsay flew back to the waiting area and called Jared. And Amanda. And Caitlin, Julie, and . . . pretty much everyone she had on speed dial.

Then she snuck into Sara's reading.

Sara was reading with Tom Welling. She stood tall, her hand on her hip, her chin up. She'd worn dusty blue jeans, loafers, a button-down shirt, and a blazer, her hair caught in a ponytail.

Lindsay watched silently. Sara didn't suck. So far.

Then Sara came to one of the most famous lines in the movie. Diane Lane had done it rushed, in a whisper, almost as though, if she said it fast enough, it wouldn't be real.

Sara's delivery was slow, dreamy. "'I could fall in love with Dallas Winston. I hope *I* never see him again, or I will.'"

She's thinking about Nick, Lindsay realized with alarm. Worse, she's . . . she's . . . fucking brilliant.

Lindsay had been so busy on the phone, congratulating

herself, she hadn't heard the rest of Sara's reading. Was it as amazing as what she'd just heard? Would she torture herself by listening in to the reactions of the judges?

Is Paris Hilton a spotlight-slut?

"What's your name again?" the director asked, interested.

"And you've never done any acting before?" This from a clucking producer. "And you're from the Texas panhandle? Near Oklahoma?"

When they got to the question "How would you feel about dying your hair red?" Lindsay vomited.

14

Beautiful People Partying

Naomi: Saturday Night, 10–11: 00 p.m.

Oh, yeah, we're goin' to a party, party!

Naomi knew the song. "Birthday," by the Beatles. Sara must have asked the deejay to play it in honor of Eliot's birthday. She was one of the few who remembered the reason they'd thrown a party. Naomi watched from her corner of the living room as Sara planted a kiss on Eliot's cheek and wished him a happy nineteenth birthday. Eliot blushed. Profusely. He tried to return the kiss, aiming for her lips, but Sara had already turned the other cheek.

Naomi chuckled inwardly. A snapshot of Eliot: His aim is true, but his target keeps moving.

None of the other partygoers, mostly guests of Lindsay and Jared, even noticed the song, or its honoree: They were too busy reveling in the fabulousness of themselves. They were packed into the living room, game room, overflowing into the backyard.

In a twisted way—she was the only one in the room, or the zip code, who'd think this—it was like the homeless shelters, crowded and loud. Just switch designer for destitute, laughter for tears, and hope for hopeless. As Sara says, we're all children of God. Just some are more favored than others; more or less entitled. The haves and the have-nots.

Tonight was all about the haves. To wit:

A night of short skirts and long beers, buff bodies and bare skin, roaming eyes and brushing fingers, teasing, flirting, the rush of being young, hot, and born to the high life. All over the house, inside and out, there was dancing—dirty and otherwise—singing, raucous laughter, clinking of glasses, kissing of asses, touchy-feely-gushy and phony. All fueled by an open bar, uppers, downers, alphabet drugs, and, she guessed, simply the kind of bubbleheaded joy that being rich and worry-free gets you.

How does it feel to be, one of the beautiful peo-*ple . . ."*

It was the Beatles song "Baby, You're a Rich Man." Had the deejay read her mind? Naomi skulked back into the kitchen, suddenly itching to get as far from the merriment as she could. Being invisible was something she had a lot of practice in. At various times during the evening, Sara, Nick, and Eliot had tried to involve her, but she'd resisted. She appreciated the effort the boys from the Midwest had made to get to know her, how they'd quickly overcome their resistance to her moving in.

But times like this, Naomi realized she knew better:

She should not even be here. She did not belong in Richie Rich's house. Naomi Foster was as far from "beautiful people" as you could be.

She knew her Beatles, though. They were tapes, not CDs, back then, that her parents used to play in the car. Her sister Annie liked to sing along, but could never remember the words. Naomi had memorized every lyric. Too bad she couldn't remember what it felt like to be happy, to feel whole, and wholly safe in that little car, just the four of them, with the four mop-tops in the tape player.

Jared's kitchen was a mess, the floor already sticky, countertops piled high with dirty dishes, stained glasses. She rolled her sleeves up, and reached for a sponge when Sara suddenly appeared, hands on shapely hips. "Jared hired a caterer, remember? They'll clean up. Come sit with us."

Naomi knew she should feel grateful, but all she felt was out of place. It must have shown on her face. Sara added, "You don't have to talk to Jared and Lindsay's friends. Me, Nick, and Eliot are sitting with Wes and Candy."

Wes Czeny and Candy Dew were Sara's—and her—bosses at *Caught in the Act*, and had been nothing but nice to Naomi. Which made her feel even less like socializing with them.

"Join us—do it for the birthday boy," Sara coaxed.

Playing the Eliot card worked. Naomi reluctantly trailed Sara into the living room, where Nick immediately scooched over to make room for her on the couch. "Have a scoop of caviar." Nick offered to spoon some of the expensive fish eggs onto a cracker. "It's salty, but hey— probably be a long time until the likes of us gets to enjoy this again."

Naomi shook her head no. In the apartment in North- ridge, her mom used to try and make Fridays festive. After dinner, she'd put out a spread of crackers and cheese, a cut-up pineapple with strawberries, cookies, pie, and ice cream. The family would sit down and watch TV sitcoms together. *All for Wong* was her sister Annie's and their mom's favorite; *Home Improvement,* her dad's and hers. It was their big splurge for the week. And that was only when her dad had picked up an odd job as a handyman, or Mom had managed to score a cleaning-lady gig. The apartment, a one-bedroom in a small complex, wasn't theirs. They were subletting temporarily, and, she'd only found out later, illegally.

"The kindness of strangers," her mom had once said. "One day, we won't have to depend on that. Our family will be the kind ones."

"One day" had never come for Laura or Lonny Foster. Naomi had long given up on it ever coming for her.

"Earth to Naomi." Eliot had been trying to get her atten- tion. She flushed. "Oh, sorry—did you need something?"

"I was asking if you did. I was taking drink orders. What's your pleasure?"

"I'm good, thanks," she replied, and turned to the exchange between Sara and Wes. "When Nick makes it as a famous model, Lionel's going to represent him, and everyone's going to want to interview him. I'd book him for *Caught in the Act* now if I were you."

Candy, already tipsy, went coy. "Nick can come in for a pre-interview any time." She rested her hand on Nick's knee—just a moment too long. Sara's face went cross for that moment.

Eliot caught it. He bolted up. "So, who else besides myself would like another drink?"

"I'll have another martooni. Make it dirty, with three olives." Candy held her empty glass up.

Wes, settled into the large armchair, seconded. "I'll go for another brewski if you've got a free hand."

Nick started to get up. "I'm ready for more beer too. I'll help carry."

Eliot looked at Sara. "How 'bout it—one tiny glass of wine or beer, anything?"

Sara didn't drink.

Nick nudged Sara. "Aw, come on, in honor of the E-man—just one won't hurt."

Something told Naomi that Nick was wrong.

Jared: Midnight–2:00 a.m.

Everybody's movin', everybody's groovin', at the Love Shack! Love Shack, bay-yaay-bee!

Mostly everybody *was* groovin' to the B52s, Jared noted as he surveyed the house—Uncle Rob's house, that is—everybody but him. Anxious that groovin' could turn to wildin', he policed the premises to be sure no one was getting into things they shouldn't, that nothing belonging to his uncle was touched. His crew was cool, but when you put Lindsay together with her friends, mixed in boisterous music and an open bar, destruction was a foregone conclusion.

Which had always been one of La Linz's more adorable qualities—except when *he* had to be the responsible party at the party. That wasn't fun. Her shenanigans weren't nearly as cute.

A week ago, she'd wanted, begged for, the party—supposedly for Eliot's birthday, but clearly, for herself.

A week ago, he'd told her, "What part of 'not gonna happen' don't you get?"

She'd cajoled, coaxed, kept him a very happy "prisoner" in the bedroom until he agreed.

Negotiations had begun the next morning. She'd won the round about having it in the house, 'cause, really, where else could they afford? He'd won the round about having it catered, with a clean-up crew, insisting she pay for half the expenses.

She'd countered that since Nick, Eliot, and Sara lived here too, they'd have to kick in. He'd said in that case, they got to invite their friends too. She'd make a face and gone, "Eeeww!" Until she realized, hello, how many Cali-friends did those three even have?

They were set, in agreement—everyone except Naomi

chipped in. Then Lindsay came home from the second *Outsiders* audition, sick, bummed, so sure she'd lost out to Sara, that she didn't want a party, didn't want to see anyone. The drama princess wanted only to "hide in her room." She could not face the world.

So Jared had become Cajole Boy, adamant that she was wrong. She hadn't lost the part to anyone yet; she'd done a kick-ass job at the audition—yes, he had heard that through the grapevine. She should be brimming with confidence. And furthermore, he actually heard himself insisting, they were so having a party. So there!

So here.

Here he was with a house full of people, the young, restless, bold, and beautiful . . . and he, acting like a nervous parent, worried that someone was gonna break into the liquor cabinet. How'd that happen again?

In the end, he'd only asked three things of Lindsay. If anyone asked, the house was hers: She was renting for the summer. No dancing on the tables. And the biggie: no inviting anyone who might come into contact with his dad, and therefore rat him out, was allowed at the party.

She'd moaned that it wouldn't be a problem. Which cool people would want to party with a loser like her? Surely no celebrities.

So what, Jared asked himself as he patrolled the backyard, were Nicole and Mischa doing on the chaise lounge? And why were Ashlee, Jessica, Lindsay, and their boy-toys in the hot tub, while the cast of *Smallville* splashed in the pool? Paris Hilton and her boyfriend-of-the-moment were playing Xbox; Nicky Hilton and her new guy were challenging them. He thought he spotted the *Desperate Housewives* teens in the loft, and surely that tiny blonde with the oversize sunglasses and beefy security guard was an Olsen twin.

Leave it to Lindsay: Her bout of self-pity had been brief, then she'd turned the house party into a tabloid's dream.

When he'd collared her, she'd waved him away dismissively. "It's Saturday night, they're only here for an appetizer. They've all got elsewhere to be. You know it as well as I do."

Heaving a sigh, Jared checked his watch, hoping the magic hour had arrived and they'd leave. So far as he could tell, no paparazzi had trailed anyone. No photogs meant no outing via any Internet sights or tabs the next day: Jared's dad would be none the wiser to his summer scam.

"Yo, Ja-*red*, wuzzup, man?" His buddy Tripp fell into stride with him as he stalked into the living room. "You're not looking too happy. Problems in paradise?" He motioned over to Lindsay, cavorting on the dance floor.

"You wish," Jared said. "Lindsay and I are good. There is no window of opportunity for you."

"Then, wazzup with the downer stares?" Tripp challenged.

"It's all good," Jared insisted.

"Well, then c'mon over. Julie can't get up, and she wants to chill with your ass."

Julie, who'd suffered a hairline fracture that night at Spider, was playing her "tragic injury" for all it was worth. "I can't dance," she complained to Jared. "I need company. Lots of it. And liquor."

"I'm here for you, Julie. What are you drinking?" Jared asked.

"A lot."

That was the theme of the night, as far as Jared and Lindsay's group was concerned. Those who couldn't, or wouldn't, dance were drinking, eating, and dishing. The talk was shop: who was up for what role, who got hired or fired, who was sleeping with the director, or wanted to; who was hooking up; who was breaking up; who was in the closet, who was about to be outed.

He'd heard it all before. Over and over. Like a loop. Jared found his attention drifting away. To Lindsay, looking hot while dancing, drinking, and giggling. He checked on Uncle Rob's belongings, the guitars on the walls, the copper bongs, the CD/record collection. No one had touched anything.

"Jared." Julie pulled him off mental surveillance. "Unknown dude flirting with your girl." She pointed across the room.

He was tall, wearing rumpled cords and a wrinkled T-shirt that read "Napster Rules." He was so not one of them. And he was all over Lindsay.

Before Jared could jump up, Lindsay led the new-comer over to their group. "Guys, this is Mark."

She was met with blank stares.

"Mark!" Lindsay squealed. "You remember, from the park." She jogged their memories. "He rescued George Clooney, and he tried out for that heinous *Heiress* movie. Neither of us got it."

Jared remembered: Mark had auditioned opposite Lindsay, and presumably Sara, for *The Outsiders*. Mark, this granola guy, was now an FOL, a Friend of Lindsay?

"Move over, guys," Lindsay urged. "Make room for us. Mark, what can Jared get you to drink?"

"Yeah, what're you having, man?" Jared grumbled, getting up to head over to the bar. He'd need another few shots of tequila if he had to hang out with this dude.

When Jared, carrying a tray full of shots, returned, Tripp was singing some old folkie song. Mark, Austin, MK, and Julie were singing along.

Jared freaked: Tripp had removed one of the guitars off the wall. Before he said anything, Lindsay leaped up. Even quasi-drunk, she realized this was a major no-no. She swiftly wrested the instrument from him and put it back on the wall.

Mark left soon after. Jared found himself relieved. A relief that lasted a microsecond:

"Body shots!" Lindsay shouted, peeling off her top—to reveal a cute cami underneath. "Let's do body shots, let's get this party movin'!"

She practically skipped into the game room, rounding up as many revelers as she could. She opened the sliding doors, summoning party-peeps inside. When she bumped straight into Sara and Eliot, she hooted, "It's your birthday! Happy—"

Eliot put his palms up. "As a birthday present, Lindsay, please don't throw up on me."

That set off a giggle-fit. Which, midway through, led to Lindsay's inept interpretation of *E.T.*—the Spielberg classic, not the TV show. She held up her finger and started chanting, "Eh . . . lee . . . yot . . . Eh . . . lee-yot . . ."

Caitlin hooted, "Wait, your finger has to glow. What's in the house that we can use to light it up?"

Lindsay, Caitlin, and Ava scouted around. Five minutes later, they returned, having glued glitter to all their fingertips. And succeeded in making Eliot turn tomato red and probably wish he really could go "Home—ET go hooomme," even as the girls were dancing around him and teasing.

The body shots had just begun: Ava was the first volunteer. Tripp had poured a tequila shot into her belly button and was first in line to lap it up. MK followed, as did Nick, then a flotilla of fellas, as Lindsay laughingly called them.

Jared felt calmer. Most of the celeb crew had split, as Lindsay predicted. No photogs had crashed the party, and so far, nothing he could see had crashed and burned.

A few body shots among friends—what was the harm

in that? As long as no one was licking liquor off his girl-friend, that is. After Ava, it was Caitlin's turn to be tickled with tongues and tequila. Even Eliot had joined in by this time: no doubt because Nick had finally made sure the E-man was sloshed. Sara and Naomi remained the tee-totalers in the house.

"Yap! Yap! Yap!" He heard it, even as he joined the line to do a shot off Caitlin, and whirled around. Lionel, Sara's agent, had arrived. In his arms, he carried a small rat-faced dog.

"George-fuckin'-Clooney!" Lindsay bellowed. "What's he doing at my party? And . . . who invited you?"

Lionel, who couldn't wait to rid himself of the runt, gave him over to Lindsay. "Good evening to you, too, Ms. Thing," he said. "Sara invited me, and I happened to be dog-sitting. Since you and George Clooney are already BFFs, I didn't think you'd mind if I brought him."

"Think again," Lindsay hissed, then drew Lionel into the kitchen, where Sara immediately rushed over to them, alarmed. "I . . . I . . . ," she stuttered. "I'm sorry, Lionel, I didn't invite you. . . ." She trailed off, unsure of what to say. Lionel was a direct link to Rusty Larson, and even Sara had pledged to keep anyone away who might report to him.

Lionel beamed at her. "I know you didn't, sweetie. I called the cell phone, and Eliot said to come on over. I have delicious news for you! And I had to give it to you in person."

Jared barged in. "Come here, man, I need to talk to you." Before anyone could stop him, he'd pulled Lionel out of the kitchen, through the living room, and out to the backyard. And told the dude in no uncertain terms: He wasn't here; there was no party; Rusty Larson would know nothing about this evening. And—urgent bulletin—whatever news he had for Sara, if it was about *The Outsiders* audition, he'd better tell Jared first. No way would Jared let Lindsay be humiliated. Not tonight, and not like this.

15

Sara Feels the Earth Move

Sunday Morning, 2–4:00 a.m.

Sara was shaking with dread and anticipation.

"You got the part! You got the part!" Naomi repeated excitedly. "Why else would Lionel be here?"

"Is that what he said?" Sara rushed at Eliot. "Is that what he told you on the phone?"

"He said he had good news for you," Eliot explained, "and he wanted you to come to the phone."

"So why didn't you come get me?"

Nick answered for his bud. "El probably said, 'Come over and tell her yourself.' Am I right?"

Eliot offered a sloppy smile. And a hiccup.

Sara bit her nails. "But . . . how could you do that, Eliot? If he's come to say I won the audition, that would mean Lindsay lost. And she'd know it, in front of everyone. That'd be horrible for her."

Eliot's bug eyes widened, and he happily slapped his

face. "Oh. I was only thinking of you, Sara-dorable one."

She sighed. She'd been preached to her whole life about the evils of alcohol. What she hadn't understood until this summer was that liquor loosened lips, acting like truth serum. She knew Eliot was crushing on her—who in the house didn't? But she didn't think it was serious. As far as Eliot knew, she was still committed to Donald. Or had he inferred the truth, that she wasn't so sure anymore?

She adored Eliot. As a friend. A true friend, one she hoped she'd have for life. It'd never be anything more than that. And now, this thing, inviting Lionel over—in front of Lindsay—that was unlike Eliot. It was just insensitive.

Naomi read her mind. "What do you care? Lindsay's been nothing but mean to you. And besides, if Lionel is here to give you this amazing news, it just means you were the better actress, the better fit for the role."

Sara found herself saying, "But Lindsay, she'll die if she doesn't get it."

"Oh, come on, Sara." This was Nick now. "She's a drama queen. She'll get over it. And get another role, too. Lindsay's determined; she's a survivor."

Did that mean Nick thought Sara wasn't? She looked at him. Her legs turned to jelly. Those charcoal eyes were smoldering. And those lips . . . no! She was not going to think about Nick Maharis now.

She stalked out of the kitchen, on a mission to find Lindsay. She didn't make it farther than the living room.

Jared and Lionel were just coming inside. Lionel rushed up to her and threw his arms around her. He glanced over his shoulder at Jared. "So is it all right if I tell her?"

Sara had not won the role—yet. The news, Lionel insisted, was almost as good. He had just got a call from Amanda, who was having dinner with the producer of the movie. They'd narrowed the search to two actresses for Cherry, and Sara was one of them. She'd audition for the head of the studio on Monday. Wasn't that the most fabulous news ever?"

Sara stared at her agent. "I'm up against Lindsay, aren't I? She's the other person."

Lionel's silence was her answer. "Come on, Sara, you're supposed to be over the moon about this news. Why the long face?"

"Does Lindsay know?"

Lionel assured her that Jared was going to find her and give her the excellent news that she, too, was a finalist. "It's all good, Sara. Now I insist you come and talk to me. I dragged all the way out here to tell you."

Numbly, she followed him, and soon found herself in the middle of the living room, with Lionel, Naomi, Eliot, and Nick. In a daze, she watched Nick's eyes wander the room: checking out the designer-decked dollies, as they checked him out. Yet he made no move to leave their little group.

Lionel leaned over, whispered in her ear conspiratorially, "You like him?"

She whispered back. "No! I mean . . . not in that way. It's nothing."

What Lionel said next disquieted her. "Are you sure he's straight?"

She jerked her head up. "What do you mean?"

"What's the secret, you two? Why are you whispering?" Nick nudged her.

"I asked Sara if you were straight."

Sara had never noticed Nick's vein, the one in his forehead that protruded when he was enraged, the way his lips pressed together, his eyes dulled. He bolted up without a word, headed for the bar.

Eliot was surprised. "Why would you ask a question like that? Nick's a babe-magnet."

"I heard about this thing called gaydar. . . ." Naomi hesitated. "Like radar."

Lionel shrugged. "No, nothing like that. It was an honest question, that's all. Just because girls like him doesn't mean he swings that way. Why should Sara waste lustful looks on someone who bats for the other side?"

Sara blushed and stood up. "I need to find Lindsay."

Lindsay found her first. Out in the backyard, Sara was walking toward the pool when Lindsay, completely hammered, called from behind her. "I have just one question for you, Sara. Why didn't you read the scene like I told you to?"

Lindsay had seen her audition? Sara whirled around. The stuck-up girl was coming at her now, guns blazing. But in her eyes, those normally dancing light brown eyes, Sara saw panic. And pain. She gulped.

"You didn't believe me, did you?" Lindsay accused her. "You thought I was tryin' to trip you up?"

"I never thought that, Lindsay. Anyways, your plan worked, didn't it? We conquered the competition, me and you."

"My plan worked. Yeah, right." Lindsay laughed mirthlessly.

Sara steeled herself. "But you're right. I didn't end up reading it the way you said. I don't know what came over me, exactly, but—I know you'll think this is stupid—I've been reading the other script, the one the policeman wrote?"

"I have no idea what you're talking about," Lindsay said.

"The one you tossed into the pool that first night? And I got it out?"

A hint of recognition crossed Lindsay's face. "*That* one? How does some hack script by some random wannabe have anything to do with *The Outsiders*?"

"It doesn't. Not exactly." Sara drew a deep breath. "But there's a character in it, her name is Kate. And she sort of is like Cherry in a way. Conflicted, you know. It sort of spoke to me. And I ended up doing the reading as if I was Kate. Funny, huh?"

"Yeah, funny ha-ha," Lindsay mumbled, then turned and walked away.

Sara took a step toward her, then froze. She wanted not to care about Lindsay. She wanted to win the role of Cherry: She deserved it. Her mom deserved it—all those years of sacrifice, all that money spent on the pageants, everything the family had poured into their only daughter. This was the payoff. This was the dream come true. She saw her name up on the screen: "And Introducing Sara Calvin as Cherry." She'd be the toast of Texarkana. Best of all? It'd be because her whole family had worked for it and she'd earned it. She should win the role of Cherry, because it was right.

Lindsay. The cute, bubbly, freckled girl popped into her head, much as Sara tried to push the image away. Lindsay had worked too—she'd spent her whole childhood supporting her family. This was her moment, her destiny, too. And that was the difference between the two of them, Sara realized. She wanted the role—desperately—but she wanted it for her family, for her town, because she believed it her destiny.

Lindsay simply wanted it for herself.

Sara hung her head.

Naomi came looking for her. "What are you doing out here? Did you find Lindsay? What'd she say to you?"

"No," Sara lied, "I didn't find her yet. I'm still looking."

She stared out over the valley. The million-dollar view, Jared had called it. At night, the lights twinkled below her, around her. And this night, the air was so clear, like someone had sprinkled it with sweet jasmine, citrusy orange, and lemon.

She didn't know exactly how long she spent staring at the horizon. She was pretty sure the music had ended and several guests had left. Lionel had stuck his head out to say good-bye, to mention he was leaving the dog, since he didn't want to drive drunk with it—Amanda would have him fired if he upset George Clooney in any way— and to apologize if he'd caused a rift.

Sara strolled around the side of the house so she wouldn't have to talk to anyone. She'd gotten around to the driveway when she heard it.

The weeping: It was heartbreaking. Someone was heaving, hiccupping, sobbing like the world had ended. She looked around, but saw no one. She didn't have to. Sara knew who it was.

It was coming from the driveway, where Jared's convertible was parked. Her eyes caught a flash of copper. Lindsay was in the driver's seat, bent over the steering wheel, crying her eyes out, hiccupping.

Sara had the urge to go over and shake her! To shout, "Stop it, you haven't lost the part. It's not decided yet!"

If she did that, she might say more. She might give voice to a tiny, persistent thought, fluttering in her brain like a darn hummingbird. And she wasn't ready to swipe it away, nor to let it sing.

Shaking, Sara turned on her heel and walked back inside the house. To a shocked Nick she said, "I'd like a vodka martini. Straight up."

It wasn't the taste she took to. It was the burning feeling, stinging, punishing as it went down her throat. She asked for another.

And another. Until the truth hit her between the eyes and she let the hummingbird sing. She would not take the role from Lindsay. She'd give a horrible reading, or better, not show up for the audition. Tell Lionel she didn't want it after all. She'd kick her own dream to the curb, because giving is better than receiving, because charity, empathy, feeling for others was part of her DNA. She would let Lindsay have this role. Because it was the right thing to do. So why did it hurt so much?

"Another, please," she slurred, and held out her glass. Eliot and Naomi had wandered off. Most of the guests had left.

"Are you sure, Sara?" Nick asked, "You've had a lot . . . for your first time drinking."

"I'm so totally sure, Nick-o-lash," she slurred.

Nick's large palm cupped her chin, forcing her to look into his eyes, those smoldering charcoal eyes, now filled with concern. For her.

"Please, sir," she belched while paraphrasing *Oliver Twist*. "May I have s'more?"

He didn't get the reference; that was okay. Sara pictured him nude as he walked over to the liquor bar, watching his thigh muscles scissor, his cute, tight butt move. *I'm in lust with Nick Maharis*. There, she'd admitted it. Or was it love? Love or lust, how could she know for sure? She'd never felt this way around Donald, or anyone. Sara didn't know you could.

She'd go home to Donald, though. A couple weeks, that's all she had left of this great summer adventure. She'd retreat, defeated by Hollywood. That's how it'd look to everyone; she'd come home a failure. No one would know that she'd turned down the role of Cherry; no one would ever know that by doing what was right, what was unselfish, she'd sealed her own fate. The tears rolled down her face only when she heard Donald's voice. "I told you Hollywood wasn't for you. Now you're back where you belong." She cringed, just at the thought of his arms around her.

Nick: Sunday Morning, 4–6:00 a.m.

Nick eased Sara's arm over his shoulder, snaked his own around her slim waist, and helped her upstairs. What choice did he have? The girl was plastered, could barely stand up. Losing her liquor virginity would either be memorable or, he hoped, eminently forgettable. No little sips of wine or beer: She'd dived into the hard stuff with a reckless thirst. Nick wasn't that good at figuring out people's feelings, but he recognized when someone was self-medicating.

Something must have happened during the party, something that'd made Sara zoom from zero tolerance to eighty-proof in the blink of an eye. Damned if he knew what it was. All he'd seen was Sara being her usual high-spirited, supergenerous self. She'd baked Eliot a cake, coaxed Naomi into joining them, and then received some amazing news from her agent.

How this became a recipe for misery was a mystery.

But, dude, girlfriend was in no shape to explain.

He led her to the loft, steadied her with one hand, and went to pull down the Murphy bed.

"No," she stopped him. "No, not here. Don't wanna be here now."

"Where do you want to be, Sara?" he asked softly.

"Your room. Let's go to your room." Her head began to loll.

She was so warm, so beautiful, so trusting and vulnerable. He wasn't blind; she'd been wanting him all summer. He stopped himself. *No, man.* He wasn't going to take advantage. Eliot was in love with her; the E-man believed he had a chance with her. He was El's best friend.

Didn't matter that Eliot had no shot with her. No way could Nick sleep with Sara either. No matter how much he wanted to.

Man, did he ever want to.

So . . . wait a minute, Nick caught himself thinking. Maybe it was her. Maybe Sara was the reason he'd ended up celibate this summer. If he'd been into her but subconsciously not allowed himself to act on it . . . maybe that's why people assumed he was gay. Was that possible? Nah.

Even through a beer-buzz haze, that made no sense.

Back in Michigan, in the rare instances he'd been rejected by a girl or had put the brakes on out of loyalty to a friend, he'd gone out and found someone else. Girls had been fairly interchangeable in his life so far. He'd never fallen for one girl so hard that he had no interest in anyone else.

Sara piped up, "I want an exercise lesson! Lesh go work out, Nicky."

His stomach tightened. "Please don't call me Nicky, okay?"

"Okey dokey," she slurred happily. "But lesh . . . uh . . . I want to ball."

"What?"

"The big red ball. Show me how to do curls. You know, the ones where your tummy tightens up and I fall off and you catch me. Can we do that now?"

"No, Sara, we can't," he whispered, while leading her into his room anyway, half hoping Eliot was there, half praying his roommate was gone. "You can't work out when you've been drinking."

"Is that a rule?" She playfully kicked her shoes off and closed the door behind them. "What other rules are there?"

"You have to treat your body kindly," he said, standing unsteadily, still holding her up. He heard himself reciting some gym-insanity. "Your body is your temple. Take care of it, and it will take care of you."

The bedroom was empty, both beds were made.

Which meant Eliot could show up at any moment. He hesitated. . . .

Slowly, seductively, she turned to face him. Their bodies were touching, then they were pressing against each other. His body reacted quickly. "No, Sara . . . ," he groaned. "You don't really want to do this."

Then he locked the door.

"God gives us only one body. Would you like to see mine?" she murmured.

It was exquisite, Sara's body. A guy could just stand there and worship it. Her full, round breasts were soft, just like her mouth, which was moist and sweet. And the rest of her—smooth, warm to the touch, and oh, had he mentioned soft? She was so soft, so pliable, willing, and wanting—he was on fire. Which totally meant he wasn't gay.

No one had ever touched Sara before. He knew, because she kept moaning it, over and over. No one had ever kissed her "in that way," "there," "for that long." He suckled her neck, traced her shoulders with his fingertips, caressed her breasts, stroked her all over. And over again.

Nick did not think he could slow down, but he summoned up every ounce of self-control he could find. Making out was one thing, and a sweet thing it was, judging by her reaction. But making out was about to lead to much, much more. He had to be sure Sara wanted this, was sober enough to make a decision, and—the realization hit him hard—if her decision was yes, he wanted to make her first time special, unforgettable.

Unlike his had been.

Sometimes Nick wished he didn't remember his first time, or that he could rewrite his sex history. It happened in junior high, the time in his life when girls suddenly noticed him, and vice versa. It was after school, under the bleachers at the football field. Christy Pennington, a cute, flirty girl, had become his first "friend with benefits," at a time before that phrase had been coined. She'd given him oral, because, he'd thought, she was into him. When he found out she'd done it on a dare—some girls put her up to it, and watched!—he felt dirty, used. Neither Christy, nor her friends, thought of him as a person; he was just a boy-toy, played with, then discarded. Exactly the way he felt modeling this summer.

Gently, he slid his hand to the small of Sara's back and guided her onto the bed. His bed, where he lay on top of her. Her eyes were closed, and he took in her long, lush eyelashes; her lips were open, waiting for his. Her arms held him close.

"Are you sure, Sara, this is what you want to do?" He hoped she didn't say no. Hoped he wouldn't have to stop.

"Nick. Oh God, Nick . . ." was all he could understand after that. And every time he thought she said "Don't," she added "stop."

"Don't stop, don't stop, don't stop."

He wanted her desperately. Not because he needed to

prove anything to himself—right? And not because he wanted to hurt Eliot. It was because she was so damn hot. And she was in his room, on his bed, with the door locked. And she wanted him. And . . . there was no going back. He would make her first time amazing—he would pleasure her, teach her that guys could be tender and giving. That her feelings were important. It's what Eliot would do in this situation.

He pushed himself off her and took off his shirt. She ran her hands up and down his chest. He started to unbutton his trou, but she reached out. "Can I?"

Her fingers were shaking as she unzipped him. She was nervous, and it made him want her more. He thought he kept asking her if she was sure; she responded by groaning, then arching her back . . . and then, there was no going back. There was no undoing what they were doing.

It was explosive, and yet sweet; she was hungry, welcoming. They were rocking and rolling: It felt like they were on a boat, being gently tossed on wave after wave of pleasure.

"I feel it," she murmured. "Oh God, Nick—do you? Can you feel it? The earth is moving."

"EARTHQUAKE!" Eliot blasted into the room, shoulder first, busting the lock in the process, screaming at the top of his lungs. "Why was the door locked, we're having an earthquake! I can't find Sara—" And then, "Oh my God . . . Nick? Sara? What's—?"

There was something worse, Nick realized in that nanosecond, than being crushed in an earthquake: the look on Eliot's face, as if he'd been sucker-punched by a thousand-ton Mack truck. He was gasping for breath, had turned ashen: Eliot, crushed by betrayal.

The floor beneath the bed suddenly swayed. It jolted Eliot into action. "Get downstairs!" he screamed. "Get the radio! Nick, turn off the gas line! Hurry!"

Panic overtook Nick. He had never bothered to locate the gas line.

16

Sunday Morning: 6:17 a.m.: The Earthquake

Jared was jolted awake by a thunderous crack. Disoriented, it took him a minute to realize where he was: He and Lindsay had fallen asleep, locked in each other's arms, on the chaise lounge in the backyard. His eyes popped open to the sight of the swimming pool bursting as if a geyser had erupted beneath it, water shooting straight up.

Then the earth moved beneath them, and the pool itself seemed to come uprooted, as if something were jostling it from underneath. Water sloshed everywhere.

"Get inside!" Eliot shrieked at them from an upstairs window. "It's an earthquake! The house is going to fall on you! You'll be buried in the rubble!"

Jared shouted back, "Get away from the window!" He grabbed Lindsay's hand, to yank her up. The rumbling of the earth had started in earnest now; deck chairs and lounges toppled and slid toward the pool.

Lindsay slipped out of his grasp, bolted up, and made for the sliding doors leading into the house.

"No!" Jared screamed. "Not that way! We have to go around front; the glass could to shatter!" He ran toward her, but Lindsay, in full dramatic panic, was already at the doors. She yelled back at him, "I have to get George Clooney!"

What? Was she bonkers?

"The dog, Amanda's dog! Lionel left it here. No time to go around front."

Before he could catch up, she flung the sliding doors open and dashed inside. The smashing sound that followed her was like a sonic boom, so loud, he couldn't hear himself, but he knew he was shouting. "Linz, Linz, no!"

And then, to his horror, the earth opened up and swallowed Lindsay.

Screaming, Jared raced around the shaking house, flew through the front door, telling himself she might be okay. He skidded into the living room with the vague thought of rescuing her, but it was too late—the walls were shaking, loosening Uncle Rob's guitars, which crashed onto the floor. CDs and vinyl records shaken from the shelves flew across the room like crazed Frisbees. Jared shielded his head, screaming, "Lindsay! Lindsay!" He heard a sickening noise from above: One of the giant beams across the ceiling was coming unhinged.

So was Eliot.

Their crisis-control king just lost it, completely! The dude who'd nagged them into preparation was hyperventilating, running down the steps with his head in his hands, screaming, "No, no! I can't! I can't!"

Jared shouted, "Stay upstairs!" But Eliot had panicked; he was too far out of control.

Nick, a half step behind, tackled him. "The poker table—we'll go under the poker table, just like you said. Come on! Sara—hurry!"

Eliot and Nick made it down, but the stairs buckled and imploded just as Sara, who was on Nick's heels, hit the top step. She dove down to the living room floor, landing, thankfully, on one of Uncle Rob's throw rugs, which cushioned her fall. Unhurt, she leaped up and ran toward the kitchen.

Nick tried to stop her. "Sara, no, not the kitchen, remember? Under the poker table—go in the game room!"

"Duck!" she shrieked, pointing up to the wooden railing of the loft as it came crashing down. It missed Nick and Eliot by inches. "The earthquake kit is in the kitchen, I have to get it." Sara was slipping and sliding as the floor shook. She flung open the door to the basement and shouted, "Naomi, stay down there! Stand by an inside wall!"

Sara whirled around the room. "Where's Jared? Where's Lindsay?"

"Help!" Jared yelled, kneeling by the coffee table, pointing to the mountain of glass that had been the sliding door, now joined by random pieces of furniture, sections of sofa that had torn off, shelving units that'd toppled—it'd all fallen atop the shattered glass.

"Lindsay's under there! Help—she's buried!"

Nick took charge. "El—you and Sara get under that table, now! Jared, get under—"

The unhinged beam came crashing down from the ceiling, slicing the coffee table, and the living room, in half, missing Jared's head by a fraction. It propelled Sara into action. With two long strides she was in the kitchen and instantly out again, carrying the kit with the flashlights, gloves, helmets, and radio. Struggling to keep her balance as the house rumbled and moved, she tossed them over the fallen beam to Jared and to Nick, who'd started across the rubble toward the other side. "Put the gloves on! Put the helmets on! Here's a flashlight!"

At that moment, another large quake erupted, knocking them all on their butts. Jared heard the front windows smash, and rolled away from what was left of the sofa and chairs.

Nick had fallen by the fireplace.

"Move, Nick," he bellowed, coughing from the sudden dust and smoke in the air. "The bricks . . ."

Nick took a falling brick on the shoulder, but crawled away before he got hit again. The next jolt sent more bricks and what was left of the furniture straight onto the pile of glass from the shattered sliding door. Another rip-ple in the ground, and the big couch, Moroccan chair, tables—every souvenir in the eclectic, cluttered living room was now atop the mountainous pile burying Lindsay even further.

Nick shielded his head from the falling debris, then managed to snatch the helmet Sara had tossed over. "Sara and Eliot, hold on to the radio and get under that table in the game room—now!" Nick commanded, and the two of them scurried toward safety.

Jared was so shaky, he fumbled snapping the helmet on, and couldn't get the gloves over his quivering hands. He felt like an impotent dunce, doing nothing while all hell broke loose around him, watching Sara and Nick take action. All he could think about was Lindsay. *Just let them get to Lindsay and let her be okay.*

"How do you know she's under there, man?" Nick called out to him.

"She ran in, through the doors—I saw them smash, and then the floor cracked open. I think she fell down." Jared struggled to keep from crying. "She was trying to find the damn dog."

Flashlight in hand, Nick carefully threaded his way over the debris toward Jared. The pile of house detritus was now easily six feet high and twice that wide. Gingerly, Nick walked around it, cupping his mouth and calling, "Lindsay! Lindsay! Can you hear me?"

Jared trembled.

All at once it was quiet. Too quiet.

"It stopped," Jared said, "The earthquake is over. I think . . . we can get her now."

"Aftershocks, man," Nick reminded him. "They could be more intense than the quake."

"Lindsay," Jared yelled into the pile, "shout if you hear me! We're gonna get you out, baby."

Nick held his hand up. "Wait . . . did you hear that?"

Jared had heard nothing.

Then, weakly, from deep beneath the rubble: "Yap."

It was no use. They'd been at it for an hour, and every time Nick and Jared thought they'd cleared away some of the mess, an aftershock rattled the walls, tossing more debris onto the pile. The bike helmets kept them from concussions, or worse. But they'd made no progress in freeing Lindsay—who'd not made a sound to let them know she was conscious.

Every few minutes, Sara shouted from the game room to assure them that she and Eliot, ensconced under the poker table, were okay. And that Naomi had wisely stayed safely in the basement. The radio was reporting a 6.1-level quake—pretty massive—that was playing havoc with the houses in the Hollywood Hills and the Los Angeles basin.

"They're saying it's gonna take rescue crews a while to get here," she yelled out. "Did you get to Lindsay yet?"

Nick responded, "Not yet. Stay where you are: We're doing good."

Then the next blast came. So loud, it rendered them momentarily deaf. It took them awhile to realize it had not come from their house. "Shit!" Nick yelled, holding his hands over his ears. "Sounds like a house blew up!"

Jared prayed no one was in it . . . but at six in the morning, that was unlikely. Then he locked eyes with Nick. Neither had to say it: They'd never looked for the gas line. No one would have shut it off.

"It's gonna be all right," Nick said, reacting to the terror in Jared's eyes.

Jared could hold it back no longer; he started to bawl. "It's my fault. I'm such an ass. We're gonna die here."

"No, you're not." A voice, steady, confident, bold, forced them to whirl around. Naomi, tiny but fierce, was standing in the doorway by the kitchen. "No one's gonna die," Naomi repeated. "I shut the gas off."

"How d-d-did you know where it was?" Jared stuttered.

"The shut-off valve is in the basement—it's next to my bed. Stay put, I'm getting a helmet and flashlight from Sara. Then I'm going to get Lindsay out."

Nick and Jared exchanged stunned glances.

Naomi returned a minute later, with a flashlight, gloves, and a surgical mask covering her mouth. "Sara and Eliot are doing okay," she reported.

"Where's your helmet?" Nick asked nervously.

She shook her head. "Won't fit. I'm going to try and crawl through the rubble to get her."

"What . . . are you . . . talking about?" Jared's teeth were chattering.

Naomi informed them calmly, "The three of us are going to clear away an opening. I'm a lot smaller than you. I'll go in."

"Are you crazy?" Nick challenged. "You can't crawl into this mound. One big aftershock and you're a goner."

"And so is Lindsay—if she's under there. That's why we can't wait."

For a moment, Jared believed—really believed—that if he blinked, he'd wake up, realize this was all a dream. A nightmare implanted in his brain by his father, to scare him into maturity. On cue, the house shook again; a broken guitar swiped his head. It was real.

Nick reached out to help Naomi climb over the mess on the floor. Gingerly, she tiptoed through the destroyed living room and over to where the guys had been trying to attack the mountain of rubble. Gloves on, she deftly and quickly started digging, shoving away shards of wood, glass, and bricks to make a tunnel through which she could crawl.

Jared babbled inanely, "If you save Lindsay, I'll give you a million dollars, I'll make sure you're never on the streets ag—"

"Shut up," Naomi said, not unkindly. "Let's focus. Keep moving these bricks out of the way. We're going to get her out. End of story."

Jared made a silent vow: If Lindsay was safe, he'd make everything up to everyone. Somehow.

A half hour had gone by, punctuated by reports from Sara, relaying info from the radio. The epicenter, she said, was in Ojai. That's where the worst damage was, and where most of the rescue teams were headed.

Another aftershock hit, sending Jared sliding on his butt toward the fireplace; if not for the helmet, the falling bricks might've killed him. Naomi and Nick scrambled right back to work.

"Okay," she determined, "there's enough room and air in here for me to burrow through and down. Give me a flashlight."

"Are you sure?" Nick asked, wiping grime and dust out of his eyes.

"It doesn't matter," she replied. "We don't have the time to make the opening bigger. Keep your light shining on me."

Thank you. You're so brave. I'm indebted to you. The words Jared wanted to stay were stuck in his throat.

"Lindsay! Lindsay! Are you okay?" Naomi's voice came from inside the cave of debris. Then, "Shit!"

"What—what is it?" Jared yelled. "Is it Lindsay?"

"I got cut," Noami shouted back. Then, "Lindsay? Are you down there?"

Then there was silence. Jared began to pace, while Nick continued to kneel by the opening through which Naomi had disappeared, his flashlight beaming.

"Why's it taking so long?" Jared felt like he was crawling out of his skin.

"Because she's gotta move slowly, man," Nick replied. "She makes a sudden move, more garbage falls on both of them."

It felt like an eternity. Suddenly, they heard music. "'Mr. Brightside'?"

"What the hell's that?" Jared demanded. "Where's it coming from?"

"Dude, it's your cell phone. Chill out."

The last thing Jared cared about was talking to anyone, about anything. Unless it was Lindsay. And what were the odds of getting cell reception buried under a pile of earthquake rubble? This must be, he thought, what hell is like. Waiting.

Then finally—it felt like an eternity—they heard Naomi. "I see her! I see her!"

"Is she all right?" Jared shouted, but Nick shushed him.

"What do you need? Can you get her out?"

Sara and Eliot appeared, she clutching the radio, he, still clutching his head. "What can we do?" Sara asked.

"Go back," Nick started to say, but Sara wasn't having it. "It's stopped. We'll be okay. We're staying out here with you. I got Eliot's cell phone; it worked, I called for an ambulance. But I don't know how long it will take."

Naomi shouted, "I've got her shoulders, but she's unconscious. I have to drag her, and pull her out backward. Nick, the minute you see the bottoms of my shoes, come in and pull."

"Is she okay? Is she okay?" was all Jared could say, on a loop.

By the time Nick had grasped Naomi and pulled both girls out from under the rubble, Jared had his answer.

Unconscious, cut up, clutching the bloody dog, Lindsay was, by far, not okay.

They hadn't been out for a half second when another aftershock rose up from the ground and a brick went flying and hit Naomi, knocking her out.

Sara, Nick, and Eliot insisted on riding in the ambulance with Naomi. Jared rode in another ambulance with Lindsay and the dog, who'd managed to survive as well. The EMT crew let him apply cool compresses to her head, which was dirty and bloodied. She'd regained consciousness soon after being freed, but was coughing from the dust and smoke. Wisely, Sara cautioned against moving her in case glass was embedded deep in her skin.

"You okay, baby?" he whispered.

Lindsay groaned, but nodded.

"You were a hero—you rescued the dog," Jared told her.

"I didn't want to lose my job—" She fell into a coughing fit.

"Let her rest," the paramedic advised Jared. "We're just about at the hospital. We'll take care of her."

Jared insisted on staying by Lindsay's side. And Lindsay insisted on trying to talk. "Naomi saved me. It was just like Johnny in *The Outsiders*—he was homeless too, and dove into a burning barn to save those children."

Good analogy, Jared thought, one a movie buff would think of.

"Is she okay?" Lindsay asked.

"I think so; she's in the ambulance in front of us. She took a brick to the head. Nick and Sara are with her."

"So they're okay?" she croaked.

"Yeah, they're good. They're fucking heroes, babe. All of them."

"Eliot. He . . . he . . . tried to tell us. Is he—?"

"He's good, he's fine. He kinda lost it, though, in the end. He just froze. I don't get it. But if it wasn't for him . . ." Jared trailed off. He had a lot of gratitude to spread, a lot of apologies.

He hung by Lindsay's gurney as long as the paramedics would allow; when they took her to be examined, he was asked to stay in the waiting area. The place was in full triage mode. Hundreds of injured were being ferried in.

Nick, waiting with Sara and Eliot, nudged him. "Dude, answer your freakin' cell phone. It hasn't stopped ringing."

"Huh?" Jared hadn't even heard it.

"It's in your pocket, man. If you don't answer it, I will," Nick threatened.

"Hello?" Jared said unsteadily.

He'd never heard his father so discombobulated. The older man was jabbering, blubbering, sobbing, weeping. "Jared! Thank God, you're safe. I went down to the school to find you—they said no one had seen you. I was sure you were—"

"The school?" Jared, still dazed, was more confused.

Until he remembered. Sara said the epicenter of the quake was in Ojai. Where the community college was. Where he was supposed to be. Of course, his father, unable to reach him for hours, assumed the worst.

"Dad." Jared took a deep breath. "I need to tell you something."

17

Aftershocks: So Busted

The share house was trashed. The structure of the cozy wood-frame abode remained intact, but all the windows had blown out. Several walls had imploded, and piles of wrecked furniture and splintered wood from tables, railings, and Uncle Rob's prized guitars mixed with unhinged bricks from the fireplace. The massive detritus of what used to be CDs, posters, shelves, rugs, and knick-knacks was scattered everywhere, all of it covered by a thick layer of dust and grime.

It was uninhabitable, so Jared, Lindsay, Nick, Eliot, and Sara had to relocate. In an only-in-Hollywood scenario, the scared, wounded, and terrified earthquake victims, who'd lost all the possessions left in the share house, vaulted from the depths of near tragedy to the heights of unimaginable luxury. They moved into the Larson mansion on Stone Canyon Road in Bel Air, guests of Rusty Larson.

Naomi, having taken a concussive blow to the head and suffering other internal injuries, remained, in the week following the quake, a guest at Cedars-Sinai hospital.

"She's going to be fine," the doctors assured Sara. "We'll release her as soon as her test results come back and we're comfortable that she's fully on the mend. Are there any family members we should contact?"

Sara had looked to Naomi, asleep in her hospital bed. There were many ways to define a family, Sara thought. "We're her next of kin."

As the biological parent closest to the calamity, as well as the one with the deepest pockets, Jared's dad Rusty played father-knows-best for all of them.

He called each and every family, Lindsay's folks in Iowa, Sara's in Texas, Nick's and Eliot's folks in Michigan, offered to fly them west if they wanted, but pretty much convinced everyone that the kids were fine, and welcome to live in his house for as long as they liked.

Rusty Larson paid for all the hospital bills accrued by Naomi and by Lindsay, who'd escaped miraculously unscathed for someone who'd fallen down the rabbit hole, as she called it. Except for cuts and bruises, lacerations and abrasions, she was "good to go."

He reached his brother Rob, filming a movie half a world away, and assured him the damage was containable, and that he'd pay for the house rehab. "There's no need to interrupt shooting the movie to come home, we've got you covered," he told his younger brother, also mentioning that Jared would explain "everything" to Uncle Rob when he got home.

That was his m.o., thought Jared ruefully. Dad would go all TCB—take care of business—then the real earthquake of his father's freak-out would come. Jared wasn't sure when his dad would kill him, just that he would.

Thirty-six hours after the quake, Jared, Lindsay, Sara, Nick, and Eliot had been treated to cleansing showers, the sauna, the steam room, and the best night's sleep they'd had all summer. They'd been served a full, delicious breakfast of French toast, pancakes, eggs, bacon, sausage, and steaming-hot, buttery rolls.

For dessert, they repaired to the great room, where they dined on heaping helpings of guilt, shame, and finger-pointing.

Eliot, whose already fragile ego had taken the worst beating, laced into Nick, blaming him for taking advantage of Sara, for betraying him, rupturing their bond of trust, and ending their lifelong friendship.

Nick swallowed it all—and asked for seconds. Eliot was right, he agreed, had been right, about everything. El had confided in Nick, and Nick had been a shit, turned around and screwed him. He didn't deserve Eliot's friendship, or Sara's.

"I don't know what happened in the bedroom," Jared said, "but we should remember, Nick kept his cool throughout the whole ordeal. If not for him—"

Eliot turned all colors. "Why don't you just come out

and say what everyone's thinking? I choked in the clutch. I nagged everyone to be prepared, but when it actually happened? I was helpless. I cried like a baby."

"That's bull! If not for your planning, all that stuff you bought, we might not have survived. It doesn't matter what you did or didn't do after that," Nick declared.

Lindsay added, "If we're looking for heroes, Naomi gets the gold—"

Sara burst out wailing, "It's all my fault! All of it!"

"How you figure?" Lindsay was truly puzzled.

Sara moaned, "God punished me. I broke my purity pledge, and He punished me."

Eliot's jaw dropped. "You think the earthquake was because of you? Do you have any idea how epically self-centered you sound?"

"Yeah, you finally sound like me," Lindsay quipped.

At which Sara started to weep piteously.

And Lindsay broke out in giggles.

Nick and Eliot told Lindsay to zip it. There was nothing funny about it.

Jared told them all to can it. "The earthquake wasn't anyone's fault; it's how we handled it. And in the competition for worst person on the scene, it's all me: I own that category."

Nick countered, "It's not a freakin' competition. No one knows how they're gonna react in a crisis. It's just live and learn, man. And thank God, or whoever you believe in, we all came through it okay."

"Anyway," Jared repeated, "we owe Eliot big-time. We were asses, man, to treat you the way we did. If you hadn't gotten all that stuff, the flashlights, the helmets, we'd have been royally screwed."

"I'm sorry I made fun of you," Lindsay put in, somewhat convincingly. "You were right all along, about everything. And if Sara hadn't brought that homeless girl here—I mean, Naomi—I'd be a goner. And the world would forever be denied my awesome talent." She looked around, but no one was smiling. "Oh, come on! A little levity. We are all okay."

Sara, still sniffling, said, "You're amazing, Eliot. I'm so sorry if we—no, if I—hurt you. You're the last person who deserves to be hurt."

"Oh, yeah, I'm such a great guy," Eliot snarled. "I'm smart, proactive, I'm"—he shot daggers at Nick—"a shoulder to lean on. I'm loyal."

"I am so sorry, man. There's no excuse—not the beers, not the party, not nothing." Nick put his head in his hands.

"Unless," Eliot said in a low growl, "you were trying to prove something to yourself."

"Prove what?" Lindsay asked.

Nick's jaw dropped, and he started up off the couch, ready to whale on Eliot. But he stopped in his tracks. Sat back down. "If that were true, it'd be Sara I owe the apology to."

"What are you talking—?" Lindsay started to ask, when Jared shushed her.

But Lindsay was still working out the tension between Nick and Eliot. Then a lightbulb went off. "Eliot thinks you made it with Sara just to prove you're not gay? Oh, come on, that's ridiculous!"

Nick flushed bright red.

"Nick, honey, if you were gay, you'd know it. You'd have known it long before you got to L.A.."

Lindsay started to say more, but Jared jumped in. "It's not our business. Eliot saved our butts—between him, Nick, Sara, and Naomi, they're the reason we made it."

Eliot challenged the girls. "If I'm such a great guy, how come I'm not good enough for either of you?"

The color drained from both girls' faces. Awkward silence ensued.

Then Lindsay cleared her throat. "I'm just so focused on my career, I haven't been looking for . . ." She trailed off, then closed her eyes, as if in pain. "I've been in love with one guy for a real long time. Even if I haven't always shown it."

Jared drew her closer to him, and she tucked into his chest.

Wistfully, Sara said, "I wish I knew what to say, but I don't, Eliot. I came to Hollywood this summer so sure of myself, my goal, everything. Right now, there's not one single thing I'm sure about. Least of all the shameful way I acted, toward you, toward Nick, toward myself. I'm so confused."

Lindsay piped up, "I hate to interrupt this confessional

moment, but I say we get up off our guilty butts and go to the hospital to check on your stray."

It's the *way* she says things, Jared thought; that's why he couldn't help loving her. Lindsay owed her life to that stray—no one was more grateful than she. Lindsay would waste little time in proving it to Naomi.

The Larson family ride, a stretch Navigator, joined the long line of limos pulling up to the valet at Cedars Sinai, the hospital to the stars. To Sara, the scene was surreal. As were many occurrences of the past forty-eight hours. Focusing on Naomi was one way of not having to ask herself the hard questions. Questions that weren't going away. They'd be waiting for her, wherever she went. There was no hurry.

Naomi looked even scrawnier in the private suite Rusty Larson had procured for her. The waif with the huge violet eyes, dark eyelashes, and choppy black hair was watching the flat-screen TV poised above her bed.

"Nice digs," Jared quipped. "This is the floor of the hospital all the stars stay on when they're having babies, recovering from illness, plastic surgery—or just hiding from the paparazzi."

"There are smaller rooms on either side of this suite for your entourage. Not to mention your security patrol," Lindsay added.

No one laughed, but Naomi offered a weak smile.

Sara perched on the side of the bed, took Naomi's small hand. "How are you feeling, darlin'?"

"I'm okay, really. I don't know why they're keeping me here."

"But they're treating you well?" Jared asked.

"Like a star," Naomi conceded.

"What are they saying is wrong with you, exactly?" Lindsay asked. "I know you had a concussion, but there's no, like, brain damage or anything?"

"I'll never be able to figure skate again," Naomi said sadly.

Lindsay blanched.

Naomi pointed at her. "Snap! That's an old joke, Lindsay. Like I ever skated! C'mon, I'm the homeless stray, remember?"

Lindsay flushed. "A near-death experience renders me gullible."

Jared slipped his arm around Lindsay's waist and drew closer to Naomi's bedside. "There's something we all have to say—no joke. You saved my uncle's house, you saved our lives: specifically, Lindsay's. For that, well, we have a lot to apologize for and a lot to thank you for. Whatever you need, whatever you want—we're in your debt, Naomi. Forever."

"Forget it. I did what anyone would have." Naomi's eyes watered, but she didn't cry.

"No way," Nick contradicted. "You did—"

Eliot startled everyone by interrupting. "You did what someone who's been through an earthquake before would have done. Someone who had lived through it, and learned what to do." He paused. "That's what I always suspected."

"Eliot! It's like you're like accusing her," Sara said, aghast.

"I meant, someone with real-life experience, who had the strength not to panic or choke," Eliot finished.

Lindsay's eyes widened. "Is that true, Naomi? Were you in that bad earthquake back then . . . but wait, how old were you in nineteen ninety-four?"

Sara grew more alarmed. "Stop it, you're harassing her."

"No, we're not, we're thanking her," Jared said. "But it would make sense if what Eliot's saying is true."

"It doesn't matter!" Sara scolded them as she squeezed Naomi's hand, "You're still pushing her, and that's not exactly a way to show gratitude."

"Time out!" Naomi coughed, raising her hand to stop them. "You're all acting like I'm not in the room. Like I'm invisible."

Chided, Sara said, "I'm sorry, we're—"

"Forget it." Naomi pointed to a button on the side of the bed. "Can you hit that, Jared? It raises the bed. I want to sit up straighter."

Would Naomi reveal herself finally, Sara wondered? There was so much she'd been wanting to ask the girl; she just didn't know how. She'd been the staunchest defender of Naomi's right to privacy, and would continue. But, of course, she wanted to know why Naomi had ended up on the streets. During the course of their nearly two months living under the same roof, the girl had said barely a word about herself.

The earthquake changed things.

The homeless girl turned out to be a hero. She'd rescued not only Lindsay and the dog but also the house itself. The questions piled up, high as the mountain of debris into which she'd selflessly tunneled to free Lindsay.

Eliot poured Naomi a glass of designer bottled water, which she gulped gratefully.

"I know you've all been wondering about me," she said calmly. "And I guess I owe you some answers."

"You owe us nothing." Sara couldn't help herself. "We owe you our lives."

Naomi waved her away. "It's okay, Sara, really. Thanks to you, I'm . . . I'm okay. You took me in—fought for me, never asked for one thing in return. You're a good person, and your parents are proud, I know it. Your God, too."

Sara began to sob quietly, but Naomi took her hand. "I did end up with a concussion, and some internal bleeding. But they've got that all under control; I'll be fine. Anyway, this is nothing compared to what happened the last time. . . ."

She drew a deep breath, then locked her eyes on Eliot. "You're right. I was nine years old in nineteen ninety-four, and we were staying at an apartment in Northridge."

Jared gasped. "No shit? Really?"

Naomi continued. "The apartment complex that got hit with the worst of it. We were in the wrong place at the wrong time."

"Your family?" Lindsay asked.

"My parents were among the fifty-five people who died," she said softly. "My sister and I survived."

"You have a sister? We'll call her!" Sara exclaimed.

Naomi shook her head. "Annie. I don't know where she is."

"You haven't been homeless since you were a kid, though?" Lindsay ventured.

"After the earthquake, Annie and I were taken in by a neighbor. We didn't stay very long. We went into foster care, a bunch of different homes, but that didn't work out either. One thing led to another, and I ended up, you know, making do. Surviving."

"In shelters? Or just . . . the street?" Sara asked cautiously.

"Both. I usually felt safer on the street. There's a kind of community out there. But the day you asked if I needed help, that was a bad day. Things had gotten dicey and I was really scared. The last two months have been the best I've had it since the quake, the safest I've felt since that time." She laughed, and clutched her stomach. "Guess I'm living quake to quake."

"Guess we all are," Sara said. There were many ways in which the earth could shake you up.

• • •

A week and a half later, a guarded normalcy had returned to Los Angeles. Only, Lindsay mused, in her case, normal was better than ever. She felt beyond comfortable lounging poolside at the Larson mansion, pampered, protected. She felt hopeful, like she'd prosper again. Wearing a new metallic bikini, she lay back on a lushly cushioned chaise lounge, a fat new issue of *In Style* on her lap and visions of glam outfits and red-carpet appearances in her head.

It was Tuesday afternoon, and she had the pool, the entire mansion, practically to herself. Nick had returned to his modeling gig; Eliot to his classes; Sara and Naomi, healed now, back to *Caught in the Act*. Jared had surprised everyone by going for an actual study session with Adam, the kid he'd hired to take the tests for him. Boyfriend had decided to play summer school catch-up, even though Lindsay was fairly sure the big face-to-face with his father hadn't happened yet.

Everyone was still obsessed with the fallout from the quake.

Online, on TV, and in the news, there were round-the-clock updates. Financially, the damage totaled in the millions. Hundreds, like herself and Naomi, had suffered various degrees of injury. Tragically, twenty-two people had died. Most were from the Ojai area, where the quake had been centered, but a few people had perished in the shaky homes atop the Hollywood Hills.

She'd come close to being number twenty-three. She

didn't remember a lot, just flinging open the sliding doors, dashing through them in search of Amanda's pooch, George Clooney, and then the sensation of dropping, falling. The earth had cracked, right under her feet, and she'd gone down. And out. Lindsay had blacked out, and so everything that happened afterward she learned about only after the fact.

The contents of the house had crashed down on top of her. She'd been buried under an eight-foot mound of glass, steel, bricks, wood, and—she giggled—knickknacks. Death by tchotchkes. She couldn't help finding that ticklish.

Here was the thing, and Lindsay faced it head on: Surviving a near-death experience had not changed her. Or at least, not so far. She understood that Eliot had prepared them, that Sara and Nick had acted coolly and courageously, that Jared had been sick with worry. And that Naomi, of all people, had bravely risked her own pitiful life to save hers. Lindsay was grateful, she really, really was. She would so show her gratitude; she'd buy each person an extremely trendy and expensive gift, right from the pages of *In Style*.

But . . . see, she knew it was wrong to feel this way, but still . . . it was over.

Been there, survived that, bought the T-shirt.

Earthquake. Rescue. Rehab.

Next.

Lindsay wasn't going to go all Oprah, or Angelina, or

even Madonna in her red string bracelet phase. Lindsay wasn't going to dedicate herself to Kaballah, or Christianity, or any other spiritual thingie.

Except for being deeply superficial, she wasn't all that deep.

At least she was real. Life would go on and *The Outsiders* would get made. Grudgingly, she accepted that Sara probably had the role; the earthquake hadn't changed the fact that twerpy little Lionel had as much as said so. Jared was all "Keep the faith, Lindsay," insisting nothing had been determined yet.

Naturally, the final audition had been postponed due to the quake. But movie schedules were being set: That tryout would happen before Labor Day, just a week away. Maybe there was something she could do in the screen test for the studio heads that would make them forget about Sara.

Those were the thoughts that occupied Lindsay's brain, and not for very long, either, as she rolled over on her belly for a more even tan. She wanted the role of Cherry, but if the worst happened, she'd survive to sniff out another acting part. Her time would come.

Desirée, the housekeeper, poked her head out the French doors. "Miss Lindsay, there's someone at the door to see you."

Lindsay squinted. "Who is it?"

Desirée shrugged. "Didn't say. But the lady is carrying a tiny dog."

Amanda? Lindsay leapt off the lounge and scooted inside.

Amanda was clad in a navy blue Prada power suit, and adorned with her armpit accessory, George Clooney, who snarled at Lindsay.

"Lindsay, darling, how are you?" Amanda air-kissed the vicinity of Lindsay's cheeks.

"I'm good. Great, in fact. Do you want to come sit down?" Lindsay calculated: If her boss-cum-agent had arrived just to thank her for saving George Clooney, no way would she hang out. If, however, there was news of the audition, Amanda would deign to stay a while.

The reason for the face-time turned out to be something different. Something awesomely sweet, and fabulous . . . and confusing as hell. Amanda settled onto the Armani sofa in the great room with the rat-faced runt and accepted a bottle of designer sparkling water from Desiree. She sniffed around. "I see Rusty hasn't changed decorators since Glynnis lived here," she noted.

Amanda had been a guest at Galaxy's parties, often staged here in the mansion, when Jared's parents were together and the agency was flourishing. Lindsay agreed. "Still, it all works, don't you think?"

Amanda nodded, though no way had she come to check out the décor. "So, my little client," she said, crossing her long legs. "It seems as though every good deed does not, in fact, go unpunished. You saved George Clooney's life—you get a tasty reward." She stroked the devil-dog, who promptly jumped from her arms and peed on the leg of the marble coffee table.

Amanda giggled. "Ooops, we'll need a little cleanup here. Anyway, I come bearing wonderful news: You got the part."

For a nanosecond, Lindsay had no clue what Amanda was talking about. "What part?"

Amanda looked at her weirdly. "Did your tragic earthquake experience render you dense? What part have you been auditioning for? What part will make you a superstar, the comeback story of the decade? You got Cherry."

Lindsay remained stupefied, way slow on the uptake. "But—but . . ."

"No buts," Amanda said. "Just yours up on the big screen."

"I didn't have the final audition. Neither did Sara."

Amanda smiled mysteriously, coquettishly. "And yet, here I am, in person, to inform you that no more auditions are necessary. You, Lindsay Pierce, will be playing the part of Cherry Valance. The announcement goes to the trades tomorrow.

Lindsay felt sure her mouth was wide open. And maybe there were words forming in her brain, on their way out. She remained speechless long after Amanda had bid her adieu, long after more air-kisses, long after, even, she stumbled to the kitchen for a rag and a can of Resolve to clean up after George Clooney.

18

Boy Confessions

Nick leaned out the driver's side window and talked into the speaker. "We'll have two double-doubles, one cheeseburger, two orders of fries, and two vanilla shakes."

"Will that be all?" came the disembodied voice from the squawk box at In-N-Out Burger.

He glanced at Eliot, in the passenger seat, looking straight ahead, lips pressed together, arms folded over his chest.

"That's it," Nick responded.

"That will be sixteen seventy-eight. Drive up to the pickup window, thank you."

Ever since the earthquake, Nick had been doing whatever he could think of to make things right with Eliot, to apologize for being such a heel. But nothing he did, or said, seemed to be enough. Nick drove El to classes each morning, picked him up at the UCLA campus each evening. He offered to buy him dinner, take him out for beers, explain what'd happened, or just shoot the breeze like they always did—anything to get their friendship back on track. But Eliot wasn't giving an inch; his shoulder was cold, turned away.

Neither had been much of a grudge-holder, but the E-man was having a really hard time letting go of his righteous anger.

Okay, Nick got it. Dude had a right to be steaming. Furious. Burned. But didn't eighteen years of friendship count for anything? Eliot's silence was killing him. Between that, his crappy job, and guilt feelings about Sara, Nick was as down as he'd ever been—lower than a pregnant ant, as his mom sometimes said.

He hadn't asked if Eliot wanted a bite to eat, just sorta kidnapped him instead of heading back to the Larson place. Nick was determined to have his say—even if he wasn't entirely sure of what that would be.

He'd driven to the In-N-Out Burger in Hollywood, remembering that Sara had gushed about it, mentioned the outdoor tables.

"C'mon, dude, let's chow down." He parked the car, hoping Eliot wouldn't be a complete jerk and refuse to move.

"Fine," Eliot answered, and followed Nick to one of

the many empty tables. Most people drove up and drove away; the only other tables were occupied by kids wearing Hollywood High School jackets.

They ate in silence, Eliot picking out the onions from his burger, checking the lettuce for brown spots. Nick gazed at the clouds floating lazily across the hazy blue sky. Back in Michigan, even the cloudy skies seemed purer, more of a crystal blue. Later, when the colors in the sky turned to pumpkin orange, raspberry, and even purple at sunset, when the air was crisp, signaling the coming of fall—yeah, that's when he liked it best.

"I'm 'bout ready to head home." He had no idea he was gonna say that. Or that Eliot would finally look at him. And agree. "I'm done with classes after this week anyway."

"Just . . . just . . . ," Nick stammered. "Look, E, I don't know what else to do. I'm sorry, man." He felt his lip quiver, and bit down hard.

"The whole situation blows," Eliot agreed.

Nick opened his mouth to say something, but to his surprise, Eliot was still talking. "I feel like I've been sucker-punched, Nick. Like, what a jerk I am. I never saw it coming."

"No, man, it's not like that—"

"Not like what? C'mon, Nick, you can stop apologizing for sleeping with Sara. Any guy would probably have done the same in that situation. How can I be mad at you for being who you are—a chick magnet? It's not your fault that I repel women."

Nick hadn't thought he could feel any worse; now he knew better. But the next thing Eliot admitted helped, a little. "It's not like Sara was my girlfriend. She's not into me, and even without that Donald guy, she probably never would be. It was a nice fantasy, that's all."

Nick wished he could wave a magic wand and bring someone for Eliot, some girl who was worthy of his best friend. "You'll find someone, E. Hey! In that college, Northwestern, things will be different. The place is full of brainiacs—the gene pool of females worthy of you will be much deeper than in West Bloomfield or here in Phony-wood."

"Yeah, I'm sure my dream-geek awaits somewhere." Eliot cracked a smile. First one in many, many days.

Nick reached into his pocked and slammed a twenty-dollar bill on the table. "Bet you the girl you get? Will be a knockout. Smart, hot—and probably neurotic, if she has to put up with you."

Sheepishly, Eliot said, "Okay, Nick. I'll take your bet."

"Anyway, we could go back early, not wait for Labor Day. We could leave, like, tomorrow. There's nothing keeping us here, right?"

Eliot picked at his fries. "You and Sara. You don't love her, do you? You won't . . ." He trailed off.

"What happened between me and Sara was a mistake, Eliot. Something, I don't know what, happened at the party and she went crazy, boozing it up, and . . ." It was Nick's turn to trail off. No need to remind Eliot that Sara had come on to him.

Eliot frowned. "That thing I said about your having to prove something. That was just stupid. I'm sorry, man. I know you're not gay—not that I'd care if you were. . . . I mean, it'd be totally okay. But it so happens, you're not."

"I know, man. I know who I am."

"It's not just Sara," Eliot said slowly. "It's what happened after. Everyone's trying to make me feel better by saying I'm such a hero. In the end, I didn't do anything. So is that who I am? Some bug-eyed geek who's all talk and no action? If a girl *was* interested in me, would I choke in the bedroom, too?"

"You think too much," Nick said, trying not to show his surprise at this revelation.

"Who thinks too much?" Nick and Eliot looked up to see Jared swinging his leg over the bench opposite them. He was carrying a tray piled with two cheeseburgers, a soda, and large fries.

"You, uh, come here often?" Eliot quipped.

"All the time. Best burgers in the West. Anyway, all that studying makes a man crave fast food." Jared admitted that he'd been on his way back from the school library, had pulled into the In-N-Out takeout line and seen Nick's car with its Michigan plates in the parking lot.

"So you're making up summer school?" Eliot asked. "Did your dad force you?"

Jared dove into his fries. "The scary thing is, I haven't even had it out with the old man yet. I know he's going to blow up at me—but so far, he hasn't. I'm trying to mitigate it by studying and taking the exams. Maybe that'll cool him off when he does erupt. Anyway, so who thinks too much? Gotta be El."

Nick gulped his shake. "We're actually thinking of heading back east. Real soon."

"Why would you want to do that?" Jared asked. "Especially now, you're finally living in the lap of Caliluxury. Whatsa matter—being waited on, sleeping on five-hundred-ply sheets, having backyard tennis courts, lap pool, steam room, sauna, and indoor state-of-the-art fitness center isn't enough for you?"

"Maybe it's too much," Nick said, dragging a couple of fries through a swatch of ketchup. "Maybe all this stuff just gets confusing."

Jared looked knowingly from Nick to Eliot. "It's Sara, isn't it?"

"No!" they both said emphatically.

Jared laughed. "The dudes doth protest too much."

"Before I got here, I never heard that expression. I hate it," Nick groused.

Jared got serious. "Look, can I say something? I don't want to pry, and you can tell me to shut up—"

"Shut up."

"That was rhetorical. Anyway, from what I can see, Nick is having a hard time with the whole modeling thing. It's making you question yourself, no?"

"No!" Nick said.

"That's what I thought." Jared kept on talking. "Here's the thing, dude. Maybe you hate the modeling gig not because you're uncomfortable with the people at the studio; maybe you hate it for the simple reason that it's boring. Maybe standing there in your tighty-whiteys, or whatever they make you pose in, maybe it makes you feel like some brainless hunk, some subhuman. Maybe it makes you feel like you have nothing else besides perfect pecs and six-pack abs. Maybe the reason you're ready to ditch it has nothing to do with which way you swing the bat. In other words, maybe the whole time, you questioned the wrong thing."

Nick stared at Jared, openmouthed.

Jared shrugged and bit into his second burger. "I'm just sayin'."

"That kind of makes sense, Nick," Eliot said slowly.

Jared pointed to Eliot. "And you—what can my psychobabble help you with?"

Nick piped up, "He thinks he's a failure, because, you know, in the earthquake, he kind of . . ."

"Froze? Oh, you mean, just like I did?" Jared inquired. "I've given that a lot of thought. Not to rationalize the way I stood there like a spoiled do-nothing rich kid, in way over his head . . ." He paused to see if they were smiling. In spite of themselves, they were.

"Here's how I'm looking at it. It was teamwork. Eliot

got us started, then passed the bat to Nick and Sara. And Naomi came in for the save. Lindsay, of course, nabbed the most dramatic part, the damsel in distress—that's who she is. And me? Well, we did end up at my house, and my dad is making reparations to everyone. So I guess I contributed my family money and clout. We all did our part, the best we could."

Eliot looked surprised. "That is the most sense you've made all summer."

Nick flashed back to their first day in L.A.: Jared's reaction to having been caught with his pants down. The guy had been so smooth, Nick had totally worshipped him. Three months later, he still did.

"I have an idea," said Jared. "Let's go catch a movie—some guy thing where a lot of shit blows up."

Nick waved his arms up and down, a worshipful motion.

True Confessions: Go, Girls

Lindsay embraced her superficiality, but she wasn't stupid. Something had gone down behind the scenes, something that eliminated the need for a final audition and took Sara out of the running.

Amanda insisted that Lindsay was more talented, that she'd given the better reading. Jared agreed with Amanda, and further speculated that maybe no one wanted to risk a big-budget movie on someone as inexperienced as Sara. Rusty claimed blissful ignorance; he was just thrilled that a client from his agency had landed a role. It meant money in his pocket.

Lindsay was left to figure it out for herself. There was something no one was telling her, something no one was whispering about: She'd checked with Caitlin, Julie, Ava, MK, Austin, and Tripp, anyone with connections and an ear to the Hollywood ground.

Lindsay's portrayal of Cherry wasn't better than Sara's: It was different. It *was* possible the powers-that-be had decided on her take. But no way would they do it without a tryout in front of the studio bosses. The director and producers were notoriously risk-averse, and their bosses dined out on the power to make the final selection. So what was up this time?

She was forced to do something totally counter-intuitive: observe Sara's behavior. The tall Texan had briefly congratulated Lindsay on hearing the news, but didn't blather on about how the best person had won, destiny, all her usual perky upbeat nonsense.

Of course, Sara was still freaked out about the earth-quake, giving up her precious virginity, hurting Eliot, breaking up with Donald, yada yada. Losing the part in the movie was probably far down on her misery list. Maybe Sara even believed she deserved to lose the part— who knew what went on in that blond head?

Still, something gnawed at her, told her Sara knew the truth. Finally, when she could stand it no longer—she'd wasted an entire day shopping and obsessing—she pounced on an unsuspecting Sara, just home from the day's work and hauling grocery bags, as if they still lived in the Hills house, as if the staff here didn't do the shopping and cooking.

"What do you want, Lindsay?" Sara tried to brush by her, but Lindsay stood blocking her way past the foyer.

"I want to know what you know." Lindsay stared into Sara's sky-blue peepers. "What Lionel told you, or what you told him."

Sara stepped to the side, attempting to walk around Lindsay. "I don't know what you're talking about. Anyway, why do you care? You won the role. I congratulated you, didn't I?"

Lindsay only caught a brief glimpse, but there was a look in Sara's eye. Of what? Regret? And suddenly, it hit her. Like a sledgehammer. "You . . . you pulled out? You freakin' took yourself out of the running! You told them you didn't want the part, didn't you?" Lindsay was incredulous. And sure she was right.

Sara tossed her hair back—a very Lindsay-like motion, it occurred to her—and stood firm. She didn't deny it, though. "What makes you think I backed out?"

"Because it's the only way I'd have gotten it without that last audition."

If she thought Sara was going to reach out to her, take her hand the way she did Naomi's so often, or say something soothing and insipid, Lindsay was wrong. Sara said nothing, just tried again to walk away from her.

"You have to tell me why you did it!" Lindsay insisted, frustrated at Sara's silence. The girl had been so open, so easy to read all summer long. Lindsay was having none of her silence now.

Sara managed to brush by her finally and head toward the kitchen. Lindsay found herself trailing the statuesque girl, feeling ever so much like a kid pulling at the back of her mom's coat, begging to be paid attention to. She didn't care, though. She had to know. "Please, Sara," she whined."I'd really like to understand what happened."

Finally, Sara whirled around, set the grocery bags down, and crossed her arms. "I called Lionel and told him I didn't want the part."

"Why would you do that?"

"Because you wanted it more than I did."

Lindsay's mouth fell open. "Well, yeah, but what's that got to do with anything?" she finally managed. "You . . . you . . . rehearsed! You told your people back in Texas—won't they be disappointed?"

"No doubt." Sara sighed.

"And you kicked ass at the audition. You really did. I snooped."

Sara smiled ruefully. Which made Lindsay feel even worse. "I did want it, Lindsay. But you needed it. That's the difference."

Sara always did what was needed. Naomi needed shelter, needed help and a friend. The house needed cleaning, the lawn needed seeding, the rent needed to be paid. Sara, ever so righteous, did the right thing. Always.

Standing there in the massive hallway between the foyer and the kitchen, Lindsay didn't try to stop her lip from quivering, or swallow the lump in her throat, or tell herself she wasn't acting. "I've been a bitch to you all summer long," she blubbered.

It was then that Sara finally touched her, cupped Lindsay's chin in her palm. "This is your dream, Lindsay. You go for it."

"But . . . don't you have a dream too?" Lindsay asked, wiping away her tears with the back of her hand.

Sara's eyes clouded over. "I'm sure I do. I thought I knew what it was, but everything went topsy-turvy this summer. I'm waiting to figure it out."

Sara had told Lindsay more truth than she'd meant to. More than she owed the selfish girl. In her heart, Sara was still the righteous girl she'd always been—and she knew she'd done the right thing. So why did it hurt so much? Her skin felt sore, every molecule ached.

"Ouch! Is it always this hot?" Naomi, trying out the hot tub for the first time, yanked her foot out of the bubbling Jacuzzi.

"Take it slowly," Sara advised. "You'll get used to it."

In a bid to cheer Sara up, Naomi had suggested an after-dinner soak in the Larsons' magnificent marble tub, which made the one at the share house look scrawny.

This was "the Gucci of Jacuzzis," as Rusty Larson had proudly bragged, state-of-the-art, featuring several tiers to sit on, two carved-in lounges, and jets shooting pulsating water at you from every which way.

"It's supposed to relax your tense muscles," Sara said.

"Or fry my skin," the dark-haired waif muttered.

Sara chuckled. "You weren't afraid to dive under the wreckage in an earthquake; you're going squeamish now?"

"*That* was all adrenaline," Naomi pointed out. "*This* is bizarre."

Sara had thought so too, back when she'd first come to Los Angeles. All these big, shiny, material things: profligate, extravagant, decadent, toys for people with so much money they don't know what to do with it.

That was then. Now? Her core values hadn't changed. But this, she kinda liked: If you allowed yourself to sink into it, to feel—and not think—it felt real, real good.

Naomi carefully slid in, pressed her back against the side. "Wow!" She giggled. One of the power jets had hit the small of her back. "This is definitely . . . weird."

"It's supposed to pound your muscles, take out the knots," Sara explained, as she sank neck-deep into the bubbles.

Sara wondered if the girl from the streets would find herself liking her first Jacuzzi experience. It was so easy to succumb (the word came to her unbidden) to all kinds of temptation, to things that made you feel good, feel important, to people who made you feel special.

No. She didn't want to go back there. She closed her eyes. What she'd done the night before the earthquake had set off a chain-of-pain reaction. Nick was wracked with guilt, Eliot was devastated, poor unsuspecting Donald got dumped—for what could she do now but break up with him? She felt responsible for all of it.

When she opened her eyes, she realized Naomi was staring at her. "We all do things out of anger," Naomi said, "no matter how hard you try not to."

The words popped out of Sara before she could censor herself. "So, what, you're a mind reader, too? Is that one of the skills you learned on the streets?" Horrified at her outburst, she slapped her hand over her mouth. "Naomi, I am so sorry. I didn't mean that—but you seemed to know what I was thinking."

"I don't have to be a mind reader to know what you've been obsessing about; it's written all over your face. And don't worry, no offense taken."

Sara considered. "So you're saying I got drunk, broke my purity pledge, had sex with Nick, all out of anger?"

"Pretty much."

"Who am I supposedly so angry at?"

"Yourself, Sara. That's who."

She wanted to say, "I have nothing to be angry at myself for." She wanted to say, "I live—or lived—a right-eous life. I did the right thing." But the words got stuck in her throat, never made it out.

Naomi continued. "Backing out of the audition so

Lindsay could win the role was off-the-chart unselfish. Lindsay isn't even worthy! You knew it. So you wanted something in return, something for you: something to make you feel good. On a visceral level—the most basic human level."

"Nick," Sara mumbled, starting to tear up again.

"You've been wanting him all summer."

"Something else written all over my face?" Sara asked sarcastically.

"Not just your face, sistah."

Sara swallowed hard. So she had been that obvious, much as she'd tried to kick those feelings away, to not name them. It'd never occurred to her, not in a million years, that she'd act on them. She turned to Naomi. "It's actually not good to stay in the tub longer than fifteen minutes at a time. You'll get dizzy."

"Let's not risk it." Naomi hoisted herself out of the water and brought over a couple of soft, oversize beach towels.

They sat on the edge of the Jacuzzi, wrapped in terry-cloth, legs dangling in the hot water. "Nick's not the right guy for me," Sara heard herself saying. "Neither is Donald. There's no future with either of them."

"Agreed."

Sara was a little surprised Naomi said that so quickly.

"Look, Sara, just because you did something once doesn't change who you are, cancel out your beliefs. You're still you, and Nick's a great guy, but on no planet are the two of you remotely right for each other. At heart, he's a simple, good-time frat-guy, more brawn than brains. You're deeper. You're always going to be searching, questioning, looking for answers. And helping other people—that's such a huge part of who you are. You're not going to stop, even if there are times, like this one, you got hurt doing it."

"Who died and made you Yoda?"

Ah, leave it to Lindsay. As if proof were needed that people, in fact, never do change. Neither Sara nor Naomi had heard her pad outside in her spa slippers. But what shocked them was not her intrusion, nor her itsy-bitsy bikini. It was the sight of Lindsay Pierce, diva divine . . . carrying a tray? With *three* fancy salt-rimmed margarita glasses and a pitcher full of the pale green drink.

Lindsay said, "Sounds like I walked in on the juicy stuff—girl-talk confessions. I am *so* all about that. Mind if I join? I come bearing gifts."

"Yes, we do mind," Naomi started to say, but Sara overruled her. "Oh, what the heck. We hardly have any secrets anymore. What's in the pitcher?"

"Margaritas: my own private recipe," the freckled girl replied, setting the tray down and pretzeling her legs. "Most excellent." She narrowed her eyes at Sara. "I assume we are still drinking?"

Sara hesitated, then shrugged. "Maybe I'll stick with only one."

Lindsay poured the glasses full and handed them out.

"So, what's our topic, besides self-flagellation? I'm not a big fan of self-criticism."

"Yeah, we noticed," Naomi quipped.

"But I am an expert on matters of the heart. And flesh."

"No kidding." Naomi again.

"And who'd guess my little savior had a sarcastic streak?" Lindsay shot Naomi a smile, grateful and genuine. "We have something in common after all."

Naomi sipped her drink. "Not so much."

"So, Nick." Lindsay grinned at Sara. "So yummy!"

Sara and Naomi shot her a look.

"Not from personal experience, girls," Lindsay assured them. "The guy is scorching! Who wouldn't want to get into his pants?"

Sara looked stricken. But she had no answer for Lindsay, who was, as advertised, spot on.

Lindsay finished her drink and poured another. "I don't get you, Sara—and in truth, I never cared that much before."

Bracing, brutal honesty: That's Lindsay. Sara wasn't the least bit pissed.

"You're like 'bass-ackwards,' if you catch my drift. I'm shitty to you, so you go all overly kind to me. You sacrifice the part in the movie for me. You go to Nick for comfort— you feel great, 'cause who wouldn't, being with him? And then you feel bad about feeling good. I mean, if you really think sex is bad, why did God make it feel so good?"

"Lindsay, don't take this the wrong way, but you

know nothing." Sara was beginning to feel the tequila.

"I know about wanting. You wanted something for you. Something . . . oooh . . . *forbidden!*" she taunted. "I don't understand what you don't understand. We all want forbidden fruit—I don't have to tell you the story of Adam and Eve, do I?"

Sara felt her jaw drop.

"You're only human, Sara. You only think you're better than the rest of us. I might not be religious, but back when I starred on *All for Wong*, we did a special Christmas episode one year. The lesson was, most people believe in a higher power who forgives your sins. Don't you?"

"I can't believe I'm saying this, but she has a point, Sara." Naomi looked shocked.

Sara slipped back into the hot tub, leaned her head against its smooth lip, and stared at the sky. "So, what do you do with those feelings? You can't give in to them every time you're attracted to someone."

"Yeah, that'd just be slutty." Lindsay giggled. She joined Sara in the Jacuzzi. "But if you're asking me personally, we'll need at least one other round of drinks."

"I'll go." Naomi started to get up, but Lindsay stopped her. "There's an intercom by the door. Hit the button and tell Desiree we need munchies and 'mas 'ritas'—that's Spanish for 'more.'"

When the housekeeper appeared a few minutes later with a tray of salsa and chips, guacamole, and another huge pitcher, Lindsay tried to answer Sara's question.

"First, you admit your feelings. They are kind of natural, by the way. You don't have to act on them. I'm all about live and let live. But since you found this out already, sex is pleasurable. I would think it has to be that way, so people would want to procreate. I mean, I don't know that much . . . I'm just sayin.'"

Damn—that is, *darn*—Lindsay. When she was right, she was insufferable. Sara didn't want to debate the Bible, or her belief in waiting for marriage. She'd always look to the Bible for guidance. But maybe, just maybe, she'd also learn to listen to her own voice. Maybe that's what this summer had taught her.

She turned to Naomi. "What about you, little one? Ever fallen for the wrong boy?"

"Me? It's more like I've put my trust in too many of the wrong people," Naomi confessed, draining her glass. "I'm in a different situation. I did what I had to, to survive. I never had the luxury of a boyfriend or thinking about who I wanted to be with." She said it without bitterness.

"You've been very sheltered, Sara," Lindsay pointed out. "You were bound to have some eye-opening experiences this summer. I hope at least some of them were good."

Sara reflected. A lot of them were not just good, but great.

The tequila seemed to open Naomi up more too. "So now that we've dissected Sara and me, what about you,

Lindsay? I mean, *really*? I know when someone's fronting. You pretend to be so worldly, like you've slept around so much. Something tells me that's bull."

Lindsay rolled her eyes. "Okay, okay, we get your point, Yoda. You know, you even look like a little troll."

Sara splashed her, hard. "That's a terrible thing to say!" But all three were laughing.

Lindsay added, "So much knowledge, spouting from the fountain of one tiny human. I do sort of, you know, love Jared."

"Why?" Sara and Naomi had to high-five since they said it at the same time.

Lindsay licked the salty rim of her glass. "Habit?"

Naomi laughed. "Like you're getting away with that! Spill."

"You can't tell us you've never thought about it before," Sara added

Lindsay drew a deep, dramatic breath. "I know he's not the hottest guy around, not like Nick. Looks-wise, I could probably do better. And he's not the smartest guy on the planet. He's no Eliot Kupferberg."

"Stop saying what he's not—and tell us what he is," Naomi demanded.

"Jared's kind of the best of both, straddling the fence between brains and brawn, never coming down fully on one side or the other. So, no lust-magnet, but he's sexy and smart enough, if that makes sense. He always knows the right thing to say and make it sound sincere. He's chameleon-like, snaky and shrewd, wrapped in a very nice glittery package."

Sara listened to Lindsay, and it was like a klieg light going off in her brain. Lindsay loved Jared because he was handsome, vapid, and cagey in a hollow kind of way. Just like the town he lived in. Jared embodied Hollywood, and that's ultimately what Lindsay saw in him. Jared can make magic happen; he's a walking all-access pass.

Sara had never met anyone like Lindsay or Jared before. She'd held her private thoughts about them, but hearing Lindsay say it out loud, admit to believing it, set off another klieg light.

"I have an idea," Sara said.

19

Jared's Big Idea

When Jared, Nick, and Eliot returned from the movies, they found Lindsay, Sara, and Naomi sloshing around the hot tub, happily sloshed, deep in the heart of "Margaritaville." To Jared's amusement, it was Sara who immediately jumped up, wrapped herself in a towel, and collared him. "Can I speak to you privately?" she asked.

Jared didn't have long to wonder what was on Sara's mind. The minute they got inside the house, out of earshot of the others, she blurted, "You said you wanted to make amends, right? After the earthquake, you said you'd do anything for us?"

"Yeah, absolutely." Only . . . Sara was pretty hammered—not quite slurring her words yet, but on the verge. "What'd you have in mind, Sara?"

"I need you to read something."

• • •

Late the next afternoon, Jared jumped into his car and drove to Galaxy's offices in Beverly Hills to see his father. He didn't have an appointment, so he waited, pacing the anteroom for close to an hour while Rusty Larson finished with his meetings and then ran a tele-conference.

The whole time, Jared gripped the screenplay tightly, as if someone walking by might rip it away from him, trick him into dropping it, giving it up. This treasure was titled *Hide in Plain Sight*; he'd read it only because he'd promised Sara. He'd totally planned to scan about ten pages, make short shrift of it, let Sara down gently. But . . . in the "who'da thunk it" department, *he* couldn't put it down!

He flipped through the 149 pages again nervously: He'd read the thing three times. Each time, he came to the same conclusion: Here was a great story, with equal parts intrigue, edge-of-your-seat action, sweet romance, laughs, and poignancy—the elements that make a movie a blockbuster. Or, expressed another way: This was *the shit*! And, the earthquake notwithstanding, the single most unexpected event of the summer.

All the stars were aligned, Jared was sure of it: The script could be had for cheap, since the screenwriter was a nobody, just a cop he'd happened across. It'd be a Galaxy exclusive, which meant his dad's company would make boatloads of money on it.

The wheels in Jared's head had not stopped spinning

since he'd finished reading it the first time. Now, as he paced, he ran through a mental list of Galaxy clients for the lead role, not unlike a list of *People* magazine's sexiest: Matthew McConaughey, Jake Gyllenhaal. Ewan McGregor could do it, potentially Jude Law—no, he's too pretty to play the cop. Pitt was possible, or you could go older, Denzel even.

For the lead female, there was no list. One person was born to play that role.

Rusty flung open the door to his executive office. "What are you doing here?" On the "I'm-so-happy-to-see-you" meter, his dad's tone was subzero.

"I was hoping we could talk." It dawned on Jared that maybe this wasn't, in fact, the best time to bust in on his old man. The scowl on his dad's face hinted that Rusty had had a crap day.

"You came here to talk?" Rusty said. "About what? What a little liar you've been all summer?" His dad wearily dropped into his enormous boss-worthy leather throne and impatiently hit delete on his keyboard.

Okaaaay, so Jared had been a little hasty just dropping by. And so excited about the screenplay, a lot forgetful that a certain volcano had not yet erupted. He tried not to flinch. He'd not prepared a speech, an explanation, rationalization, or even a bald-faced lie. "Uh, yeah, that was part of the reason I came. I want to apologize."

"Bull," Rusty muttered. "You came here because you

want something. I'm so sick of your lies, Jared. Do you ever tell the truth?"

"Only the parts that matter."

The quip was cribbed from the TV show *Entourage*: He and his father had laughed hard when the wily agent had said the line. Now? Not so funny.

"How could you be so disrespectful?" Rusty demanded. "I'm your father. I sent you to summer school to make up your lousy grades and you just blow me off, do whatever you want. Where do you get the balls?"

Jared lowered his head. He knew from rhetorical questions.

"And don't give me any crap about me and your mother being divorced, and some other 'poor misunderstood rich kid' garbage. I've read all those scripts. They all stink."

Jared hadn't planned on going there. Nor would he interrupt his father's soliloquy. He knew when to "hold 'em."

"Besides," Rusty growled, "if you think you ditched school to screw me, you're not as smart as I give you credit for, 'cause you only screwed yourself. And then squatting in your uncle's house and charging those people rent—what were you thinking?"

Not that he'd be outed to his father by Mother Nature, that's for sure.

Rusty echoed his thoughts. "Obviously, you didn't

count on an earthquake." Suddenly, his dad went emo, teared up. "If you had been at that school, and if something had happened, I'd never have been able to forgive myself for forcing you to go there."

Yeah, Jared thought. Now you're off the hook, you can go on blaming me. Thoughts unmuttered were often best.

"I want the raw truth, Jared. This is your moment. Don't blow it. What possessed you to do this?"

Jared deliberated. There was too much at stake here. He went with full confessional: "I've been trying to tell you, Dad, for a long time."

"I'm listening now." Rusty put his feet up on the desk, crossed his arms behind his head, and leaned back. Jared talked. And talked, babbling on like some James Cameron movie desperately in need of editing.

"It's not that I don't respect you, I just don't agree with you, Dad. I don't belong in school. I belong here, at Galaxy, with you. I thought if I made you believe I'd pulled it together this summer, got good grades, and at the same time did something to help the company—"

Rusty's hand went up in a stop motion. "You think Galaxy needs help?"

Jared swallowed. "Well, doesn't it?"

"We've had better times," his dad conceded. "What has Lindsay been telling you?"

"Nothing." The one lie he told, he told for her. He rushed on. "I know you think I'm a slacker, I'm lazy. How many times have you said I'm just like Uncle Rob? Take the easy way out, never live up to my potential?"

It was his father's turn to remain silent.

"And I am"—Jared's lip trembled unexpectedly—"I am lacking in a lot of ways. I messed up this summer, but not in the way you think. I was stuck up, I misjudged people big-time. I belittled Eliot when he tried to prepare us, I made fun of Sara, and I tried to kick Naomi out. Naomi! If not for her . . ."

He couldn't continue.

Rusty offered him a tissue but remained silent, listening.

Jared wiped his leaky eyes. "Lindsay might not have made it. 'Cause she was buried, and I was no help. Everything I have—money, access, style, everything that made me so self-important, me, the ultimate cool Hollywood insider—it all turned out to be worth nothing. I wasn't brave or smart. I was a sorry-assed wimp whose main contribution was whining."

Truly, truly, truly, he told himself, opening up like this to his father had not been premeditated. In no way had he meant to butter up the old guy so Rusty would forgive him, so he'd . . . oh God . . . be in a prime position to make his pitch. To get Rusty excited about *Hide in Plain Sight*. It was his moment; he had the floor, and his dad's full attention, and empathy. Jared blew his nose, wiped his eyes.

"I didn't go to school this summer, but I learned a pretty big life lesson. And I hope that counts for something. I'm no hero, and I suck at school—but I do have talent, and I know this business, show business. I live and breathe it. And I . . . Dad, I found a screenplay. . . ."

20

Finding Naomi

"This is a joke, right?"

Five heads shook in unison. Jared, Lindsay, Sara, Eliot, and Nick were serious as a heart attack. Naomi had been in the bedroom, sitting in the window seat (imagine!) reading a book, minding her own business, when they ambushed her, just flung open the door, brandishing a dozen long-stemmed red roses, a bottle of champagne, and a proposition—one at which they assumed she'd jump.

She stood still. "Guys, this is so sweet. But there are other ways to say thanks. You don't have to offer me a part in a movie. It's overcompensating."

"Asking you to star in *Hide in Plain Sight* has nothing to do with gratitude," Jared assured her. "It's—"

"*Brasheet*," Lindsay interrupted. "That's Jewish for 'It's meant to be.'"

"It's Yiddish," Jared corrected, "and it's pronounced *beshert.*"

"It's ber*serk,*" Naomi told them with finality.

Had it only been Jared or Lindsay pushing this insane idea, it would've been easy to dismiss them. But they had allies—Eliot, Nick, and Sara—and she was feeling seriously ganged up on, under pressure to explain herself. 'Cause no way, no how, not ever would she consider their beyond-ridiculous proposal.

Nick put a friendly arm around her. "This is a big movie, Naomi. Most people would think they've died and gone to heaven, to be asked to star in it."

Most people—did she really need to point it out?—were not her.

"A month ago, Lindsay and I would've fought you for it!" Sara exclaimed.

"And so would Naomi Watts, and Reese Witherspoon, and any of the Kates—Bosworth, Beckinsale, Blanchett, Winslet, Hudson—you name 'em," Lindsay put in.

Naomi rolled her eyes. Had they all gone bonkers? Was she the only sane one in the room? And how had everything suddenly moved into warp speed? Listening to them made Naomi dizzy.

Just a few days ago, Sara had asked Jared to read *Hide in Plain Sight.* In the span of seventy-two hours, he'd read it and taken it to his father, who'd agreed that the screenplay was pretty wonderful. Galaxy quickly secured the rights from an overjoyed Officer Ortega—now, officially, a screenwriter! Because there are no secrets in Hollywood, word got out quickly, and the whole showbiz community sniffed out the new "buzz-worthy" screenplay. In swift succession, a producer and director signed up. Paramount Pictures snapped it up, and *Hide in Plain Sight* got "greenlit"—Hollywood-speak for happening. The casting process was about to begin.

Jared refused to allow any actresses to audition for the starring role until Naomi took a shot at it. Which she stubbornly refused to do.

"You read the script," Sara reminded her. "And somewhere deep inside, you know you're perfect for the part of Moxie."

"Why don't you want to even try out?" Eliot asked.

"Hello? Not an actress—remember? Or did the earthquake give you all amnesia? Girl from the streets. Sara's stray. A homeless ho," Naomi fired back.

"Ooops." Lindsay genuinely blushed. "You heard that, huh?"

Naomi narrowed her eyes at Jared. "Just two months ago you thought I was a crack-head killer. Now you think I'm a movie star. Make up your mind."

"Who said you couldn't be both? They're not mutually exclusive."

It was Lindsay's quip, but Jared elbowed her in the ribs. "A lot can happen in two months," he said. "A lot did happen. I was exposed as the jerk, the asshole, any horrible thing you can think of: Fill in the blank. But I'm still an opportunist, and if it helps you to see it that way, go for it."

"What he's saying—" Lindsay started, but Sara stopped her.

"He doesn't need you to interpret. What Jared means is, if you agree to read for the role and things work out, Jared wins too. It makes him look good to his father and raises his stock in the biz. It's win-win, Naomi."

Naomi arched her eyebrows. Sara on Jared's side? What had the summer come to?

"It's totally quid pro quo," Lindsay put in. "You saved our lives. We give you a part in a movie where you'll earn millions. The movie makes billions, we save Jared's dad's company. We're all heroes. It's so Hollywood! See?"

Naomi did not see. Their idea was harebrained, insane. And impossible. What were they thinking? This wasn't some fantasy, and she wasn't their own Eliza Dolittle, or Julia Roberts in *Pretty Woman*. The homeless waif from the streets becomes a rich movie star? That only happens in the movies. Not in real life, and certainly not in *her* real life.

After the quake, when Eliot had guessed she was a survivor, she'd told them about her past. The version she gave them was abridged. If she went along with the crazy idea to read for the role in the movie, and if she actually got it? Too much info would surface. She couldn't take that chance.

For the first time since Sara had taken her in, Naomi felt caged. She pressed her back against the window-seat wall. "As much as I want to help you look good, Jared, I can't do this."

"Can't? Or won't?" Eliot said it gently.

"I can't! I can't be famous. I'm an under-the-radar person."

"That's in the past. Everything's changed now," Sara said soothingly.

"How do you even know I'd be good?" Naomi challenged. "Just because the role calls for a kid who runs away and ends up on the streets? If that's the criteria, why not go to Hollywood Boulevard, pick up any homeless girl, and offer her the part?

"Eeeww!" Lindsay couldn't help herself.

"Only you can play this part," Sara said. "You have so much soul. You look like you've seen so much sadness, like you're wise beyond your years. It comes across in your eyes. That, and your fierce determination—we saw that during the earthquake. It's like you were someone else. You were born to play Moxie."

"And," Lindsay noted, "you'd come cheap."

Jared shot darts at her.

"Well, she wouldn't cost what a Cami Diaz would, or Reese, or Charlize. Even Nicole Richie—God forbid!— would charge more. That's meaningful to the studio."

"How 'bout you don't say any more," Nick suggested.

Lindsay furrowed her brow, then turned to Naomi. "Wait a minute. I get it. You don't want to do the role because you think people will find out you were really homeless? And look down on you?"

"Gee, Lindsay, I wonder why she'd think that?" Eliot said sarcastically.

"You're so not seeing the big picture, Naomi. Rags-to-riches stories are classic—they never go out of style, they're totally on trend. It's like a full hour of *Oprah*! It's the cover of *People*. You'll be America's sweetheart."

Naomi shuddered.

A light went on in Jared's head. "Oh, crap, there's more, isn't there? You haven't told us the whole story."

"She doesn't have to tell us any more than she wants to." Sara fell right into default mode, defending Naomi.

Thoughtfully, Jared said, "Not to sound like more of a jerk than you already think I am, but, Naomi, whatever it is, whatever you're hiding that you think is so terrible it would keep you from this—I bet I can fix it. Spin it so it's a good thing, not a bad thing."

"That's what's so sick. You really believe that." Naomi's laugh was bitter.

Jared took no offense. "I'm not Superman. But there are things I can do, places where I have influence. Let me—"

"Save me? Let you save me like I saved Lindsay? Did it ever occur to you that maybe I don't need saving? Maybe I've been saved one time too many."

A plunging sadness gripped her as she packed her few belongings. She finally got them off her back by agreeing to think about trying out for the role.

She'd lied. Naomi didn't need to think. None of them would ever, ever understand what her life had been like, that to have people know her name—to be in the spotlight, to be exposed? It was unthinkable.

The days after the 1994 earthquake were a blur. She'd gone in and out of consciousness; all she remembered was waking in a strange place, asking her sister Annie where Mom and Dad were. She'd come to understand she was in a motel with Annie, saved by Mr. Knepper, the tall, kindly man who lived in the apartment above theirs. Annie was eleven; she was nine.

Over the next several weeks, Mr. Knepper explained what'd happened. The earthquake had demolished most of the apartment complex, and many of the people who lived there, including their parents, had perished. For a long time, Naomi was incapable of comprehending more. She'd never see her parents again. That was too big; it blotted out everything else.

The story Mr. Knepper told the girls got worse. The apartment, he alleged, wasn't even theirs legally. "Your folks weren't paying rent; they were squatting. Their name was never on any bills. So it's not like you gals can make a claim or anything." He told them if they tried to contact the police, everything would be exposed. Their parents would have died criminals, and they themselves would go to jail, to juvie.

Annie and Naomi believed him. They were kids, just dumb, terrified kids who, in the blink of an eye, were orphaned. They didn't have other relatives they knew of—they'd spent most of their lives on the road with their parents. They didn't know how to search for potential kin. Mr. Knepper saved their lives, dragged them out of the rubble, he said, fed and sheltered them. They thought they were safe with him; that's what he told them.

When he asked about school, they told him the truth: They'd been home-schooled. He vowed to continue their training, right there in the motel.

They rarely left the motel. They didn't know they could. When he told them he'd always wanted daughters and he felt like a father to them—that's when the sisters began to be uneasy in his presence.

They knew it was wrong when he began to act more than paternally toward them. Annie hatched a plan. Naomi never knew exactly what her sister had done to immobilize Mr. Knepper, how she'd gathered food, some clothes, stolen some money—planned their escape.

They made up different names, different birthdays. They'd stayed in Griffith Park for a while but were soon picked up by the LAPD. Having no identification, no one to claim them, no one who had filed a missing persons report, they were turned over to child services.

It wasn't until they landed in foster homes that they were separated. "Never tell," Annie had tearfully warned her. "Never tell what happened. We'll get in bad trouble."

"Why?" Naomi had asked. "We didn't do anything wrong."

"I did," Annie said. "I had to. Swear you won't tell. If anyone finds out what I did, I'll go to jail. Or worse."

Naomi swore. She believed that, one day, after they were out of foster care, they'd live together, be a family again. But that's not how it worked out. Naomi ended up in a string of foster homes, and eventually she ran away for good, never finding Annie. A part of her believed that if she stayed on the streets, Annie would find her. It'd been years now. Still, she clung to that belief.

And now here comes Jared Superstar. A rich kid with resources, money. Giving her this hooey about making her a star—and maybe he could. Maybe Annie would find her. But if she went public, Annie's secret—Naomi now believed Annie may have done something bad to Knepper—it would come out. She'd go to jail.

"She's gone!" Sara scurried down the elaborate staircase of the Larson mansion, calling out to the others. "Naomi bolted."

"What do you mean, she's gone? Gone where?" Jared appeared at the bottom of the steps, Lindsay, Nick, and Eliot on his heels.

"Her room's empty, bed's made—like no one ever used it," Sara reported.

"Did she leave a note?" Nick asked

"She's not suicidal, you dunce. Jared just scared her away," Eliot declared. "You moved too fast, you overwhelmed her. Of course she ran."

"Who made you the expert on all things Naomi?" Jared demanded. "When's the last time someone got offered a movie role and reacted by running away? Get real, Eliot."

"You shouldn't have come on so strong, man." Eliot looked at Lindsay and Sara. "You either."

"Enough, all of you. We have to find her," Sara decided.

"Hopefully, she didn't get too far—if she's on foot, we should be able to catch her. If she took a taxi, that's another story," Jared calculated. "I'll get the car. We'll go after her."

"No!" Lindsay crossed her arms.

"No what? We don't try to find her?" Nick asked.

"Not you guys. Sara and I will go. We'll have a better chance of finding her, 'cause we're smarter than you, and when we do, she'll open up to Sara."

Jared handed Lindsay the keys to the Lexus. The girls made a left out of the long, winding driveway, keeping their eyes peeled for a small, thin girl with choppy black hair and huge violet eyes.

"I think she'd probably head for the main road," Sara opined after they'd circled the area a few times. "She's more likely to find a taxi there."

Lindsay turned right, toward Sunset Boulevard. "I hope she isn't trying to hitch a ride. You never know what kind of jerks are on the road."

Sara pressed her lips together, her eyes darting left and

right as Lindsay drove—remembering her first day in Los Angeles, when those sleazy guys tried to lure her into their car. If *she* had enough sense not to go with them, Naomi surely would resist, no matter how desperate she was.

"I don't get it, exactly," Lindsay mused. "Why would she run away? Why not just say thanks but no thanks, I'm not interested in your movie?"

"I'm guessing she figured we wouldn't let up on her, we'd pressure her. And I'm also guessing that running from scary situations has kept her alive all these years."

"How can you compare our offer to make her a movie star with scary street situations? That's ridiculous."

"To you, maybe. Who knows what goes on in her head," Sara pointed out.

They had no luck finding any pedestrians at all along the winding, palm-tree-lined Sunset Boulevard, so they headed east toward the shopping district. They wound up and down the side streets, checking coffee shops, bookstores, any place Naomi might've gone into. No luck.

"What about turning onto Hollywood Boulevard," Lindsay suggested, "where you first found her?"

They rode in silence for a while. Every so often, Lindsay's cell phone rang: Jared asking for an update.

Hollywood Boulevard was crowded, commuters coming home from work, shoppers out and about—tourists, skinheads, the usual carnival of weirdos, beggars. No Naomi.

Out of nowhere, Lindsay blurted, "I'm not going to try

and force her to do this movie. I owe her, Sara. I owe her everything. If she wants to stay underground, I owe her that, too. But I'd like to give her money, at the very least, so she can do what she wants. And I want to her to know that she always . . ."

Silently, Sara finished the sentence: *that Naomi always has friends. People to turn to. Always.* Sara reached over and squeezed Lindsay's shoulder. "I know. Me, too."

They passed Big Al's Tattoo Parlor, Bondage Babes Leather 'N' Thongs, Off-Track Betting, take-out places. "Where would she go?" Lindsay said for the eighteenth time.

"She'd go where she feels safe," Sara said.

"Oh, my God!" Lindsay exclaimed. "We're such duh-heads. We should have thought of it right away!"

In the middle of traffic, in a completely illegal move, accompanied by the outraged horns and curses of dozens of cars, Lindsay slammed on the brakes and made a U-turn.

Naomi was sitting at the property's edge, several feet from where the pool had once been.

Lindsay had managed to squeeze the car between the huge yellow-and-black CAT construction trucks, which took up half the winding street in front of 5905 Chula Vista Lane. It was nearing sunset and the workers had gone for the day, but the big cleanup trucks had remained.

Without exchanging a word, the girls threaded their way around back. The quake had caused an upheaval in the yard, Uncle Rob's property now ended in a mini-cliff. Naomi was on it, her legs pretzeled under her; she leaned back on her arms for support. She stared out into the valley.

Naomi didn't seem the least bit surprised to see Sara and Lindsay, who settled on either side of her.

For a few peaceful moments, no one spoke. The valley spread out below them, the hills all around, and the sun, a big red rubber ball floating in the sky, brushed the top of the mountains.

Lindsay murmured, "Awesome view."

Naomi nodded in agreement.

"It's so great that Rusty is getting the house rehabbed," Lindsay noted, "so when Rob gets back, he won't have to deal with the mess."

Sara gazed at the sky. "Nature caused the earthquake, but look what nature gives us. Nothing can take away the glory of this landscape."

"These past two weeks," Naomi said quietly, "at Jared's house? It's the first time in my entire life I ever had my own room. But I was happiest in this place, in the basement. Funny, huh?"

"No, not at all," Sara said. "I feel completely out of place at the Larson mansion."

Lindsay whipped around. "Really? Not me. I feel right at home there."

"Will you live there some day?" Naomi asked Lindsay.

"Oh, I don't know. I'm not thinking that far ahead."

"But you'll end up with Jared, right?" Sara asked. "You love him."

"You two are made for each other," Naomi put in.

Lindsay had no quip. She seemed to mull whether she should say anything. Finally, she said, "Remember that night in the hot tub, you guys asked what I saw in Jared? I didn't tell you everything. I love him because, at the end of the day, he'd do anything for me. He's crazy about me. He accepts me even when I'm selfish, and snobby, and—"

"You? Selfish? Come on!" Sara jabbed her, and they all laughed.

"Jared has seen me at my worst. And he loves me anyway."

"Then why do you sound so mournful?" Naomi asked.

"Because . . ." She took a breath, "Because I hurt him once before. And I could hurt him again. At least I think I could. If something came up and, say, Jared wasn't in a position to help me, career-wise? I could leave him. I could do that."

Sara glared at her. "You're full of shit, Lindsay."

Naomi and Lindsay gasped.

"You . . . you . . . cursed!" Naomi stammered.

"Well, I'm tired of hearing Lindsay talk trash about herself. You do, you know! You make jokes out of everything, pretend to be heartless and selfish, and, okay, I'll grant that in some ways you are. But when it matters, you've got a heart of gold, girl. You really do."

A tear streaked down Lindsay's cheek. "If you ever tell, I'll kill you."

"Your secret's safe with me. Now, go on and tell Naomi what you came to say." Sara smiled knowingly.

Lindsay sniffed. "I'm sorry we freaked you out, Naomi. You don't have to read for the movie; you can forget about it, if that's what you want. You don't have to tell us why. But—"

"No buts," Sara scolded mildly.

"Just let me finish, okay?"

Lindsay looked into Naomi's eyes. "Here's the thing. Whatever's going on in your head, whatever you need—for whatever reason—we can help you."

Sara said, "We became like a family this summer, Naomi. All of us. And family help one another. If you need money, if you need to stay under the radar—whatever you need, we're there for you."

"You don't have to be alone again. Ever." Lindsay and Sara leaned in and hugged her.

You'd expect huge, gloppy tears to fall from those ginormous anime eyes. When Naomi cried, they did.

21

October: *Beshert*–What's Meant to Be

"What's the word from our guys in the Midwest?"
Jared asked Lindsay, who'd just shut her cell phone. The
pair were lazing in Jared's backyard on a balmy Saturday
afternoon, with Linz looking exceptionally luscious in her
metallic bikini—so "in," as she advised him, and so perfect with her copper hair, golden brown eyes, and faded
rusty freckles.

A stab of pain shot through him. Lindsay would be
leaving soon for the location shoot in Oklahoma for *The
Outsiders*. After much haggling, the movie studio decided
to remain faithful to the original, in setting at least. She'd
be gone for three months, and though Jared would visit
as often as possible, he missed her already. He'd be busy,
doing double-duty. As part of the big Larson compromise,
Jared had agreed to really go back to school, to take
classes, and to work part-time at Galaxy.

From her lounge chair, Lindsay leaned over and gave him a peck on the cheek. "Nick's at college. He joined a fraternity—and big surprise, he's already got a girlfriend. He thinks he's gonna be a business major. I think we convinced him he could open a chain of fitness centers one day. I'd invest in him."

Jared laughed. "I bet you would, cutie-pie. And with all the money you're gonna make on *The Outsiders* and the plans I have for your career, you'll have lots of money to invest."

"Bet on it," she said dreamily.

"And Eliot, our neurotic-genius friend?"

"Emergency El is doing fantastic," she reported. "I got an e-mail. That school in Chicago is like his dream environment. He's even got—are ya sitting down?—a girlfriend!"

Jared punched his fist in the air. "Yessss! Awesome!"

"I texted him; he's gonna send a picture. I told him we could probably all get together over Christmas. I mean, I'll be in Oklahoma—how far could that be from Chicago and Michigan?"

Jared chortled. "That's my Linz. Don't ever change, baby, okay?"

She narrowed her eyes. "I think you just made fun of me."

He reached over and cupped her chin. "Never. I'd never make fun of you." The kiss was tender, and sweet, and lingering.

"Mr. Jared, a delivery came for you." Desiree's voice wafted from the French doors. She held up a large manila envelope.

Jared knew what it was—he'd asked Amanda to please send it over on Saturday so he could surprise Lindsay before the rest of the showbiz community saw it on Monday. He opened it in front of her.

Lindsay's hand flew to her mouth, her eyes went wide. "Oh, my God, Jared! That's . . . that's . . . where did you? When will this come out?"

They were staring at a poster, the first draft of what would eventually be used on billboards, magazines, and in TV ads to advertise *The Outsiders*. The final version wouldn't be released for many months, but Jared and Amanda had fought for the wording on it, and Jared wanted Lindsay to see it.

The poster pictured the seven male stars standing shoulder to shoulder—included among them were Tom Welling, from *Smallville*, and Mark Oliver, the young actor Lindsay'd met in the park—their names listed beneath the photograph. On the side, in her own spotlight, was a profile of Lindsay's sparkling face, with the words, "And starring Lindsay Pierce as Cherry."

She gulped. "You did this for me."

"Well . . ." Jared tried to hide his grin. "It was really your agent, Amanda, who did the heavy lifting. But, yeah—as the son of the owner of Galaxy, I put my two cents in. C'mere, you." He held his arms out.

Lindsay joined him on the chaise lounge, tucked herself under his arm.

"And you know, Ms. Pierce," Jared said, "this is only the beginning. Galaxy and I have big plans for the likes of you."

Through her tears, she giggled. "Tell me again."

"We're gonna pitch *Leave It to Lindsay*, a half-hour TV series, and it's all you. It's you being single and funny and free in L.A.. It's you being clueless and brilliant at the same time, it's you being self-centered and intensely generous. It's you and your coterie of friends—it's *I Love Lucy* meets *Sex and the City*. You should be planning that Lindsay Pierce doll now."

"And the perfume," she sniffed. "Everyone has a scent."

"Okay, you two, get a room!" Sara sashayed into the backyard, wearing capris and a snazzy V-neck top accessorized with a golden cross necklace.

Lindsay bolted upright and gave Sara a huge smile. "Wuzzup, Saint Sara?"

Jared looked from his girlfriend to Sara. A strange feeling overtook him. He had the distinct feeling Lindsay knew why Sara was there. Which intensified when Lindsay, who never could contain her excitement, suddenly shot off the lounge chair and started prancing about, circling him.

Sara laughed and pulled something out of the Hermès Birkin bag that Lindsay had pressed on her.

She'd only agreed because in her new job—while still auditioning for acting roles—she was always toting around scripts and papers.

Sara had not gone back to Texarcana, not gone back to Donald. She'd decided, after much deliberation, to stay in L.A., to continue trying to find acting gigs and to work with Naomi. Once the formerly homeless girl accepted them as true friends, as family, she'd opened up. Told them about her missing sister, her fears of finding Annie, or of not finding Annie.

Lindsay had offered to help. Jared's family had the resources to be discreet, to be sure no harm came to anyone, no unwanted publicity. They hadn't found Annie Foster yet, but they had earned Naomi's trust. In short order, that trust had led her to audition, finally, for the role of Moxie in *Hide in Plain Sight.*

The newbie actress needed a manager, someone to protect her, look out for her interests. They created that job for Sara at Galaxy.

"Well, come on!" Jared was getting antsy. "What are you and Lindsay up to?"

Slowly, just to mess with him, Sara extracted a rolled-up poster from her bag and gave it to Jared. "Unroll it."

Jared did not enjoy being stealthed. Warily, he slipped off the rubber band and unfurled the poster.

"It's a first draft," Sara warned. "It's not final."

"But the wording is!" Lindsay squealed.

It was Jared's turn to tear up. McSmoothy became McMush. The poster was for *Hide in Plain Sight*. And it wasn't the billing, "Introducing Naomi Foster as Moxie," that moved him to tears. It was the top billing:

"A Rusty and Jared Larson Production."

Epilogue: One Last Laugh

Later that night, Lindsay and Jared were still out-doors; hadn't moved from the chaise lounge. They had one more surprise visitor.

"Uncle Rob!" Jared exclaimed. "You're back! You're . . . here!"

Indeed he was. The tall, craggy, forever-hippie Robert Larson, Jared's favorite family member, loped into the backyard. He'd be bunking here at the mansion, he told them, until his own house at 5905 Chula Vista Lane was fully operational again. He stretched out on the chaise next to the couple and turned to Jared.

"So, nephew, how was your summer?"

Jared shrugged. "Oh, you know, nothing exciting. Same old, same old . . ."

Lindsay began to giggle. The giggle became a guffaw, which morphed into peals and peals of staccato laughter, bouncing off the canyon walls and through the valleys, around the hills, drifting into the perfect California night.

RANDI REISFELD

is the author of dozens of original series and
novels for teens, including three *New York Times*
bestsellers. A seasoned Summer Share writer,
she has already contributed *CC (Cape Cod)* to
the series. Her new trilogy, Starlet, reflects her
lifelong obsession with all things Hollywood.
About Summer Share: *Partiers Preferred*, also set
in Hollywood, she says, "This book is my all-
time personal favorite. I hope you have as
much fun reading it as I had writing it!"

Randi lives in the New York City area with
her family, two cats, and one exuberant puppy
whose paws always manage to land on the
"delete" key every time she's written a really
good chapter. Visit www.randireisfeld.com.

PULSE **it**

Did you **love** this book?

Want to get the
hottest books **free**?

Log on to
www.SimonSaysTEEN.com
to find out how you can get
free books from **Simon Pulse**
and become part of our **IT Board**,
where you can tell **US**, what **you** think!

SIMON
PULSE

Let's get this straight . . .

Jonathan Parish is seventeen, out and proud—and accidentally winds up in bed with a *girl*? Yup—an inebriated lapse of judgment leads him to sleep with a member of his angsty-straight-girl posse at a party. Word soon gets around that hot-but-previously-unavailable Jonathan might be on the market. And his school's It girl makes him a proposition: if he pretends to be her boyfriend, she'll fly him to London to attend a Kylie Minogue concert.

With his eye on the prize, Jonathan will do pretty much anything to see his beloved pop star Kylie up close and personal. Even if it means acting like he's straight and going back into the closet. . . .

the straight road to Kylie

Nico Medina

"I can't get this book outta my head."
—RACHEL COHN,
bestselling author of *Gingerbread*

From **Simon Pulse**
Published by Simon & Schuster

Printed in the United States
By Bookmasters